NEW KINGS
of
TOMORROW

J.M. CLARK

FRATERNITY ROSE
PUBLISHING

SUMMARY

Twenty years ago, Jacob lost everything. Just as he was starting to figure out life as a college freshman, his world was suddenly shattered when a devastating illness destroyed the world he once knew and claimed the lives of everyone that mattered to him.

Jacob and the other survivors of the pandemic were transported to the Palace Program. Housed in a quarantined modern facility, the Palace is a perfect community designed to protect them from the sickness that wiped out ninety-five percent of the world population.

The Order, which has risen as the new ruling power, believes the desires of the Old World were responsible for its collapse. They appoint Sirus, the program director, to rehabilitate the survivors and continue with the reproduction of mankind.

As the years go by and Jacob's relationships in the Palace become more complex, he slowly begins to see that the man-made utopian society is nothing close to a perfect tomorrow, but is instead an unfathomable deception.

Join the mailing list and receive free giveaways and exclusive content:

Website: http://www.writtenbyjmclark.com
Email: writtenbyjmclark@gmail.com

BEFORE

CHAPTER ONE

Jacob

THE CLASS LOOKED UTTERLY EMPTY TO Jacob—pathetic, in fact. A few students were sprinkled in the seats here and there, when customarily just about every desk was filled. Professor Dansbury's philosophy class was one of the most popular courses on campus. An easy A and some good discussions to boot were nothing to sneeze at for a college freshman.

As a kid, Jacob didn't shy away from philosophical discussions with his father. They'd talk about good and evil, perspective, and how a specific point of view could determine the subjective nature of good and evil. Jacob's father would always remind him to stay in the moment and never forget to think outside the box. "The man who stops thinking creatively is cursed to live a life of monotony and repetition." One of his favorite self-appointed quotes.

Sitting at a desk-chair combo with its small pork chop–shaped slate of wood just big enough to fit a book and a pencil or two, Jacob looked around and noticed that half the class hadn't bothered to show up that morning. His Philosophy 101 class was held in the basement of this building. It was a decent-sized room built in the manner of a small theater; red drapery hung on the walls, and a podium stood in the center of the floor for the instructor. The seats for the students descended in rows sloping down at an angle, with the exits at the top of the stairs. Typical lecture hall design, nothing special. Seen one lecture hall, you've seen them all.

Jacob realized that out of those who had bothered to show up, no one was paying attention to the lecture, and everyone seemed to be glued to their phones more than usual. Texting, reading, then a swipe, more texting and reading. In most cases, the instructor could manage to hold the attention of students with his lectures and classroom debates, but today no one seemed to care.

Danbury raised his voice as he said, "One of the most tragic things I know about human nature is that we all tend to put off living." He placed one hand on his heart, the other firmly on his desk, like he was being sworn in to testify in court. He had a flair for public speaking. Always moving and talking like he was live on Broadway.

His graying hair lay flat on the sides of his balding head, the crown of which reflected the fluorescent lights on the ceiling. Looking toward the back of the room, he proclaimed in a loud booming voice, "We are all dreaming of some magical rose garden over the horizon instead of enjoying the roses that are blooming outside our windows today."

He dramatically dropped his hand from his heart for effect, letting it hang by his side. With the other hand, he reached into his back pocket and retrieved a handkerchief to wipe snot from his upper lip and nose. Dansbury went on to say, "That's a quote from Mr. Dale Carnegie. Isn't it a wild thought though? We tend to get so caught up in the end game of the hunt that we do not pause to be in the moment. We rarely stop and smell the wildflowers, listen to the sounds of nature, and just be. We forget to just be, and that is the shame of it all, right?"

He turned to face the wall behind him and sneezed, wiping his nose once more before turning back to face the class. "Guess we are a people of repetition, never learning the error of our ways until those very ways deliver doom to our doorsteps." He released a contemplative "hmm" with a hunch of his shoulders.

Ironically, Dansbury stopped his lecture to stare at the tablet lying face up on the podium. After a few seconds, he pushed a button on the side of the device and swiped it off. He stared at the ground for a time, his handkerchief held to his lips in thought.

The professor then shoved the tablet into his carrying case along with a bunch of papers and notebooks as he hastily ordered the class to read chapter fifteen and give their own ideas on what it meant to be in the now. By that time, Jacob and another guy were the only ones left in class. Everyone else had packed up and left. Why hadn't he noticed?

"Okay guys, I'm releasing you early today. Almost everyone who cared to show up has left by now anyway, and I'm needed elsewhere. I'd urge you gentlemen to contact your loved ones right away and make sure they are okay. Things seem to have gone awry in the world today." Professor Dansbury paused and regarded Jacob and the other kid still staring down at him. "Get out of here while you can."

What is he talking about? Jacob thought as he watched the professor do a slow gallop to the door. Dansbury reached back into his pocket and retrieved his handkerchief for another loud nose-blowing before he vanished into the hallway.

Jacob stuffed schoolwork into his book bag and grabbed his phone to text Leanne as he walked out of class. They had plans to hit the campus Starbucks while she quizzed him on a math test coming up tomorrow. Walking up the staircase of the basement floor, he swiped the phone to unlock it, and there it was.

In came a rush of notifications for missed calls, text messages, social media messages, and news updates. Jacob knew right then something was indeed "going awry" as Dansbury warned just moments ago.

LEANNE: *6:45 a.m.* I'm not going to be able to make it this morning J, I feel terrible and I have to take my mother to her doctor. Must be something going around. Love you.

7:01 a.m. When you get this please call me. I don't feel good enough to drive. Can you take us to the emergency room? You know I'm a big baby when I'm sick, lol.

7:11 a.m. Jacob, seriously call me right now. I'm beginning to get scared. My mother is throwing up all over the place.

5

7:22 a.m. Something is very wrong. Check on your parents and please let me know that you are ok. Are you seeing what the news is saying? Why aren't you answering? Just text me and let me know you're ok.

Jacob picked up the pace and began to speed walk to his car in the southern parking lot, thumbing through more messages as he walked.

Logan: *7:15 a.m.* Hey man, I'm gonna have to cancel on basketball tonight. I just can't make it. I feel like shit bro. I'll hit you up later if I'm feeling better.

Mikey: *7:17 a.m.* Have you been watching the news homie? WTF!!!

Kate: *7:21 a.m.* Did you see the news this morning? What the hell is going on?

Autumn: *7:26 a.m.* Jacob, call your mother. She just reached out to me and is feeling terrible. Take care of my sister. Call home when you get this, then call me. Love you.

MSNBC pop-up notification: *CDC Announces Death Toll Climbing*

JACOB BROKE INTO A BRISK JOG, anxiety setting in. At that moment, it all started to make sense to him as he made his way to the parking lot. *A lot of students seem to be missing from campus today, class was half empty.* Moving through the campus grounds, he didn't see very many students. Much less general loitering. There should have been groups of students studying outside on this warm early-fall day. And there was no music playing. There was always music playing in the courtyard, but today, nothing.

He looked up to see that the few people who were on site today were doing the same thing as him. Staring down at their phones and hauling ass to their cars. *Are they reading the same types of messages that I am? Are people in their lives getting sick as well?* Jacob jogged past the campus Pizza Hut to see no one working today. Didn't look like it was ever opened at all. A tall lanky kid with curly red hair who reminded him of a hipster Ronald McDonald threw down his book bag and broke out into a full sprint, leaping over a bench along the way to the southern parking lot.

CNN POP-UP NOTIFICATION: *Stay Inside Your Home or Risk Deadly Flu Bug*

Jacob continued to scroll through his messages, trying his best to push the budding panic from the pop-up news notifications to the back of his mind while jogging to the parking lot. He was afraid of what he would read next, but he just couldn't stop.

Dad: *7:31 a.m.* I need you to come home after class, and bring some Theraflu and NyQuil please. Thank you.

7:35 a.m. I think I'll just drive up to the hospital. Valerie is not doing so well. I think she needs to see a doctor. Lol maybe I do too. Take the trash to the end of the street when you get home. You forgot last week.

7:57 a.m. Call me when you get this message. Please answer your phone Jake.

FOX NEWS pop-up notification: *Is Flu Bug the Work of ISIS?*

HE SPOTTED the Blue 2009 Chevrolet Impala his father bought him just a few short months ago. It was easy to find since there were very few cars left in the parking lot. He shoved the phone in his pocket and snatched open the car door. *Please let this whole thing be an overreaction. Please, please...*

He threw his book bag in the back, spilling pencils and planners out all over the floor, and slid into the driver's seat. He slammed the door closed and frantically searched his pockets for his keys, but he couldn't seem to figure out where they were. Jacob's mind was disheveled, and he was panicking. He stopped moving and just breathed in and out for a few seconds. *Relax Jake, just relax...breathe.* His mother always told him that he just needed to breathe to control his anxiety, to control his temper.

After a few short moments of allowing himself to be calmed by his own breathing, he lifted his ass up off the seat and patted the sides and back of his jeans. Nothing. Anger came boiling back to the surface like molten lava spilling over the lip of a volcano set to erupt.

"C'mon! Where the fuck are my keys!" he screamed in the quiet car, the quiet parking lot, the quiet city of Cincinnati. There was no response but that of his own echo, the sound vibrating in his ears, mocking him, feeding the fear that had begun to form in his brain. How could the world be this silent?

Jacob caught a glimpse of a young woman wearing a burnt orange peacoat. Her long black hair bounced behind her as she ran past his car to a group of vehicles parked behind him. His eyes followed her, and he saw that she was crying. Watching her get inside of her car through his back window, he remembered that he put the keys in the back pocket of his book bag. Reaching into the back seat, he grabbed them out of the bag and started the car.

Jacob pulled out of the parking lot, driving with one hand and calling Leanne with the other. He needed to hear from her, to make sure she was okay. Hell, just to hear her voice would be enough right now. Some form of normalcy this morning would suffice; he needed to feel like the entire world hadn't moved on without him. The phone rang once before she answered; she was crying and sobbing uncontrollably. Leanne's tears were not a comfort, but her voice was, distraught or not.

"Jacob? Oh my God, Jacob, are you okay?" she asked before her words were swept away in a coughing fit.

"Yes, I'm fine. Tell me what's going on. I just got out of class, and everything is going crazy all over. No one showed up to school today," Jacob replied.

"I don't know, Jacob, we are just really sick. Everyone is. Are you okay? How do you feel?" Before he could answer, she coughed again. The deep, hacking sound scared Jacob. "It started last night with my mother," she went on. "And now Dad is sick too. I'm feeling like crap. I don't know what happened. We were fine yesterday afternoon, and now it's hard to even get out of bed. I wanted to take my parents and myself to the emergency room to be treated, but I honestly don't have the strength. Have you seen what they have been saying on the news? Something is going on, and I don't think it's good." Leanne cried into the phone.

Jacob could hear the scratching sound in her voice. It sounded like it was painful for her to even speak. He could hear the short, wheezing breaths struggling to find their way in and out of her lungs, like she was all clogged up with mucus. He thought that she sounded the way he did when he had to be rushed to the ER years ago with a severe sinus infection. He was popping antibiotics like M&M's for two weeks before he was able to leave his bed.

"Listen Le, I just need you to calm down. Please baby, just try to calm down for me. I'm running home to check on my parents right now. They say they aren't feeling well either." Jacob spoke in the calmest voice he could muster. He was nervous enough to scream though; none of what was happening made sense to him.

Leanne began to cry even louder into the phone, as if his words about his parents further cemented what she was already thinking. "Jacob's parents are sick too," he heard her yell to someone in the same room. He assumed one or both of her parents.

Jacob spoke in a low tone, "Baby, listen to me. Are you listening?"

Huffington Post pop-up notification: *National Guard Deployed Amidst Deadly Flu Bug*

"Yes, I'm listening, Jacob," Leanne replied with a raspy cough. "I'm sorry—this is all so fucked up!" she yelled into the phone. "Jacob, everyone is sick, nobody is answering their phones, and—"

"Listen to me, Leanne, stop talking and listen." Jacob smacked the steering wheel hard enough to make the horn blare. "Just call nine-one-one. They will send someone to help you guys out if you can't drive. Take whatever meds you have in the house until they get there to help you. Do you hear me?" Jacob skimmed the curb of Reading Road. He was driving too fast, but he could go as fast as he wanted; there were no other cars on the road with him.

Leanne coughed up what sounded like phlegm before saying, "I just called them, and all I'm getting is a busy signal. I called my uncle Bailey afterwards, and it went through fine. He is in Erlanger, and he is sick as well. He's going to head over this way once he is feeling a little better. He just left the urgent care and the line was out the door. I'm so afraid, Jacob." Leanne continued to cry and violently cough into the phone.

"Please, just keep calling nine-one-one until you get through. I'm going to check on my parents, and then I'll be right over to drive you wherever you need to go if your uncle or the ambulance hasn't shown up yet. I promise, baby, just hold on, please." Jacob began to cry then, feeling helpless to those he loved most in this world. He couldn't help but to sob with her. He knew that it wouldn't help the situation and would probably make her even more upset. The last thing she needed to hear was her boyfriend blubbering into the phone like a wimp.

Jacob and Leanne had only begun to date six months ago. Young love was a thing that did not require a maturation process, so as far as he was concerned, his one true love was dangling from a bridge right at that moment. And he could do nothing to save her. The feeling of being absolutely useless hurt him to the core. Made his stomach turn in fact.

"Okay Jacob. I'm holding on, and I'll keep calling. But please hurry if you can. I hope your folks are okay. Please let me know something as soon as you make it to them."

"I will, baby, I promise. Keep calling nine-one-one. They have to pick up eventually, right? You will get through at some point, and I'll be there in no time. I love you," Jacob responded. He thought briefly about how this could be the last time they spoke, but he quickly shoved that fear deep down. He couldn't let his mind go there if he was going to be of any help to anyone.

He called home over and over as he barreled down the highway. No answer. All the while he tried not to see the notifications constantly popping up from different news outlets.

"Don't look at that trash. They sensationalize all that stuff. It's meant to getcha going," his father would say while they drove home from some sports practice of his. Mathew was a great man, a great father. Thinking about him made Jacob even more panicked, remembering the fearful tone of his father's text message. He pushed down on the gas harder, hitting seventy-five miles per hour.

He wanted to turn on the radio and find a news channel to break the silence, to stop his mind from running in circles, but his brain wouldn't allow his hand to do so. He drove in fear, his anxiety consuming him like an infant swaddled in its first blanket from the hospital, and he had problems seeing the road clearly. His hands were shaking, and he felt the beginning of a twitch in his left eye. A lump the size of a tennis ball clogged his throat as beads of sweat rolled down his forehead, his stomach was a mess—he thought he may need to pull over to collect his thoughts and calm down, but he couldn't. He had to get home as fast as possible. He sped up to eighty, tearing down the road like it belonged to him. Only him.

I could just turn on the radio and hear about what's going on. No harm in knowing the facts. But he knew that wasn't true. He knew his current reality was best-case scenario. He also knew that what could be waiting on the other side of door number two was much worse, maybe something he couldn't handle.

He hadn't opened any of the pop-up notifications on his phone for the same reason he wouldn't turn on the radio. Not knowing could be as helpful as knowing sometimes, depending on the situation, and he had deemed this situation the "not knowing" type. One crisis at a time. Right now he was dealing with the immediate issue of checking on his parents. He could deal with the rest of the world later.

Instead of checking the news sites, Jacob drove to his parents' house in pure silence. For that little bit of time, he could still pretend that all was well. *It's just a nasty flu bug going around. People will get treated with meds. Nothing to worry about.* After all, he was feeling perfectly fine. He wasn't sick, so that meant not everyone was sick. That realization comforted him a touch, and he clung to that bit of hope.

The empty streets could be a sign of people staying home for the day maybe. No police, no ambulances, so maybe that was a good sign that things weren't so bad. If things were terrible, there'd be more cars on the road, right? Instead, there was virtually no traffic, and the day was beautiful. Terrible things like this didn't happen on beautiful days. Terrible things like this didn't happen at all.

Jacob brought the car to a steady pace. The last thing he wanted to do was get pulled over by the cops (who were nowhere to be found), which would delay him getting home to check on his parents. *No cops are pulling anyone over today, Jake,* the most honest portion of his psyche reminded him.

He slowed down and turned his music on through his smartphone and AUX cord. The music was on, he heard it, but he could still be driving in silence and wouldn't notice the difference. He thumbed through his phone, avoiding news notifications like landmines until he got to the music app. He turned on a playlist Leanne had made for him. It was a good song list, but Jacob's mind was elsewhere.

Jacob squirmed in the car seat, his stomach a ball of unraveled yarn frayed at the ends. He drove like this for maybe thirty minutes, but to him it seemed like three hours. Hell, even three days. It was hard for him to explain the thought process of wanting to get somewhere as fast as possible but at the same time never wanting to arrive.

He did arrive though, and when he did, all the adrenaline came surging back into his body. His family needed him. His girlfriend needed him. And he needed them all to be okay, because if they weren't okay, nothing would matter anymore.

Jacob pulled into his driveway. He was almost out of the car before the key was out of the ignition. He slammed the door shut and ran through the grass, jumping over a small flowerbed to the porch and then bursting into the house. He came home to find the same gruesome scene that most survivors found on that quiet Monday morning in the month of October, 2019.

CHAPTER TWO

Trevor

O N THIS MONDAY AFTERNOON, THE SUN was high in the sky, and life couldn't be better in Northern Kentucky. Trevor David Cox sat at the register of his shop, which had stood on Lester Avenue for five years. After leaving the Marine Corps, Trevor had built the shop plank by plank with the help of his brother-in-law, Gerald, and his father.

Now forty-two years old and gearing up for a heavy winter's snow, Trevor was waiting on a shipment of goods to stock the back room. They always came later in the day, so he knew that today would be a long one. Branden, the clerk he'd hired to work afternoons, had called in sick that morning.

Trevor read through the paper while he waited; the sports page to be exact. He puffed on a Marlboro Red, flicking the ashes into an empty blue coffee mug. Everything was online these days, so you couldn't help but follow the leader in most things, like online banking, Facebook, and purchasing just about anything you could imagine from Amazon. He thought that some things should remain...vintage, so Trevor still insisted on getting his sports the way his father did; with a cup of joe, a cigarette, and the local newspaper. The Cincinnati Reds still sucked. The Bengals were still flirting with a playoff win—business as usual.

The general store that Trevor and his wife, Amy, owned wasn't a big shop, but it was one of the more popular in their town. They sold general products, from toilet paper to candy, all the way down to the *Time Magazine* that Mrs. Nelson came in to purchase every month like clockwork. She also bought pot from a few of the local teens, but of course her secret was safe with them. Traffic flowed like a river on most days. Today was different though.

Trevor was reading an article on the Bengals' new tight end when Tommy from up the road on Montana Way came walking into the store. Tommy lived in a spiffy double-wide trailer with his girlfriend, Carla, and their two children. His lady worked at a daycare in Florence, and Tommy collected unemployment, going on his second year. He liked to build useless shit to sell on Craigslist. After a few beers, Tommy would claim that if you clocked into a job for The Man, then you were probably a chickenshit and not a man at all. Men don't work for other men. He was that guy.

"Hey Tommy, what can I help you out with today? You catch the game last night?"

Tommy waved his hand in a "hold on" motion. He walked down the medicine aisle, coughing up a lung the whole way, and began to rifle through all the medicinal options. He grabbed one of each available option and made his way up to the register.

Trevor stared at him. Lots of people had been coming in that morning to get medicine. Something must be going around. He felt fine though.

Tommy's face was swollen and red, his eyes baggy and irritated. The look you get after rubbing your face raw for an hour to stifle the runny nose and watering eyes that accompanied any good congestion. He shuffled up to the counter and used the corner of it to steady himself with one hand, clumsily dropping the medicine on the counter.

Trevor stood up. "Are you doing okay, buddy? You don't look so hot today."

"Man, me and the ol' lady are really feeling it this morning." He paused to rub his nose with the palm of his hand. "She thinks we have the flu or something." Tommy pulled a tissue out of the back pocket of his blue jeans to wipe his hand clean. He leaned against the counter to balance himself once more.

"Well alright man, I guess it's good you are getting some medicine then, right? I've had a few people come in this morning to get some of the same stuff. Must be something going around. I'm sure this will knock it right out." Trevor began bagging the products.

"Let's hope so." Tommy balled the tissue up and placed it back in his pocket.

"But hey, let me ask you something, Trevor. Have you looked at the news this morning?" Tommy stared at Trevor with the most serious look he could pull off considering his face was swollen twice the size of its original form.

"Outside of this paper, I don't think that I have, Tom. Why do you ask?" Trevor placed both hands on the counter and gave the sick man his undivided attention.

"I think it would be a good idea that you get around to it. Something crazy is going on, it's all over the news and stuff. Carla was on the internet all mornin', scaring the hell out of me with the stories. The president was on there talking about it, and the news channels been sayin' the same thing, so there must be something to it."

"Really?" Trevor raised a brow, wondering if Amy had heard about any of this.

"She sayin' a lot of people all over the country are gettin' sick. Some folks in other countries have even died." Tommy paused to sneeze again. "Them folks on the news was sayin' that a lot of people might die if they don't see a doctor. Said a lot of people done already died." Tommy stopped to wipe his nose again, this time with the back of his oil-stained hand.

"They had Mr. Trump on television this mornin' telling people to stay in the house until they can figure it all out. That's what I'm doing in here now, gettin' some medicine and stuff so that we have some. Carla told me that the hospitals is all packed full of people and such… but you seem to be alright, right? How's Amy and the kids? They sayin' that kids are getting the worst end of it. Our two crumb-snatchers are just as sick as Carla and me."

Fear jumped to the front of Trevor's chest like a rabbit out of a hat. He hadn't spoken to Amy since last night. He woke up early to go on his morning run and then came straight to the store to open. Now that he thought about it, he remembered hearing her cough up a storm in the middle of the night, but she was always catching colds around this time of season, so that wasn't a reason for concern.

The day before though, their son, Michael, was sent home from school sick. His food wouldn't stay down last night before bed, and Amy had to rock him to sleep. She hadn't had to do that since he was a baby, and he was nine years old now. He could have gotten Amy sick.

Oh my God, Trevor thought.

"My wife and kids are fine, thank you very much. What the hell, man?" Trevor demanded, lashing out at the sick man for reasons he couldn't understand. "What are you tryin' to say, Tom? You coming in here with this conspiracy shit and asking about my family and carrying on." Trevor was calling upon an authoritative volume he'd mastered in the Marine Corps, and it made Tom stand at attention.

"Well, I'm sorry, Trevor. I meant nothing by it, you know that. No disrespect meant to you and yours. I was only asking because a lot of folks seem to be getting sick, like I just told ya. That's all, man, I meant no harm by it." Tommy took a step back from the counter.

Trevor grimaced. He'd been working on his temper, but he still had a propensity to lose it at a moment's notice. War changed you. Even when you came home and got a chance to pretend that you didn't live through hell...you were still different. It didn't take much to send him back to that familiar place.

"I'm sorry too. I shouldn't have come at you in that way, buddy. But like I said, my family is fine, thank you. Is there anything else I can do for you? My lunch break is overdue." Trevor placed the change on the counter for Tommy to pick up.

Trevor didn't want to touch the man's hand. One look at Tommy's expression showed that he knew it, too. What was understood didn't need to be explained. Tommy gathered the change and his bag of medicine before shuffling out of the store without another word, coughing and sneezing all the way to his vehicle.

Trevor waited until Tommy's white pick-up truck was kicking up rocks on the gravel parking lot before he grabbed the store phone and tried to call home, but there was no answer. He tried once more on his cell and got the same thing. *Now why would Amy not answer the phone?* She should be up by now, Tricia should be at school, and he knew Michael was home sick. It was possible that she had taken him to the doctor though. She did mention that last night before bed. In his mind, Trevor was able to easily justify why Amy wasn't answering. The alternative was still unthinkable at this point.

Trevor got up from the counter and walked over to the medicine aisle to take a quick inventory of what had been purchased. It was funny to see that when he wasn't focused on a certain thing—in this case the mass number of meds purchased among other small crap like drinks, chips, and magazines—he could easily overlook something important. He noticed that the only items left in the drug area were a bottle of Pepto-Bismol and one box of off-brand Sudafed. He had never seen the inventory in this section get so low.

Damn. He knew that this area had been replenished last Thursday when the supplies came in. Walking back up the aisle, he noticed an ambulance racing up the road with sirens blaring. That jogged something else in his memory. That was the second time he'd seen the ambulance come past there.

Couldn't say that it was odd, but he also couldn't remember the last time he had seen that happen. Things were normally quiet in that area. When you weren't looking for an anomaly, it was easy to let it stare you in the face without ever giving it a second glance. That made him wonder how many other things he had overlooked since last night. *What if Tommy was right?*

Without another thought, Trevor walked over to the door and flipped the *Open* sign to *Closed*, grabbed his car keys from the side of the register, and ran out of the store. He almost forgot to lock up, but he turned and quickly locked the door before jogging to his truck. Something inside was telling him that he needed to get home. Needed to check on his wife and kids.

It would be okay if someone would just answer the damn phone, but when he called and got nothing once again, it fueled the illogical fear in his mind. And with his background, all fear was to be taken seriously.

I'll just run home and check on them, make sure no one needs anything, and I'll come right back to the store. Maybe see if Amy needs me to pick up dinner tonight since she may not be feeling well. Maybe some fried chicken or even McDonald's. That's it, no big deal, he thought as he got behind the wheel of his black GMC truck. Trying to calm himself down with a mundane task like planning dinner worked...but only a little.

The drive home was short. The shop was only a few miles from the ranch-style home they had built about ten years prior. Peeling into the driveway, he scattered the crunchy fall leaves from the cement into the grass and barely managed to brake before hitting his garage door. He began to take the key out of the ignition but came to a sudden stop. Then...he just waited. He couldn't be sure what he was waiting for, but he sat there in the driveway and didn't make a move.

Alone in the car, he noticed that the keys dangling from the ignition was the only sound outside of the wind blowing and tossing leaves around. Trevor needed to get up and go, but still he waited, like some invisible force kept him glued to the seat.

Maybe he was waiting for Amy to come out of the house with a smile. Maybe Michael would even look out his bedroom window and wave, like he would do so many days when Trevor would get home from work. Maybe Tricia would come running from the backyard with her friend Hailey from next door to ask for a ride to the mall...

But nothing happened. Trevor felt alone there in the car, but he felt safe. Safe from what could be, what he feared was waiting for him behind those doors.

The golden leaves rolled up and down the driveway, dancing in the wind, unbothered by the tribulations of man. Nothing in his world had changed just yet, and really, at moments like this, that's all that really mattered. For this little bit of time, he would enjoy that.

Trevor stared at the garage with his hands on his knees for what felt like hours. But it was probably only five minutes. He didn't know for sure that something was terribly wrong...but he did. *Tommy said lots of people were dying.* The need to help his family took priority over his fear, and he decided it was time to face whatever was going on inside of his home.

Trevor reluctantly opened the door to his truck and stepped out, guiding the door shut behind him. He walked up to the front door, turned the knob, and reluctantly stepped inside of his home.

Amy came racing out of the kitchen. She was running full speed with a handful of towels, in an actual sprint, right toward him. She was looking in his direction, but she was also looking through him, past him. She didn't say a word, and neither did he. When she got about three feet away from him, she made a sharp left at the steps and began taking them two at a time.

Trevor couldn't remember the last time he saw Amy move that fast. For all intents and purposes, she was growing older and wasn't in the shape she once was, but she took the steps like the track star she was back in high school. Trevor stood frozen at the front door, staring at the staircase his wife just went bounding up like a frantic deer. He stood still, terrified to follow her—afraid of what waited for him up those stairs.

What the hell was going on? Her panic terrified him, and he had a pretty good idea of why. Trevor began walking up the steps, his right foot landing in what looked like vomit, right there on the steps. There was also vomit on the banister. "Oh God," he said aloud.

He carefully went on walking up the steps until he made it to Michael's room, where he could hear Amy mumbling to herself. He couldn't make out a single word she was saying, and he stepped into the room to get a closer look at what she was doing.

After three tours in Iraq and Afghanistan, there was not much that Trevor hadn't seen. From blown-off body parts by way of IEDs, rape, murder, and everything in between. If there was an atrocity that could be imagined by the human brain, he'd likely witnessed it throughout his time in the military. Not a bit of that prepared him for the sight inside of his son's room. It was a whole new ballgame when the terror resided in the comfort of your home.

Amy was kneeling over their nine-year-old child in his bed, mumbling and wiping, over and over. She wiped the sweat from his brow and then used the same towel to wipe the vomit from his mouth.

With one hand, she pressed an ice pack to his small, still chest. The same wiping and applying over and over. *Why does she keep doing that?* Both her hands worked automatically like a broken robot, performing the same task repeatedly.

Trevor noticed all the bedding had been stripped from the mattress and thrown onto the floor. He could smell the sour perfume of vomit in the air; it had soaked into the tan-colored carpet, saturating a small area on the side of the bed nearest the door.

He could see that Amy had been walking in it with her bare feet and spreading it throughout the room, even where he stood now in the hallway. She was likely the culprit of the vomit all over the steps. Trevor looked across the hallway behind him at Tricia's closed door. *Maybe she is at school.*

Trevor could not bring himself to step closer to the bed, where his wife was doing the same wiping ritual that never ended. He felt helpless and weak. With all the years of military training and real-world experience, he was still rendered absolutely useless when his family needed him most. He was afraid.

Michael's face lay hanging off the side of the mattress, mouth protruding open with a slack-jawed look, almost like a fish caught on the hook. Bile leaked from the open end of his mouth, falling onto the mattress. Amy continued mumbling to herself, still not seeing Trevor there, still not noticing her husband. She was in shock, he could see that now.

There was no rhyme or reason to why she was doing what she was doing. In moments like that, sometimes people needed to feel like they did something when the time came to do something.

At that moment, Trevor broke out of his paralysis. He went over to grab Amy and pull her out of Michael's room. Enough was enough; he needed to take control of the situation.

His hand grasped her elbow and he pulled, but she just turned and looked at him, through him, and spoke incoherently. He couldn't make out exactly what she was saying, her hand still clutching the vomit-soaked towel and wiping at the air. The other hand, still holding the ice pack for his chest, had given up the fight and was dangling by her side.

"Amy, c'mon darling, you have to come with me," Trevor said to his wife, trying to remove her from an inevitable situation. He had seen enough death to know when it was at someone's doorstep, and he knew that Michael had opened that proverbial door, allowing death to waltz in and make himself at home. It was far too late for their son.

What should I do? he asked himself. He could save Amy from wiping and poking at her deceased son—even that was something. He had to remove her from the situation. That's what a good man would do, a good husband and father. He went to grab Amy's arm again, more forcefully this time, but she looked right at him, abruptly sneezed, and began speaking in a way that was somewhat understandable.

"Gotta, g-g-gotta clean Mike...Mikey, Mikey up. He has school, has to get to school," she stuttered.

"No Amy...darling c'mon, Mikey can't go to school today. Come with me, please. Let's go downstairs. We can go pick up Tricia from school. Please, let's just get out of here." Tears began welling up in his eyes, not just because of what happened to Michael, but because of the state Amy was in. Michael was gone, but she wasn't aware of it, wasn't aware of reality at all.

"Gotta...g-gotta wake Mikey up. Wake up, Mike." She went back to wiping at the air with her free hand. Wiping that air clean. The look on her face was not sadness, but more concern. Robotic concern, if a robot could express such a facial expression.

He tried to jerk her arm to remove her from the room, but she didn't budge. He tried to pull her a bit harder, and still she didn't move an inch. She just kept staring at him and repeating herself. He had always heard about this amazing strength a woman could summon when life-or-death situations arose regarding her offspring, but he always thought it was an old wives' tale. That day in his son's room, he found out it was actually true. He could not get her to budge from Michael's bed no matter how hard he pulled.

Trevor finally let Amy's arm go and screamed at her. He didn't know what else to do other than what he would do if he were still in the marines. "Dammit, Amy, we have to go! Let's go find Tricia. We have to get her from school. And we'll go get Mikey some help." Their son was gone and couldn't be helped, but he tried the lie in a desperate attempt to get his wife away from there.

Amy's robotic expression transformed into an almost devilish grin. Sexual, even.

"Don't be silly. Tricia is in her room, stayed home sick too, too. She's still asleep too, won't wake up." That's when she began coughing. Trevor backed away from her. Tears began to fall from his eyes then.

At that moment it dawned on him. Tricia was in her room, dead as well. *Oh my God!*

He left Amy with Michael, and she went back to her job of wiping sweat from his head, then sopping up the puddle of vomit from the bed.

Trevor took off out of the room, across the hallway, and swung the door to his daughter's bedroom open.

CHAPTER THREE

Juan

Driving up Thirty-Ninth and Fleming Road, all Juan Morales could think of was his daughter. He knew that she was sick; everyone was sick. He also knew that he and his family needed the money, so even though it hurt that morning to put on his uniform and leave her in the house with a stomachache, for her sake, he had to.

He and his riding buddy, Eric, were both feeling terrible, popping two Sudafed per hour. The dosage said to take no more than six in a twenty-four-hour period, but he'd gone over that limit at least two hours ago. Add to that ibuprofen and a gang of other meds that he probably shouldn't be mixing together. They could both lose their jobs if the boss knew they had been popping pills like a couple of college kids, but today was different.

Juan couldn't seem to shake the body aches. He was distracted, halfheartedly paying attention to the road as he thought about getting home to his family after this shift. Marie had asked him not to go to work, but besides the obvious paycheck, the truth of the matter was that people needed him this morning. Maybe more than ever. Yesterday was a day like any other, and today the sky was falling. When duty calls...right?

Some type of crazy flu bug had been running rampant, and people were destroying the phone lines with emergency calls. At this point, many weren't even able to get through to dispatch. There had been deaths, lots of them in fact, but some managed to make it to the hospital, which was quickly becoming too packed to take any new arrivals.

Looking at the clock on the dashboard, he noticed that it was 11:30 a.m. He and Eric had already been to at least ten homes throughout the city. Juan took a glance in the rearview mirror; Eric was sitting in the back of the ambulance, talking to his mother on the phone.

"After this shift, I'm coming right over, Ma, I promise."

Eric listened intently to the voice on the other side of the phone as he stared out the window, tapping it with his free hand. Juan heard the crinkle of a plastic bag in the back. Eric had been spitting mucus in a small trash receptacle for most of that morning.

"Not much I can do though. I have a few friends there, but this is an emergency, and I can't get in contact with anyone there to get you seen any faster." He paused to listen to her speak, then pounded the window with his fist in anger. "I'm gonna keep trying. You just gotta hold tight, Ma."

Juan could see in his peripheral vision that Eric was wiping tears from his eyes. He heard the desperation in his friend's voice. "You've gotta remember that a lot of the nurses and doctors are out sick as well. For the most part, the people that are working this morning have been there since last night. I swear they are going to take care of you. UC is the best hospital in the area. Hell, one of the best in the country."

Eric was quiet for a minute while he listened to his mother's complaints. "Okay, Ma, I hear ya, I do. Me and Juan are super busy trying to help folks out. You know I'll be up there to see you right after my shift, but I should go...Okay Ma...I love you too...Bye-bye."

They drove in silence for the next few minutes, other than the constant coughing and throat clearing and the endless wail of the siren.

"She deserves better than this," Eric said suddenly.

"You're doing all you can," Juan said, the words scratching against his sore throat. When you share the small space of an ambulance for three years with someone, you get to know them. Eric's father walked out on their family when he was a kid, and his mother raised him and his brother all on her own, even worked two jobs to pay for Eric's EMT classes. Classes that he had struggled to pass. Even after finding out that he had passed, Eric still continued selling marijuana during his first few years as a paramedic.

"She's been through enough already." Eric's response was punctuated by his loud, hacking cough.

Juan knew there wasn't much he could say about that. It was the truth. Eric's older brother ended up getting arrested for sexual assault when he was seventeen years old and caught a few other charges while doing a two-year bid. It had been five years since then, and he was still locked up. It had to be painful for Eric to not be able to get his mother the care she needed, especially with the things they were hearing about this nasty flu bug.

Juan felt the same way about his family. They'd been driving around for hours helping others, but were helpless when it came to being there for the ones they loved. Kind of a cruel torture when you think about it. For every person they were able to get to the hospital, that was more time their own family members were suffering with no help.

Juan focused on the road ahead, trying to ignore the cry of the sirens going off in their ears. He wondered if he'd ever be able to turn them off. They had not driven without the sirens on since they started the ambulance up that morning. There was so much he wanted to say, but with no reference point for comparison, he couldn't even begin to understand how to start chipping away at the layers.

Being charged with helping people who couldn't help themselves when you were going through the same thing was a hard pill to swallow (no pun intended). But someone had to do it.

Eric chugged a bottle of Robitussin DM, laid down, and placed his hands over his face.

"We will be at the next home in a few minutes, bro. Try to get some rest until then." Juan turned onto Winton Road, and in the rearview mirror he saw Eric lift his head.

"We can't do this all day, Juan. You do understand that, right?" Eric replied. Juan heard him throw the empty bottle on the floor of the ambulance. "We just can't."

Juan didn't respond, pretending not to hear him over the sirens.

He'd begun to think the same thing himself a few hours ago, but he didn't want to admit it just yet. *Are we even helping anyone? Does this even matter? How serious is this pandemic?* Juan opted to go with denial.

"Stop reading that junk on the internet, you know they hype shit up to get views and stuff, man. It's never as bad as they make it seem," Juan said. He could just make out Eric scrolling up and down the screen of his smartphone.

"I hear ya, but no bullshit bro, this flu thing is everywhere. Like literally every country in the world. I wouldn't call this click bai—" Eric began coughing up a lung. After spitting more mucus into the receptacle, he said, "You have to take a look at it. The president has given a speech about it and everything."

They drove in that contemplative silence for a few more minutes before Juan decided to double down on a second helping of doubt. "I'm thinking it's gonna be just like that swine flu thing from some years back. It will get a bunch of attention, scare the shit out of people, and boom, it's gone. Ya know? The flu bug thing is probably being used to distract us from something even worse, like more of our rights being taken away." Juan rolled down the window to spit an ungodly amount of snot onto the passing road.

"I hear ya, Juan, I hear ya," Eric replied.

Juan picked up his phone from the cup holder to see if his wife or daughter had updated him on anything. Forty-six notifications sprung up on his phone the second he entered the unlock code, and it was all the big boys.

Headlines from *The New York Times*, *Washington Post*, *USA Today*, *Wall Street Journal*, and *Boston Globe* were dark—some really dark shit. He had tried to avoid them. *Why?* he thought to himself. *Because reality was only what you experienced.*

It was easier to pretend when you were ignorant to the facts. If you didn't see it or read it, did it really exist? Of course it did, but you didn't have to deal with it...at least not at that time. Everyone was guilty of that throughout their lives, some more than others.

Juan swiped away from the notifications and checked his text messages. Nothing. No texts. He dropped the phone back into the cup holder and took a right on Reading Road.

Eric lifted his head up from the back of the ambulance once more. "What's the point? Honestly, like, why are we even doing this?"

Juan considered his response. *Answer honestly, or play the doubt card again?* Ignorance card it was. Three strikes, right? Go out swinging, Juan Morales.

"What's the point in what, Eric?" Juan was getting pretty annoyed before he had a sneezing fit for what felt like ten minutes straight.

Eric allowed Juan to finish sneezing about a hundred times in a row, then answered, "You and I both know that the people we can even transport to the hospital won't be seen. There are not enough nurses or doctors to help them. My mother just told me that the line of people needing help at UC is out the door. Out the fucking door, Juan. I'm not sure about you, but I feel like death. And judging by the amount of shit you keep spitting out the window, you can't be feeling much better. Let's be real with ourselves for a second. I take my job as serious as the next professional, but c'mon, man. It's pointless." Juan remained silent.

"People are dying all over the place. I'm sick...you sound like shit up there. Why not take this ambulance back to the hub and go home to our families? News stations are broadcasting that we are in a state of emergency. Why doesn't that go for you and me? We got families, we matter too, know what I'm saying?"

Juan picked up his phone again and checked the messages. Seventeen additional news notifications had popped up, but no new messages though. He thought there might be some truth in what Eric was saying. Maybe he should go home and check on his family. "How about we do this last pick-up; we're almost there. After we drop them off at the hospital, we can ditch this shift and get home to our families. We will deal with the boss tomorrow. It's not a bad idea, Eric."

"Good deal," Eric responded through a gnarled cough. Juan heard him rustling around on the gurney in the back before settling down. He knew his partner wasn't doing well at all. *Hold on buddy, we are gonna call it quits here soon.*

Juan grabbed his phone once more, avoiding the notifications as he made his way to the phone app to dial his wife's cell. When she didn't pick up, he decided to leave her a message. He thought that perhaps she could still be asleep, but in the back of his mind, he didn't really believe that.

"Baby, I'll be home in about an hour," he said to her voicemail. "Me and Eric are gonna clock out early today. I know you guys need me there. I feel bad for not being with you both, so I'm coming to you. Be dressed and ready to go to the hospital. UC is a mess, so we'll go to Mercy West. Kiss Sofia for me and tell her that Daddy is coming home."

Juan swiped the screen and laid the phone on the passenger seat before making a left onto Circle Ave. He took his eyes off the road for a second to check on Eric in the back. Even with the siren going, he could hear that Eric's breathing was becoming harsh back there, his chest rattling like a bird desperately trying to escape a cage.

MARTIN POWELL COULDN'T WAIT for the ambulance another minute. He had to get his family help *now*. He loaded up the kids and his wife in their large Cadillac Escalade and slid into the driver's seat. He loved that damn SUV. He never could have afforded a vehicle like that without his wife's income to help with the purchase. At that moment though, he didn't care about anything but getting them the help they needed.

Martin drove sixty-five in a twenty-five with his wife slumped over in the passenger seat. She was comatose and running a temperature of one hundred and five degrees, and he feared that her brain had begun to slow broil from the heat.

In the back seat, one of their kids was screaming while the other mirrored his mom's position perfectly. Everyone always told them how beautiful their sons were. The consensus of every middle-aged mom in the grocery store was that they would grow up to be heartbreakers. Mixed-race children were so gorgeous, people would say. But today... today the young boys looked like death warmed over.

Martin gunned the gas of his SUV in a panic, overwhelmed and determined to get his family the help they needed as fast as possible.

As any self-respecting good man would do, he was taking control of the situation. The fear, anxiety, and urgency had his adrenaline in over-drive, and he found it difficult to focus on the road. Martin looked in the back to check on his children. "Put your damn seatbelt on, Damon. And help your brother with his."

When he turned back to the road, he saw the ambulance before he heard it. He wondered for a brief, fleeting moment why he hadn't heard the sirens. *All that adrenaline rushing through my head,* he thought as he realized he was going far too fast to even try to stop. The last thought he had before smashing into the ambulance head on was, *Maybe this is better.*

Martin was thrown from the vehicle; he hadn't been wearing a seat-belt. He felt his waist being wrapped around the bottom of a telephone post. His spine was instantly severed, every rib cracked or crushed. And one of those ribs had broken off and punctured a lung.

He laid on the curb, bleeding out of his mouth, attempting to get his breathing to catch up to the speed of his heart. It was pumping so fast he thought that it would come bursting out of his chest. With every beat, he could feel blood filling his mouth. The SUV had landed on its side in someone's front yard. It was smoking, totally crushed. Martin caught vague images of the pieces of his children, now leaking from the door openings of the back seat. Both children were crushed instantly from the impact.

His wife, a labor and delivery nurse for Jewish Hospital in the city, sat in the passenger seat, which had found a new home in the back seat. Her beautiful face was crushed against the cracked glass. She seemed to be staring out the window at him. No lights were on upstairs in that house though. His dead wife gaped at him through the glass with one eye.

She would never look at anything again in this life. Half of her face had been torn off or peeled down to the neck. Exposing bone and an empty eye socket, the flap of skin lay on her chest, the missing eye on the floor of the Escalade, lying next to Damon's Baby Bop sippy cup.

Just before Martin's world faded to black, he thought about how his wife reminded him of that character from the Batman comics he would read as a child on his grandparents' deck in the summers of his youth. The guy would be angry one minute, then cool the next. He had a big coin he would flip to decide what he would do next...She reminded him of that guy.

JUAN NEVER MADE it home to his wife and daughter. That was for the best though. He would have arrived at the small two-bedroom apartment to find them both dead, cuddled together in bed. The flu got them a few hours before he met his fate head on with the formidable Cadillac Escalade.

On the corner of Circle Ave and Reading Road, there was no sound —no one screaming, no one running out of their homes to witness the screeching accident. The sirens from the ambulance had retired for the day, and there would be no more sirens begging for all oncoming cars and pedestrians to move out of the way. Juan's shift did indeed end early.

No one needed special care that afternoon. Juan Morales died instantly, with a steering column smashed inside of his chest. It burst his heart, but he didn't feel a thing. Good for him. Eric, who was lying down in the back of the ambulance, broke his neck during the crash. He never knew there was an accident, and for that he could count himself lucky.

Most everyone else in that city—in every city, state, and country of the world—would not be so fortunate. Juan and Eric never had the chance to find out, but the fever claimed millions, even billions of lives that same day.

CHAPTER FOUR

Jacob

SOME THINGS YOU JUST KNOW. SO many of us have felt that strange sensation where we can predict something before we know it to be true. Before Jacob burst into the front door of his parents' home, he knew what he would find, but all the same, he had to see it. He had a duty to uphold as far as a son, even as a decent human being, so even though he knew he would find his parents either so sick that death was imminent or already dead, he would witness it anyway.

Everything in his being told him that he should get in the car and drive away. Drive to Leanne's, or maybe to Logan's—really anywhere but his parents' home. Something compelled him to stay though, and so he did.

He was right. No one was in the living room, or in the kitchen. The home he grew up in felt utterly empty and cold. There were no televisions playing, no food cooking; there was nothing at all. *They are in the bedroom.* He tried to believe it, but even then, he knew that he was only going through the motions of what an optimistic son should think in this kind of situation.

He walked slowly down the hallway, using the wall to balance himself because he needed the help. Pictures of his childhood memories decorated this hallway. School pictures, summer vacations, Christmases, and sporting events with his father. They were almost hard to look at while Jacob made his way to their bedroom. The bedroom door stood open; he didn't need to walk inside to see what he knew he would find.

From the hallway he could see his mother, Valerie, lying in the bed, staring up at the ceiling. His father, Mathew, was crumpled into a pathetic version of the man he once was, lying on the floor next to the bed in a morbid-looking fetal position. A picture of the family laid next to his head. The frame had vomit all over it. His father had finally decided to wear the gym shoes Jacob had bought him for his birthday a few months back. Funny how you notice the most irrelevant things at the most inappropriate times.

Maybe those little thoughts were due to his brain attempting to retreat from the moment, from the trauma. To find normalcy at a juncture that felt anything but normal.

Jacob walked into the bedroom and touched his mother's chest, just in case she was still among the living. She wasn't. But again, Jacob knew that.

He did not repeat the test with his father; he knew the man was gone. His father's tongue protruded from his mouth, and his eyes were as big as the moon. No son should have to find his parents like this, in this sullied and horrific state. But the reality was, there were no specific laws of nature that would rule out the unthinkable.

Surely that was better than the opposite. They always say no parent should have to bury their child. Odd that it was viewed as somehow easier for a child to bury the beings who bore them into this world. To Jacob it felt like a god dying—he imagined that it felt that way for all children who went through the same thing.

In any event, his parents would never have to realize that horror, so apparently there was some silver lining involved in the mess Jacob found himself in.

He didn't cry though; the shock was far too heavy to allow tears. He couldn't even fathom what the hell was going on. He and his dad were just talking about the game yesterday, and his mom was planning a lady's trip to Mexico with some of her church friends. That wasn't twenty-four hours ago. Today he found them both dead, lying in their own mess.

He thought briefly that this could be a dream. But even nightmares had some semblance of mercy, as the fear would wake you up when things went too far. No dice on that day.

There would be no waking up to reality. Jacob was left to deal with the realization of the day: that this *was* reality. And he was not mentally equipped for that task. But what human would be? He laughed to himself, and it instantly felt wrong to be laughing.

He stopped laughing abruptly, wondering if perhaps he was going insane. He grabbed the comforter and covered his mother up with it. Then he opened the ottoman at the bottom of the bed and got another blanket to cover his father. That was better, and more respect-ful, he thought. Jacob walked out of his parents' bedroom, closing the door behind him.

He collapsed in the hallway outside of his parents' bedroom, across from his own room, and finally allowed himself to sit in the moment. To accept what had happened. He had been able to see this through, knowing the outcome but still doing what was right. His father would be proud of him. Jacob buried his face in his hands and allowed himself to finally cry.

CHAPTER FIVE

Trevor

NINE-ONE-ONE WAS STILL BUSY. AFTER ABOUT forty-seven calls (according to his cell phone call log), Trevor decided to give up on help. He placed his phone on the coffee table as he walked over to sit in his favorite chair in the living room. He remembered his wife bought him this chair from the Value City down the road. What was it? About two years back, as an anniversary gift. He had eaten every dinner in that chair since the day it showed up on the moving truck.

Trevor pushed the latch down on the right side of the chair and reclined back. He stared at the ceiling, following the blades of the fan going around and around. That had always calmed him, and this afternoon he needed to be calmed. Life would not, could not ever be the same. He had just lost everything...but...but...

Amy could still be heard upstairs, mumbling to Michael about waking up. She was telling Michael's body that he couldn't "schleep" through a whole school day. She was on a constant loop and had been for the last hour or so. It was useless to try to stop her, so he stopped trying. After closing Tricia's bedroom door, Trevor had tried to go back into their son's room to pry her away from the bed, but still she wouldn't budge. He thought it best to leave her to it, let it play itself out.

Nothing could prepare you for the horrors of seeing your children die, as Trevor had witnessed this beautiful autumn afternoon. On a normal day, a day unlike this one, he would still be at work, talking to customers about the football games yesterday. Trevor wondered how many NFL players were alive today. That was an interesting thought. *Bet that money couldn't save you from this.* He put his hands behind his head and tried to relax the anxiety residing in his heavy heart. One moment you could have the world, and the next you could have nothing at all.

Trevor thought that he would raise his children from infants into adulthood. He'd put his hopes and dreams into them, investing so much time and money into these little people that he'd helped Amy create with his own body, only to watch them fade away before his eyes, suddenly and painfully

Trevor just sat there, staring at the ceiling fan and listening to Amy mumble her words, which were beginning to sound like a song to him. There would be no more Little League baseball games with Michael. No more football. Tricia would no longer bug him for money to buy clothes (the kind of clothes he rarely approved of) anymore. They would never sit in the living room together and watch television programs while eating dinner again. That was all terrible and hard to cope with, but Trevor felt guilty about the thing that hurt him the most.

Amy would never be the same again, and he hurt for her the most. He felt like trash for feeling the way that he did, but he loved her so much.

Clearly, she'd snapped, and he had begun to doubt she would ever leave that room. He knew that eventually he would come to terms with what had happened to his children, and he would move on. As hard as it would be, he would do it. But if Amy didn't make it through this, he knew that he wouldn't either.

Before there were kids to be loved and nurtured, there was just her. Amy had been his reason for living for so long, he knew that going on without her was not possible. So he would not allow that to be the case, no matter what.

All those years away from her overseas while he was in the service, he had never touched another woman. And there had been ample opportunity to do so. Amy had always been the only woman for him, so even now, he would wait for her. As long as he needed to wait to see if she would snap out of it and come walking down the stairs.

Who counted time anyway when the world was ending? Until she came to him, he would lie back in the chair his wife bought for him and stare at the blades on the ceiling fan while she continued to wipe the face of his deceased son and sing her little song.

CHAPTER SIX

Jacob

J ACOB SAT IN THE HALLWAY WITH his back against the door to his parents' room, as if he were trying to make sure nothing came out. As if he could trap the memories inside that would one day come back to haunt his every moment of sleep. He'd finished crying and had now made the decision that after calling Leanne's phone over a dozen times to no avail, he should stop avoiding the inevitable and get a clue about what the hell had happened to his town, his city, to the world. He was in no condition to drive right now, but he could educate himself. Or torture himself.

After an hour or two of reading every notification from every news outlet—from Fox News on the far right to CNN on the far left—he now knew that life as he knew it this morning was over. There didn't even seem to be a plan in place. They were just telling folks to stay in the house.

That didn't help my parents, he thought to himself. *How many people are dead?* There were thousands of reported deaths, and even more people were getting sick and being rushed to the hospital. So many that the hospitals were full and there were no beds left. Most of the nurses and doctors were sick themselves. The CDC had opened help centers at the sports stadiums in different cities to help the hospitals with the sick.

Had Leanne and her parents made it to US Bank Arena downtown to get some help? Maybe that's why she hadn't answered. He bet she didn't put her phone on the charger like he'd said to do. According to the news, it wasn't clear if this was chemical warfare from an enemy of the US, but the president was blaming it on North Korea or possibly Russia. He'd even mentioned terrorist sects from the Middle East.

Jacob didn't think any of that made sense, because every country was being affected by this flu bug. Why would Russia or anyone else infect their own countries with such a ravaging pandemic? They wouldn't...right? He banged the back of his head on his parents' door as he tried to collect his thoughts. It was all so confusing, and really, it didn't matter anyway. It was only a matter of time until he would get sick and be among the dead.

The notifications stopped updating suddenly. Pretty soon an hour had gone by, and nothing was coming up from any of the media outlets. Made him wonder if they were sick and dying as well. *If those that provided the news and told us what to do were no longer living, then how could anyone get information?*

Jacob tried calling everyone he knew, but no one was answering. Either the line was busy, or his calls were going to voicemail without ringing even once. He wanted to get up and go over to Leanne's house to help her, but he was afraid. Afraid to see her the same way he had to see his parents. He couldn't do it again. Dying sounded like such a better idea.

Leanne not answering his phone calls or text messages was enough to tell him that she was either at the hospital, getting help, or had suffered the same fate of so many people that day. He felt like a coward for not wanting to go see if she was still alive, but a man could only take so much in one day, and Jacob's mental cup runneth over.

One thing that Jacob could not seem to reconcile though, was the "why" of his own physical situation. Why was he not sick? Everyone he knew seemed to be ill or dead—what made him any different?

He flipped his cell phone over and over in his hand, unable to make sense of what had transpired. He was afraid, confused, and feeling lonelier than he had ever felt in his life.

He wondered if Mr. Dansbury was sick as well. He was doing an awful lot of coughing and sneezing that morning. He didn't look like he was going to die though. The flu bug was clearly airborne; if it weren't, people wouldn't be getting sick so quickly and so easily.

Jacob had no idea what to do next. Everything he saw said to stay in your home if you were there. Or to stay at the hospital if you had been fortunate enough to get inside of one of them. There was supposed to be government aid coming to every city to help people that were still alive, and to aid those that were suffering from this flu.

Jacob got up, left his phone on the floor, and walked down the hallway to his own bedroom. He closed the door and laid in his bed, crawling under the covers and pulling them up past his lips, just underneath his nose. He lay there like that, staring up at the ceiling and trying to find sleep. He hadn't done that in bed since he was a child, hoping the boogey man stayed away.

After another hour of listening to the sound of silence outside of his window—no sirens, no one talking, crying, nothing at all—he eventually dozed off to sleep.

When he awoke that evening, Jacob went back out into the hallway to retrieve his phone and to look in on his parents. (To see if they were still dead, he supposed.) Yes, his parents were still dead in their bedroom. Leanne still hadn't returned a call or text message. No one had, for that matter, and there were no updated news notifications. Jacob dropped the phone and went back to his bed, lay back down, and did the only thing someone could do at a time like this...he waited.

The following morning, he awoke to the sound of footsteps in his cold and empty home. Help had finally come, or so he thought. Before leaving his bedroom to see who was in the house with him, Jacob looked through the blinds to see if it was the police, or maybe the National Guard. There was a long white van parked in the driveway, and there were people packed in the back.

TWENTY YEARS LATER

The Palace

CHAPTER SEVEN

Jacob

JACOB WOKE AT 7:00 A.M. LIKE CLOCKWORK, just as he'd done every morning for the past twenty years. He got up, stretched, and got a drink of water. Then he made a beeline to the bathroom to wash his aging face. Time had been kind to him; Mary always told him that he had aged so well, for whatever that was worth. Maybe he looked decent for his age, but he didn't feel like it. Time had not been kind to him physically or emotionally.

Jacob walked to the living area and sat on a bright white love seat to have breakfast. A meal that he did not prepare. No one here had cooked for themselves since they arrived all those years ago, but still, they ate heartily every day. Upon waking up, all Jacob needed to do was stumble over to the nutrition dispensary, lift the latch, and grab the silver tray, upon which his breakfast would be warm and ready. The breakfast that appeared would be based on the option inputs from the day before. This morning he had six strips of bacon, two sausage patties, and scrambled eggs. A favorite dish for him, but he had long grown tired of it, and most other things here.

In the living area of his appointed pod, a forty-five-inch television screen was mounted in the western wall next to the door. The only thing ever televised was a live feed of Sirus during dinnertime. At any other time, the screen displayed the ever-present message: "Please Wait." Everyone had to tune in to watch the daily word from Sirus; it was seemingly the only function of the televisions. To Jacob, it always felt like a waste, but the sleek, modern screen added a certain feng shui to the efficiency-style pod. Most everyone there thought it was a way for the Order to spy on them. Jacob didn't care either way.

He finished his glass of water and gently returned it to the silver tray with the remnants of breakfast scattered along the plate. He mostly picked over it all, a bite here, a bite there, moving the eggs around the plate until he was satisfied with the visual that made it appear like he had eaten enough. Jacob placed the tray of food back inside of the nutrition dispensary on the left wall of the pod. The dispensary would do the magic that it did while he was out of the pod. He didn't know how food came to be there, or when or how it was taken. It just was.

He stretched a bit as he made his way to the bathroom, taking long strides and winding his arms in wide circles as he moved. The creaking of his joints was audible in the quiet pod. With age brought the slowing of metabolism and aches from seemingly natural movements. He turned the water faucet from cold to warm.

Feeling it heat up over his hands, he stared at himself in the mirror above the sink. Jacob grabbed a washcloth and dipped it beneath the warm running water before applying it to his face to wash away any fragments of sleep from the night before.

Water went dripping from his forehead and past the age lines leading to his pale blue eyes, traveling along the curves of his nose until finally finding a home in his mustache and the forest that was his beard. Jacob rubbed the beard down into a point. Over the years, his beard had been slowly invaded by more and more gray strands. He liked the gray, it looked good on him. Reminded him of his father. The thought made him look away from the man in the mirror.

He folded the washcloth neatly into a small square and placed it in the top right corner of the sink (as pod rules directed him to do). A cleaning crew would come to pick up the rag and any other dirty clothes lying around the pod.

They came to clean the pods when Palace members were away at morning enrichment classes and other learning or stress relieving activities. That was life here: no working, no wars, no fighting, no killing... although Jacob was skeptical about some of those things. He'd heard stories about things happening.

After drying his face with a towel, he stopped to look back at himself once more. Someone wise once told him to stop and be in the moment. He could barely remember that man now, but every day he made sure to do that. Or at least he tried too. The Palace sapped his energy. Made it hard to stay in the moment when every moment seemed identical to the one before.

So much time had passed, yet nothing had changed outside of his appearance, and his blood pressure. His eyes had begun to form bags that did not go away once he had been awake for a few hours. *Oh no, Jake, these bags are here to stay.* His father always called him Jake. He could sometimes hear his dad speaking in his head.

Jacob smiled and laughed to himself. He was still a good-looking man though, and he was aging well. At least, Mary thought so. Mary was special to him; they probably spent more time together than the teachers would prefer. He fancied himself a rebel of sorts in the Palace, and for that reason, she was drawn to him.

He gave himself a sarcastic wink. "Today is going to be a wonderful day," he said aloud. Being positive was the medicine for the illness of repetition, and the Palace provided this ailment in abundance. The subject for morning enrichment today was his favorite, entitled "The Mistakes We Allow."

His favorite teacher would be holding the lesson. Teacher Phillip always had a way of getting his point across that enabled everyone to understand, and he allowed them to share their thoughts equally. The central idea of this communicative exercise was that "the true gift of ignorance is actually not knowing how ignorant you are, because only in that state can you truly be the intellectual powerhouse you believe yourself to be."

Teacher Phillip was so good at making tough ideas come across easily. He reminded Jacob of a scientist from the Old World by the name of Neil deGrasse Tyson. Jacob's mother and a girlfriend of hers went to see him speak in California one weekend during his freshman year of high school.

Wonder if he is still among the living? Jacob thought while gathering dirty clothes and towels from the bathroom.

He walked back into the bedroom with its white sheets, white comforter, white walls, and white furniture. If he never saw the color white again, he wouldn't miss it at all. Everything inside of the Palace was white. Reminded him of a hospital, a very posh hospital, but still, a hospital. Jacob stopped in the middle of the immaculate room to reflect on the ignorance lesson of the day. He threw the clothes, towel, and washcloth in a soggy heap by the pod exit.

It kind of makes sense when you think about, he told himself. Only a fool believed himself to be all knowing. An intelligent man would never believe himself to be the authority on any subject, because an intelligent man knew that he knew nothing. This idea came from a philosophy he learned a few years back called the Socratic Paradox, and Jacob had taken to it: "I know that I know nothing." Really, in the end, that was the truth. Reality was what you made it, and this could be different for everyone. He learned to not feed into the bullshit that the teachers shoveled into their gobs twenty-four hours a day, but that particular lecture had been a good one. If he had to be here, he may as well learn a thing or two.

Jacob sat on the edge of his bed and bent over to touch the tips of his toes, stretching his back in the process and grimacing the whole way while thinking over this idea. Over the years, Jacob had become much more of a cerebral person, at least more so than when he lived out in the world.

Prior to the sickness, he would fit into the jock stereotype: big, strong, stupid jokes, quick to anger, and in Jacob's case, being a dick to anyone who cared about him. A lot about who he was made him ashamed to think of it now.

Today...well, he was still quick to anger, but he did a much better job of controlling it. One, it wasn't allowed here, and two, he had learned better coping mechanisms, and he did thank some of the teachers for that. Things that had happened in the past fueled his thirst for knowledge. The whys, whos, and ifs were like ghosts of

Christmas past for Jacob. Except they showed up in his dreams every night to torment him about the past that he couldn't change. While he had learned so much about himself and the human condition, the answers that he desired still evaded him. And at this age, this point in his life, he was beginning to think that those questions mattered less and less.

Jacob thought back to when everyone in the world thought they could go around polluting the oceans, pumping toxins into the sky, and doing things that only served themselves. They believed that they could do this until the end of time because the world belonged to them, a possession to do with as they pleased. He had felt the same way, and he was not proud of that, but he was not ashamed of it either: he was a product of what society came to deem as normal.

He could only hope to get into the Greater Understanding Program one day and change things when he got back out there. This Palace Program was only meant to be a one-year solution; it was past time for him, for everyone, to be on the outside, living beyond the eastern courtyard. Here he sat, twenty years later, still going through the motions. His confidence was beginning to waver.

All of humanity had thought the planet to be a non-thinking, non-self-aware object, a plaything even, for the beings that inhabited it. This wasn't the case though, and everyone found out that they were lacking the fundamental truth looming in the background of their faults. They did not own the planet, the planet owned them, and it would fight back against the cancer attempting to drain the life from its core. *As it should have*, Jacob thought. Sadly, this happened before enough people could wise up to the damage being done, and they had all paid the toll. Both the dead and the living.

Jacob stood and removed his white pajama pants and underwear, throwing them both in the dirty clothes pile. He walked past his bed, returning to the bathroom to turn the shower on.

The pods were all identical in layout. The bed was the centerpiece of the pod, and the bathroom was just to the right of the bed. A love seat sat a few feet away from the foot of the bed, just before a short white table and the TV in the wall. To the right of the love seat sat a smaller table and three chairs surrounding it, which could be used to host other members. The left of the bed held the closet. The doors were of the sliding variety. On that same wall, just further up, you would find the nutrition dispensary. The exit door stood on the right side of the dispensary.

The pod belonged to him alone, so having a small space worked out fine. There were just a few couples in the Palace—those who had arrived with their significant others. Unfortunately, because of the sheer number of deceased, most of the world's population didn't make it. And if they did, their spouses didn't.

Standing outside of the now steaming shower with body wash and shampoo in hand, Jacob recalled one of his childhood vacations with his parents. It was funny, but he couldn't remember where they'd gone exactly. He could, however, recall jumping into a steaming waterfall. They had fun, took all kinds of pictures, and once they got back to the hotel, they ordered room service and pigged out all night. Those small returning memories, jogged by things like smells, sensations, and voices, always made him feel like he wasn't in this facility, hidden away. For a time at least.

Some Palace members hated the memories that came charging out of nowhere from time to time. They preferred to just deal with the here and now, and Jacob understood that point of view too. It was heartbreaking to realize that the things from that forgotten world would never come back. *That's life though*, he thought as he stepped into the shower.

While allowing the hot water to beat down on his body, he thought of the outside—imagined how it must have changed these past twenty years. While he had been outside, they only got a hundred-yard radius in any direction outside of the Palace. The quarantine zone was marked by small red flags in the grass. Unless one wore a protective suit, anything outside of that would mean certain death. The sickness was still active, and until it could be fully contained, this Palace served as his home. Indefinitely.

Jacob proceeded to wash and think about everyone he'd lost twenty years ago. Just like he had done every morning, every shower, on every day before this one.

CHAPTER EIGHT

Trevor

"IT'S BEEN SO LONG, KID. IT'S really hard to recall, but I'll try," Trevor told Ethan.

He crossed one leg over the other and tried to conjure memories from the time before. As the years went by, it got harder and harder for him to pull off that trick. The sun beamed down on him and the young man. It was indeed a beautiful day.

"I'd be so thankful to you, sir," Ethan gushed as he sat crisscross on the ground in the courtyard of the Palace. The teenager rested his weight on his hands behind him as he waited for story time with Trevor, a big goofy smile on his face.

Trevor had become the resident storyteller in the Palace. He was among one of the older members at sixty-two years young. All the Palace-born folks come to him or other members who had once lived on the outside to get insight into what the world was like before the sickness. You could only get so much imagery from morning enrichment, lectures, and imagination.

Trevor felt uncomfortable at this eager display from the young man. Ethan was maybe sixteen years old, but he still acted like a damn child. *Stop smiling at me like that,* he thought. All the new ones were weird, and it gave him the creeps.

"Alright Ethan, before the sickness, people could go anywhere they pleased—"

"We know that much, Mr. Cox." Ethan gave Trevor a quizzical look. "What I'm asking is more about the types of places you would go and the things you would do. These things are never in the teachings," Ethan whispered with a mischievous grin. He gave Trevor a look that said, *Now start over, Grandpa, and give up the good stuff.*

Trevor smiled uneasily and readjusted his sitting position on the park bench. It was one of twelve park benches positioned in a big circle that surrounded a statue of the earth here in the courtyard. Water shot up around the statue on every side. Looked like something you would have seen in a nice outdoor restaurant or a park, even a shopping mall from back then. This was a location within the Palace grounds that the older members would come to walk, talk, and just get some fresh air. It was also the *only* place you could go to get some fresh air.

The courtyard was located just outside the east exit of the Palace. There was no security at that door, like at the main exit. Anyone could see the red flags in the grass from the courtyard; they weren't very far away at all. The surrounding areas were fields and dense forest—so the Palace members were in a big beautiful structure seemingly made just for them, hidden in the woods.

"Well," Trevor said, staring at Ethan and searching through his mental rolodex for memories that would please the young man's curiosity. "We would go all kinds of places. There were these buildings called grocery stores. I owned a property that served the same purpose of a grocery store."

"That's a place where you would buy food that wasn't really good for you?" Ethan said with a big grin, cutting Trevor off again. "Like fake food, right?" he said.

Trevor laughed and said "Yeah, I guess you could call it that. But back in those days, that's just the way things were. You could go to these places, and they had all kinds of food. Some 'fake,' as you would say, but some of it came fresh from the earth. They had other things as well, like home products, medicine, and clothes. Some even had banks in them. There was a grocery store in my hometown that had a US Bank inside of it. On payday you could go get your money and shop for food at the same location."

"You mean US, like the old regime? United States?" Ethan lit up. The kid was enjoying this. His smile widened with self-satisfaction.

Since arriving to the Palace, Trevor had problems trying to reconcile what had happened with what this New World meant. Humans were very adaptable creatures; he was not necessarily unhappy. He had accepted what was, and he counted himself lucky to be here today, and with his wife.

On the other hand, he had also fought, watched friends die, and gave up years of his life that could have been spent with his family for the United States of America, which had become a thing of novelty, a relic, something suspended in history. It was not Ethan's fault, or anyone's for that matter, but that didn't change the fact that it still felt like yesterday to him, and to the other people who had lived through it. Some things you couldn't get out of your head no matter how much talking, probing, and good days you had.

"Yeah, it stood for the United States," Trevor said, giving a nod and spoon-feeding the young idiot a helping of "good boy." These story time sessions always got Trevor eternally boiling. He tried not to show the irritation on his face. Sometimes he failed, but over the years, he had gotten the hang of putting on a good face.

"Banks were places where you could get money? Or currency? To buy things at the grocery store and other places, correct? So you could just go in there by yourself and pick up things to take home, as long as you gave them those little pieces of paper or the plastic card?" Ethan asked his questions with a hint of hubris in how things were today, and, adversely, how dumb things sounded before. Trevor wanted to kick the kid square in the chest, knock him into the flowerbed behind him.

He knows what money and credit cards are. The little shit fancies himself better than me, better than us. Trevor thought it, but he wouldn't say it. "I know it sounds crazy, but yes, you had to pay for things that you got back then. We didn't have a fleet of cooks to bring us food, or cleaning crews to pick up after us, or anyone to hold our hands through life. We actually had to work and pay for all we received," Trevor said with a prideful wink to Ethan. Throwing that short jab made him feel better, regardless of how immature it might have been. Trevor had never been above being petty to prove a point.

"Hmmm I see, I see. But who would make children of the earth work to enjoy what the earth provides to all for free?" Ethan replied.

This made Trevor pause. Nothing was free; it all came at a cost to both the planet and those that were in charge. But in charge of what?

Trevor had sat through hundreds of morning enrichment classes, lectures, and general talks with Palace members and teachers, and he now understood that the ways of the world pre-sickness were wrong. But there was still that small part of him that also understood the premise of the free market, so he tried to explain in the most basic way to someone who hadn't experienced the Old World and how things worked back then.

It was frowned upon to talk about the rituals and ideals that destroyed the Old World. Trevor couldn't lie or omit truths. He thought that lowering his voice to give the information served as a good enough compromise.

"If we all could just take and take as we wanted with no rules or order, then the strong would lord over the weak. Currency or trade made it possible for a weaker man or woman to have the same things as those who were physically stronger. It helped to differentiate humans from animals," he said to Ethan, hoping this would suffice to feed the young man's curiosity.

Ethan's entire face lit up like Christmas on Times Square with an ah-hah look. His eyes got smaller as he tilted his head to the side a bit. "But isn't that exactly what happened, Mr. Cox? Didn't the top one percent of the population end up lording over the other ninety-nine percent?"

Trevor sat back on the bench, caught off guard. He looked up into the beautiful blue sky, leaving Ethan to wade in his river of success. To Ethan, making a legit point to the old guy about a world he himself had never seen was a great success. Part of that fact angered Trevor, and the other part made him think deeply on the subject.

He shrugged and thought to himself, *Kid has a point.* These Palace children were sharp. The world had indeed changed, and yet Trevor had not. In that moment, he felt prehistoric, being given a subtle lesson on logic by a child that had never left the confines of this hundred-yard radius in all his life.

"Well yeah, I guess you are right, Ethan. And that's how we ended up here," Trevor said, touching him on the head.

"Don't worry, Mr. Cox, we are going back out into the world soon, and we will take it back. Sirus has been saying that most of the sickness has passed." Ethan looked up at Trevor with a light of hope in his eyes that could light the darkest cave.

"Yeah, that's what they say, Ethan." He didn't mention the fact that they'd been saying that since the Palace had been created twenty years ago. "Any day now, I'm sure we'll be out." Trevor returned the hopeful smile to the Palace-born teenager. He didn't believe they'd be out any time soon, but he hoped for it just the same.

Ethan got up from his sitting position, dusted the dirt and stones from the back pockets of his blue jeans, and shook the hand of one of the oldest men in the Palace. He thanked Trevor for the talk then mentioned that he had a lecture coming up and relations exercise that evening. Trevor wished the young man a joyful day and watched him walk back inside the Palace.

For the next hour or so, Trevor sat there in the courtyard, surrounded by the beautiful shrubbery, flowers, hedges, and small ponds. He could hear the laughter of others in the area as he watched the kids running and jumping over the ponds, playing tag and ball games. He could even spot his still-beautiful wife, Amy, walking the trail with her friends. Some of her girlfriends were young, some as old as himself. She enjoyed walking out in the courtyard, and he still lived to see her smile.

The Palace—or the prison, as Trevor called it when he was alone with Amy in their pod—had all a man could want. Great weather, food, socializing, sex, learning, and safety. If you asked him though, he would still choose the Old World over this nonsensical fake stuff. Negativity ran rampant in the Old World, and that was okay to an extent, because it was real, it was genuine.

Trevor didn't feel things were genuine here; he never had. From the very beginning, it felt off somehow, but what was the alternative? He thought about how much things had changed—and how much things had stayed the same—as he went back to watching Amy.

CHAPTER NINE

Rachel

R ACHEL SAT ON THE WHITE COUCH inside of her very own pod and did what she did every morning before getting her day started. She woke up and had a chilled glass of orange juice. Every night before bed, she input the usual breakfast order into the nutrition dispensary so that it was ready when she awakened: a bran muffin, butter, and a sharp knife to spread the butter. She never had much of an appetite early in the morning, but Sirus and the teachers constantly said that breakfast was the most important meal of the day, so she never missed it.

Even at sixteen years old, she was a good listener and prided herself on taking direction. She would like nothing more than to reach the level of Greater Understanding and be released out into the world to help repair what had been broken for so long. She was committed to it —they all were.

Since the age of ten, she had occupied this pod alone, and the accreditations lining themselves up in her personal file were a sight to behold. Teacher Luke was always telling her that he wished more of the Palace-born were like her. He seemed to have taken a liking to her as of late. He was a really nice guy, and he often came and checked on her to make sure she was doing well. Sometimes he even checked her sheets to make sure they were properly fluffed. "You have a way of taking everything in stride, so even-keeled," she remembered him saying. He was utterly wrong, but she appreciated the sentiment. It made her smile, and Rachel took pride in her ability to stand out in a class of hopefuls. Since her days in the child center, she had been touted as a leader.

After finishing her bran muffin, she walked over to the nutrition dispensary and set the saucer on the silver tray along with her now empty glass and the remaining butter. "Waste not want not" was one of the major tenets of the Palace, and for good reason.

Standing in the center of the living area of her pod, she looked around happily. There was a lot to be appreciative of. Without the Order and all that they had put together in hopes of sustaining life, who knew where everyone would be today. They had teachers to help them prepare for the New World, cleaners that came to pick up after them, and the security squad that kept them safe.

Rachel clasped her hands together in front of her face and spoke Mother Earth's prayer in her mind: *Thank you for breathing life into every man, woman, child, and lifeform that you deemed fit to walk on your skin, drink of your bosom, and eat of your fruit. We are thankful, and we shall never take your gifts for granted, O Merciful Mother Earth. Amen.* No day was ready to be tackled without Mother Earth's prayer. Teacher Luke always said that.

Rachel knew the white color scheme of the pods symbolized the fact that they were a pure people, a renewal of humankind, free of all the filth, greed, and selfishness that had plagued the last generation and brought the sickness upon the earth. Dirt and grime showed easily on the white, and they had to be reminded of filth's presence when it is present. Both spiritually and physically. This small pod housed Rachel's entire life within it. This was home, the only home she had ever known.

In the Palace, there was no such thing as parent/child relationships, for no one person belonged to another. This concept wouldn't be foreign to any Palace-born person, but those from the Old World found it hard to deal with. The teachers taught that possession breeds selfishness, which in turn breeds vile thoughts and leads to rot of the soul. She agreed; you had to get those thoughts out of your body as soon as you felt them boiling deep inside of your being.

After growing up in the child center until age ten, they released her to a single pod, a process called level ascension, to begin common life in the Palace. This consisted of morning enrichments, activity time, lectures, and relations exercises (sex for its health and social benefits, which would not begin until one was biologically capable). But above all that, the most important point of focus for each Palace member was the internal war within to be the best person one could be.

The various Palaces were only meant to be temporary annoyances, but when you were dealing with the survival of the human race, you must make sure that every *i* was dotted and every *t* was crossed. The old people were becoming irritated with how slowly things were going, but better safe than sorry.

Rachel stepped into the bathroom outside of the eye in the television screen (there had been rumors about hidden cameras). All was not meant for the eyes of everyone, not even the teachers. The journey of greater understanding was mentally taxing, and all should be allowed the time to...*defuse* in the manner that they saw fit, so long as it didn't hurt others, the earth, or her natural resources.

She set the knife used to spread butter next to the sink and began to remove her clothes. She folded her white tee shirt and placed it just outside of the bathroom on the white carpet. She wriggled her small, lean body out of the white linen panties and laid those on top of the tee shirt. Now fully nude, she grabbed the knife and stepped into the shower.

She closed the glass sliding door behind her, then turned on the water. Steam began to fill the bathroom, and the water felt lovely against her skin. She would get a chance to clean her body afterwards. For now, there were more pressing matters to attend to if she was going to make it through this week. *Thank you, O Merciful Mother, for I am a child of your doing and of your will.*

Feeling the droplets of water raining down on her long brown hair, she closed her eyes and took it all in. The feeling was almost euphoric, the anticipation was always the best part. She wondered if anyone else in the Palace defused in this way. They had activities on the eighth floor to help relieve stress, but those never worked much for her.

Rachel raised her right arm to the ceiling of the bathroom, head still pointing down toward the shower floor. She didn't need to look up and watch the knife go about its work; she'd been doing this for the past two years and could do it in her sleep. Holding the knife in her left hand, she touched the blade to the soft, damaged skin just above her armpit, which had just begun to sprout hair a year ago. Rachel held the knife on her arm, feeling the blade dig into the skin but not cutting yet. The coolness of the metal felt good to her in comparison to the hot water.

Slowly, she began to slice vertically down her arm, just like she had once a week for the past year or so. Even though the hot water from the shower came beating down on portions of her body, she could still feel the warmth of blood running down her arm and onto her chest.

The weight of blood was different from water; it was heavier, more meaningful. The difference became noticeable to her. She never looked up to see it though, for this would be a vile deed, and she was not a bad person undeserving of Mother Earth's love. Even so, the sensation forced her mouth to curve into a smile. It felt orgasmic, and her eyes squeezed shut as she bit her bottom lip in ecstasy. Rachel's left hand dropped to her side, still clutching the knife, before the pleasure forced her to drop it. Her body weakened and slumped a bit.

She took in the feeling of what she would call defusing from the mental and moral Olympics that went hand in hand with training to be a soldier on the front lines of healing the earth. She was game for the battle to come; it would not be easy to fix what became broken out in the world, and it would take strength and resiliency. She prepared herself for the rigors of future responsibility by cutting herself, by releasing.

The water on the floor of the shower had become pink, with darker red loops and patterns swimming around within it. It looked like the loops and lines of red were chasing each other down the drain. This war would not be won with guns, bombs, or any kind of violence. That didn't work. That thought process got humankind in this mess to begin with. This war would be won with kindness, selflessness, and compassion.

I'll hurt myself before I hurt another, she thought as she picked up the knife and raised it a second time. Her right hand was still raised to the ceiling, fingers bent, dripping water from the shower. She carved another piece of her arm in the same area as the first cut, but considerably deeper this time. She wanted to touch her arm bone with the blade if she could.

The pain-pleasure dropped her to her knees. The fall would most likely bruise her knees, but right now that wasn't important. She collapsed like a baby deer learning to walk, legs splayed out in two different directions beneath the weight of her small body. She dropped the knife again and sat there, now opening her eyes to watch the blood go tumbling down into the drain. It was darker this time. The pink water turned to red water, and she could see all the stress that had left her body. *That's my confusion, that's my pain leaving my body; that's the weakness of my being leaving me.*

This act of defusing always left her feeling a tad lightheaded after a while—that was when she knew it was time to get on with the shower, dry off, and bandage the wounds. If she didn't take that cue from her body, she would surely kill herself from blood loss. She was mindful of that though, so she never went too far.

After dressing the wounds and putting on clothes for the day, she went back to the bathroom to retrieve the knife from the shower. She made sure all the blood and any evidence of this week's defusing session were gone from the sight of any teacher that would come into her pod to clean while she followed her daily schedule.

To be caught self-harming or having any sign of mental instability would be a cause for mental evaluation, and that would go in her personal file, which could set back her course toward the Greater Understanding Program. She would not have that.

All was well though. She returned the clean knife to the silver tray with the glass and saucer, and the shower beamed its white glow, as it had before she'd dirtied it with her defusing method. Rachel put on a jean skirt with a long-sleeve red shirt, tied her hair up into a ponytail, checked her face in the mirror, and flashed a big beautiful smile at herself. "Today is going to be a wonder-filled day." She grabbed her notebook and pen and walked out of the pod. All was perfect.

CHAPTER TEN

Sirus

"HOW ARE YOU DOING, MR. BENEFORD?" Sirus glared at the small balding man sitting on the opposite side of the massive oak desk. A small gold statue of Earth sat dead center in the middle of the desk. The office was dark, the only light coming from assorted candles all over the room. The curtains were drawn, giving the room almost a mournful atmosphere. A plethora of assorted papers and folders were scattered on Sirus's side of the desk, and the folder on top of that pile had Aiden Beneford's name on it.

"I'm doing fine, sir, thank you for asking. I'd like to say how truly honored I am that I get to speak with you." The man twiddled his fingers together. No one got to speak to Sirus. They knew him through feeds from the television screen in their pods at dinnertime, and that was it. Sirus noticed the anxiousness falling off the gentleman like sweat beads rolling down the forehead of someone sitting in a hot car on a summer afternoon. The man forced a weak smile, but Sirus saw the small quiver in his bottom lip.

"Are you nervous, Mr. Beneford? I assure you, there is no reason for that. I want you to be calm. It's really a pleasure to meet you." Sirus glanced across the desk with a warm smile, the kind a mother gives her child when he comes home with all As on his report card.

"No sir, not nervous at all. Maybe a little excited, yes. I've been told by Teacher Paul that you were considering me for the Greater Understanding Program. I've been working hard to realize this moment since we all arrived here, and frankly I'd like to hear more about that, if that's the truth of course. It's very likely that my excitement is getting the better of me, and that's coming across in my behavior. My apologies," he replied.

Sirus continued to smile but didn't speak. He held his stare for a few seconds, then got up from his seat and pushed the wooden chair with dark brown leather armrests into the desk. Letting the words drift in the room, he built the man's anticipation for his response. Sirus walked over to the window and opened a slit in the curtain. He stared out into the Palace courtyard, leaving Mr. Beneford to sit anxiously, awaiting the words to come.

"Well, Mr. Beneford, if Teacher Paul said that, then there has to be something to it. My men do not lie, that's not how things are run here." He stopped looking out the window and turned to the gentleman sitting at the desk. He stared into Beneford's eyes, making sure that his words were being taken seriously. He was establishing control of this dialogue, and he wanted to make sure that Beneford knew that. "Have you enjoyed your time in the Palace, Mr. Beneford?" Sirus asked in a friendly voice as he turned back to the window. "I'd imagine so, considering the alternative."

Mr. Beneford adjusted his sitting position in the chair. "Of course, you'll want to answer honestly," Sirus prodded. "We all know that absolute honesty is an important tenet of the Palace." He watched as Beneford glanced at the grandfather clock in the corner of the room. It was a big, beautiful clock that ticked loudly. One like they had back in the Old World, but even those were antiques back then. Many other things in Sirus's office were objects from the Old World. There was even a pack of baseball cards on the bookshelf.

"Hmm, for an older guy like myself, that's a tough question to answer, Mr. Sirus, sir. I did live in the world prior to the sickness, so while I do appreciate this beautiful place, I long for things to go back to the way they were. Without the negativity and destruction of the earth's resources...of course."

The man crossed his legs and sat up straighter in his chair. Sirus could tell by Beneford's expression that he believed he'd answered the question in a way that the teachers would expect.

"It's not a tough question, though. Either you have enjoyed the time you have spent in this facility, or you have not found it enjoyable. There would be nothing wrong with either answer. Of course, I'm asking because I care about how you and every other member of this Palace, and every Palace outside of this one, feels. I want to know how people are adjusting over the years." Sirus let a hand caress the oak-brown curtain as he spoke. "So please, spare me the long-winded explanation."

"Very understandable, Sirus. I did not mean to be vague," Mr. Beneford said, bowing his head forward slightly.

"It's important to the government to keep you all safe and happy while we are making things safe and stable for our return to living on the outside. But when it happens, it will be a New World, with upgrades to our thinking and society building. I won't bore you with that though. You have been studying for the last twenty years, so I'm sure you could teach me a thing or two on the ideology changes of our species."

Sirus turned and looked at Mr. Beneford with that same smile, the calming smile, as he glided back over to the desk. Sirus knew that everything he did screamed of flare—it was part of what made him so charismatic, part of why the Order had appointed him the program director of the Palace.

He was a good-looking man by any standards. He had short brown hair interspersed with grays, the color of burnt umber and ash. There was also a touch of gray in the middle of his trim beard, and he wore a nice pair of reading glasses, which had no chance of concealing his light-blue eyes, almost the color of freezing ice. Sirus quickly learned that his six-foot-four frame could be intimidating in the Palace, even with his slender build. But he had a nice physique for a man of his age. Even being on the greater end of sixty years old, he had quite the fan club...especially among the female Palace members.

"Well I would s—"

Sirus cut him off mid-sentence. "Do you know why you have been in this place since the...the events that took place so long ago? I mean, do you really know? You take me as a man of relative intelligence. If you don't mind me saying, I've read over your file."

"I know what we were told and have been told since we arrived." Mr. Beneford looked puzzled by the question.

Sirus placed a strong hand on the gentleman's shoulder and gave him a grin that begged to let him explain a bit more. He sat on the edge of Mr. Beneford's side of the desk and paused to choose his words carefully.

"Allow me to give a bit more clarity, sir. I've been the liaison between the people and the few in government who still control what's left of the earth. Believe me when I tell you that there are very few government officials still among the living. We are all truly lucky to still be alive, Mr. Beneford. Do you understand?

"There was no precedent set for such a pandemic outside of those from before the twenty-first century. You know the culprits, the Black Death of 1347, American plagues brought into this very country from Europe—we could even go back to the Antonine Plague of 165 AD, which boiled down to nothing more than a plague of smallpox and measles." Sirus stopped abruptly to think, then he let out a bit of a chuckle.

Mr. Beneford watched Sirus with a befuddled look, seemingly caught off guard by the laughter.

"Forgive me, sir, I do not laugh out of cruelty. Please don't take it the wrong way. I'm terribly sorry. I get inveterately tickled by that last bit in my soliloquy." Sirus touched the man's knee in a joking way that said, *Lighten up, buddy*.

Mr. Beneford just gave a confused smile and shook his head. "Of course not, sir."

Sirus, now quiet, continued to study him with his chilling blue eyes. "Good...good." He went on. "I'm sorry, I laugh at the pure foolishness of these plagues in relation to where we are today as far as sidestepping them with the ease of avoiding a parked car on a brisk walk. All three devastations I named, and many others that wreaked havoc on this earth, are all curable by antibiotics or some other simple method today, but all the same, millions, maybe even billions of souls, have perished due to these types of things over human history.

"Now how is that? I'll tell you. Even a simple thing can become a troublesome thing if you don't know how to combat the scenario." Sirus winked at Mr. Beneford and lightly tapped his shoulder with his fist in a pounding motion.

"To the credit of this country and few others, there were brilliant scientists and government officials who foresaw something of this nature coming and planned accordingly. Again, I won't bother explaining the science of it all, it's not as exciting as it may sound, but we did anticipate something happening. Long story short, plans were made in the years leading up to the sickness. There were FEMA camps set up, underground places to live, things like that. Most of which never came into play because of the sheer death toll. This illness went off like an atom bomb all over the planet."

Sirus put his hands together and moved them away from each other, making the gesture of a bomb blowing up. He mouthed the word *BOOM* and looked up at the ceiling of the office, as if following the blast radius. Mr. Beneford's eyes followed. Sirus then placed his hands into his lap and returned his gaze back to Mr. Beneford.

"Herbert Hoover once said, 'Older men declare war. But it is youth that must fight and die.' The mistakes of those from the past cost the new generation their lives, their homes, their planet. It's all so ridiculous, sometimes all you can do is laugh. Wouldn't you agree?"

Mr. Beneford visibly relaxed his posture. Sirus could tell the poor guy was putting a real effort into trying not to look scared. "Yes, yes, I would agree that it's all very ironic. You make a great point, sir."

Sirus got up from his makeshift seat on the edge of the desk and began to walk circles around Mr. Beneford at a slow pace while continuing his dialogue. He truly enjoyed hearing himself speak. He could do this all day. Crowd or not.

"You see, there were very few of the world's leaders still among the living, which called for the members still in existence to band together for the sake of the survival of all mankind. You would be surprised to see how fast nations that once hated each other come together for the sake of survival. This is important, wouldn't you agree, sir?" Sirus broke out of his rant to reconnect eye contact, regarding Beneford with a soft, empathetic look. Then he continued to move around the desk again.

"Yes, Sirus, it's of the utmost importance that life is able to continue." Mr. Beneford's eyes followed Sirus and his constant circles around the office, as though he were the predator circling its prey, which was of course Sirus's intention.

"Good...good. But I ask you, when you say life is able to continue, what do you regard as life, sir?" He again stopped pacing at the opposite end of the desk, behind his own seat, and placed his arms across his chest. Sirus looked deeply at Mr. Beneford, the way a child looks at something he doesn't quite understand.

"Well, human life, and all life on Planet Earth."

Sirus nodded his head in agreement and uncrossed his arms. He placed his hands in the pockets of his black dress pants and continued his circles once more.

"The hierarchy in which you gave your answer is important. You are still placing humankind outside of the other lifeforms on this planet. While we are different, mostly based on how our brains function, we are not to place ourselves ahead of or beneath any other form of life here. For we are all one.

"But we have become a cancer here, and Earth is similar to any functioning living form of life in the way that the planet will try to fight off whatever is killing her, same as your body would do if you began to develop a tumor. Do you follow?"

"I do follow you, Sirus. I must admit that I'm now wondering why you are telling me this. Have I offended or done something wrong?" Mr. Beneford looked at Sirus with confusion painted all over his face.

"Please allow me to finish my thought," Sirus said gently while raising a hand. "We have always fancied ourselves the origin and reason for the existence of all other things, and that's just not the case. We must all come together and function as one entity. This is what we have been trying to teach everyone in every Palace, in every forgotten country and corner of the world. If we want to get back to living on the outside and living in peace with all of life on this planet, we must change the way we see things. We must retrain our thought processes."

Sirus conjured his winning smile and sat back down in his seat on his respective side of the imposing desk.

"I understand. I misspoke, sir."

"Did you? In most cases we say exactly what we mean the first time. Your subconscious will betray you every time, Mr. Beneford," Sirus replied, almost in a whisper.

"Yes, I misspoke. I've been taught better, and my haste to answer your question got the bet—"

"I ask because it's been brought to my attention that you have been talking about some of the old ways of thinking and behaving," Sirus said matter-of-factly, smiling even bigger than he had been. "You have been in the Palace since its inception, so I don't need to explain to you why that's not a good idea."

Mr. Beneford looked away nervously.

"I've been told that you were speaking about night clubs. A mention of strippers and cocaine? We don't talk like that here. Those things have no reason to even be mentioned in the Palace. It's filth, sir...you know that."

"Oh no, sir, I may have spoken to a few of the older folks in the courtyard—very innocent in nature, I promise. Ya know, just reminiscing about the old days. I'm the first to say that I appreciate everything about the Palace and all the new teachings. I've studied all the new literature for twenty years, taking part in every morning enrichment, new and old. I apologize if Teacher Paul regarded my words as troublesome. That's who the report came from, correct? I did not mean for my words to come off that way, I swear it." Mr. Beneford's voice cracked, and tears began welling up in his eyes.

"Calm yourself. It's not important who the report came from. We hear all and see all. While you may have been speaking to people from the outside like yourself, you do understand there are Palace-born humans everywhere, and they could hear you...and maybe someone did." Sirus paused for effect, the smile on his face fading.

"I do not mean to verbally discipline you. That is not my job here —all discipline is carried out by authorized security. Nor is this a meeting about discipline or even a bad mark on your file. I'm just making sure that everything is working out for you, making sure that your time here is favorable to yourself and everyone who encounters you. You know what they say about one bad apple."

Sirus flashed from his cold stare back to the smile like a flip book. That fast.

"You are not that bad apple though. We know this and wanted to express how important it is to have members from the Old World in the Palaces. You have a wealth of knowledge for the Palace-born humans to call upon, and that's to be respected and cultivated. You have been a model member of this Palace, and that matters to everyone."

Sirus grabbed Beneford's folder. "Your informational studies and contributions to the Palace are documented, and there are no negative marks on your record. Very impressive for a twenty-year span, sir. If there's a man qualified for the Greater Understanding Program, it would be you, Mr. Beneford. And we would like to offer this to you today." Sirus stood and walked around the desk to shake Mr. Beneford's hand.

The man before Sirus looked confused, anxious, excited, and terrified all at once. "Oh my, oh shit. Excuse my language, I'm sorry. I'm just so happy. Thank you so much!" He began to bounce up and down in his seat like a child who was just told he gets to go to the fair with his big brothers. Tears fell down his cheeks, and he wiped them with the sleeve of his shirt.

"Thank you so much, Sirus. I've been doing my best, trying to help everyone as much as I possibly can, and it's paid off. I can't thank you and the Order enough. When do I get to leave? Where am I gonna be stationed at? Oh my God, so many questions, I'm sorry."

Sirus could read the man at a glance. Being accepted into the Greater Understanding Program for someone who's been there for twenty years was like being told you get a new chance at life. You died an ugly death, and boom, you get a second shot at it all.

"No need to thank me, sir, you earned this. In this Palace, in every Palace, we keep our word about the Greater Understanding Program. You fit the criteria, and we could use a man like you out in the world, helping to make the environment safe for everyone again. Just make sure you keep that dirty talk to yourself in the future."

Sirus pointed at him jokingly. "You have completed all the training, you have made leaps and bounds with your mental assessments, and you have helped the Palace Program in ways that you couldn't understand."

Sirus motioned for Mr. Beneford to stand up before giving the man a hug. Sirus patted his back, then took a step back to look him over. "You have done well, my friend, and fortunately you will be leaving in the next few minutes. A teacher is waiting outside of this office with a protective suit and your belongings from you pod. The protective suit is engineered to protect you from getting sick upon leaving the quarantine area, so he will help you get acclimated to it before you leave."

Sirus leered at Mr. Beneford sadly. "You will be given your instruction en route to your post. As you've been taught before now, we can't have you go back through the Palace. Obviously this isn't something that happens often here, and we've found that it can upset others to the point that they become severely depressed or even envious. Such an emotional imbalance can interfere with other members' focus on their own personal goals. As you are well aware, upsetting the balance in such a way does far more harm than good."

Mr. Beneford nodded furiously. His eyes were dreamy and far away. It was obvious that not saying goodbye didn't faze him one bit—his yearning for the Greater Understanding was that immense.

"The others will be alerted of your ascension to the Greater Understanding Program, and you will be used as a benchmark of what can happen when you devote yourself to the Palace Program. Thank you, Mr. Beneford. I will show you to the door, and to the man who will take you through security for departure."

Sirus walked the giddy gentleman of sixty-one years of age to the office door and opened it with one hand. Mr. Beneford, who couldn't stop smiling, still clutched Sirus's other hand.

"Again, sir, thank you for your service to this Palace. I know you will do wonderful things in the Greater Understanding Program. I've forwarded your name to some of the leaders there, and they will be looking out for you when you arrive. You deserve everything that's coming to you."

"Thank you, sir. Thank you so much." Mr. Beneford rushed to the exit, more than ready to leave the Palace forever. He could be heard still crying and talking as he walked the corridor with Teacher Simon.

Sirus closed the office door on the nineteenth floor of the Palace, located somewhere in old Indiana, in a country formerly known as the United States of America. He walked over to the desk, gave the golden globe a spin, and sat down in his seat. He was about to have dinner with every member of every Palace via live stream. This was a tradition within the Palace; the final meal of the day was not served without the words from Sirus. Traditions should be followed, and followed strictly, so that good habits would not devolve into unpleasant habits. Unhealthy habits brought terrible outcomes.

CHAPTER ELEVEN

Jacob

TEACHER PAUL WAS PRESENTING THE LECTURE for today's morning enrichment. He was a small, gaunt, balding man, and looked every year of his late forties. Unlike Jacob, who, at close to the same age had a full head of hair and a strong, fit body, Teacher Paul appeared sickly-looking in comparison. Deep lines sculpted his face, and his eyes seemed to be sinking into their sockets.

There wasn't a bit of facial hair on Teacher Paul's withered face. In all the time that he had been at the Palace, he had never even had the growing stages of a beard or mustache. Despite his haggard looks and slumped posture, he was one of the kindest people you would ever meet. He was always willing to help with anything, and he was very patient with the sometimes clueless Palace people. Teacher Paul also conducted the mental evaluations when anyone would have a mental slip or a lapse in judgement.

Jacob always attributed the teacher's gift of calming to his voice. So smooth and gentle. In the early days of the Palace, Jacob had quite a few "mental evaluations." Most of the people from the outside world did in the beginning.

Today's enrichment class covered the topic of "Love and Loss," as understood by the old ways of thinking about relationships and the loss of those relationships. Not one of Jacob's favorite topics to tackle. Despite all the years that had passed and all the hours of counseling, he still had not found a way to heal from the trauma of his past, and he had accepted that he never would. Sometimes it was best to not revisit such things.

Out of sight, out of mind, right? Waiting for the morning enrichment hall to fill up, Jacob spun a black ballpoint pen in his right hand and tapped his foot to an old beat that he had always loved. He couldn't quite remember the name of the song. "Bling," or something like that? By that musician guy, Drake? Every year he forgot more and more from the Old World.

Trevor walked into the room and headed for the seat next to Jacob. Since coming to the Palace on day one of the evacuation, Jacob and Trevor had been close. They had both been one inch from insanity, sitting in that van coming from the US Bank Arena. Trevor had been raving about his kids, family members, his wife, and how the government had perpetrated it all. They had to hold him down to ensure everyone's safety in the white van.

That was long ago though. It felt like a different lifetime. Funny how time worked in that way, turning your real-life episodes into dream-like scenarios that you could hardly materialize into actual memories after a point. Then again, there were those memories that sat right on the surface of Jacob's psyche, rising up every day regardless of how long ago the experience happened. That Monday in October all those years ago remained that way for him. For everyone here from the outside. They all had that metaphorical patch emblazoned on their jackets. Sure, they could learn coping mechanisms; they could try to fill the holes with sex, socializing, food, fun, and knowledge. Some holes had no bottom though, no matter how you tried to fill it.

When his mother allowed him to stay home from school, they would always watch the *Dr. Phil* show together. The TV therapist would say something to that extent. "No matter what you put inside of that hole, you will never be able to fill it. This ain't my first rodeo..." Or something like that.

"Hey there, playboy." Trevor patted him on the shoulder as he took his seat next to Jacob. The older man relaxed, sticking his right hand in his back pocket. Trevor had always done that. He'd been like that since they got there. Jacob never bothered to ask him why though. Maybe he just didn't know what to do with his hands.

"Hello, Gramps. You feeling alright this morning, or we needing to grab your cane so you can make it back to your pod after morning enrichment?"

Trevor let out a huge bellow of laughter and slapped Jacob on the back, maybe a bit harder than necessary. "Funny guy over here. You ready to get your brain scrambled a bit for breakfast?" Trevor said under his breath.

It was an inside joke between the friends about morning enrichment classes. Trevor liked to call it indoctrination. Jacob wouldn't go that far, but he thought everyone was a bit brainwashed to some extent. It really depended on the message. The teachings weren't religious in nature or anything like that.

The Order had outlawed religion. The teachers sent from the government taught that religious institutions were a huge part of where things went wrong in the Old World. It had always been a crutch of mankind to create deities that were empathetic to them. Having a scapegoat to justify killing and thievery didn't hurt either.

The morning enrichment (also known as ME) lessons were discussions about healthier ways of thinking and reconciling emotions in a beneficial way. Trevor always called it "egghead bullshit." He had a way with words. Those who had a propensity to fly off at the mouth about the teachings and lectures would be seen as volatile and in need of mental evaluations. Which would then lead to negative marks on their files, and that would ultimately make it harder to get into the Greater Understanding Program. Such behavior could even result in banishment from the Palace, and everyone knew what that meant.

Jacob had everything he could want or need here, and somehow, he still found himself unhappy more than he would like to admit. Trevor had expressed the exact same feeling. Lots of depression, but because you get your head tampered with if you say too much, most never do.

He'd seen depressive behavior in some of the other Palace people. Like his friend and usual relations partner, Mary. A girl of about twenty years old, beautiful face, high cheekbones, and long black hair that reached down to her bottom, she would have been modeling in some-one's magazine in the Old World. But that world was gone, so instead she spent her days learning to try to be a perfect person, talking his ear off about the Old World, and having the occasional sexual encounter with Jacob or any other male that suited her fancy. Mostly Jacob though; they broke the rules together in that regard quite a bit. Relations exercises were only once a week with an appointed partner, and anything outside of that would be considered sex for the sake of sex. This was not allowed.

The sex act itself had been flipped on its head in the Palace. Sex was no longer what it was before for Jacob: something that involved passion, sometimes love, and excitement (if he was lucky). Relations exercises served the purpose of either reproduction or health benefits. He thought there was more between him and Mary though, and he didn't know how to feel about that. Jacob hadn't felt anything for any woman since Leanne. It was complicated for him because that rela-tionship seemed to be in limbo. He had never found out for sure that she had died, and the possibility that she was in some other Palace somewhere always floated in the dark recesses of his mind no matter how much he tried to convince himself that she was gone. Palace members could only be in contact with members from their own Palace. There were no phones or internet access to communicate with anyone on the outside.

"Apostle Paul gonna get started here soon, or can we go back to our pods?" Trevor whispered to Jacob with a short elbow stab to his ribs and a smirk.

Jacob leaned in closer. "Better keep it down before someone hears you. Lots of ears around in here." He looked straight ahead as Teacher Paul entered the room, wearing his carefully ironed black suit complete with dark blue tie and shiny black dress shoes. This attire served as the uniform for all the teachers. There were no female teachers in the Palace, but there were females in high positions and in the child center. Even in the security squad.

"I don't give a shit," Trevor whispered as he sat back in his seat.

Jacob almost laughed out loud, He choked back the giggles and kept his focus on the front of the room.

"Hello family," Teacher Paul began. "I'm giving thanks to Mother Earth today for allowing us the chance to be here with one another in this moment, for every moment is precious and nothing is promised. It's great to see you all, and I'm very excited for today's topic. Is anyone else excited?" Teacher Paul ran his small bony hand through the few scraggly strands of graying hair on his head and stared out into the room.

Forty pairs of eyes sat in white chairs facing him. Each Palace member came with a notepad and pen in hand to take notes on the lecture. The entire room was white, from the walls to the white marble flooring. It was the trademark décor in all the ME session rooms. Long beams of light on the ceiling illuminated the room, making it brighter than necessary.

"We are," the entire room responded, like a choir singing about the good Lord. Always "we are," because there was no longer an "I" from the collective.

"Good, good. I like to hear that." Teacher Paul came from behind the desk and stood in front of the class. He stared at every single person in the session, not saying a word, just looking at everyone for what seemed to be a minute or so. Jacob could see the cogs turning in his head.

"If I were to ask you, 'Why do you become angry or sorrowful when someone that you care for passes away,' what would you say?" He began to walk up the center aisle between the seats. Everyone stared at him, following his movements and voice.

"You would probably say that you were sad to lose that person, or that they were too good to be gone so soon, right? In the Old World, people praised different gods. Theoretically, these gods would be waiting for you upon your death, and you would live with them in happiness, doing whatever it is that humans do with gods after moving on to the afterlife, right?"

Teacher Paul reached the back of the classroom and turned to head back down the aisle. He had a way of making the rhythm of his words match the rhythm of his movements. The type of man who knew when he had an audience paying attention to his every word.

"Now, if we really believed what we say we did as far as the afterlife, back in the Old World that is, why would we be so guilt-ridden and overcome with pain when those we loved died? According to the old teachings, we should be excited for them, elated even. Sure, our best friend may have just smashed in his cranium while driving drunk, but that's okay, because now he gets to be in the afterlife with insert idol god's name, right?"

Jacob wiped a tear from his eye, hoping that no one saw him, and went back to jotting on his notepad.

Why are you crying, you big idiot? He didn't know why he was shedding tears about shit that happened so long ago. He should have been over it by now. He wasn't though, that was clear. He was a forty-year-old grown man and still hadn't dealt with the loss of his parents and everyone else in his life. Leanne in particular was a soft spot. Thinking of her made him ashamed of what he did. Or better yet, didn't do.

He never got the chance to go see her after finding out she was sick. She had probably died alone while he sat in the hallway of his parents' home, blubbering like a child. She deserved better than that; she deserved better than him.

"You see, we never got excited about the untimely deaths of our loved ones because somewhere in a dark corner of our hearts we all knew they weren't in heaven...or hell for that matter. They were just gone, no longer around, and this was enough of a reason to cry and mourn. That person becomes a memory, and then at some point even that goes away, and they become forgotten. And that's what we fear, becoming like that person, a memory...forgotten."

Teacher Paul sat down in his seat and opened the floor up for discussion. The session was lively, with many different speakers giving their two cents and probing teacher Paul for more gems on the topic. Jacob didn't take part. For the remainder of the time he jotted down things here and there, but he was still thinking about Leanne and the day his life changed forever. These morning enrichments were meant to bring old memories and mind-sets boiling back up to the top of your brain, forcing you to deal with them. He could deal with most of the lessons in the Palace, but having to think back to what he lost and would never get back was too much.

He and Trevor were alike in that way. Jacob didn't hear him

speaking either. When he turned to look at his friend, he was staring down at his desk. Trevor had been like that for the majority of the session. It hurt Jacob to see the man like that, but somewhere inside, they all were "like that." The important question now was: How deep could you bury those feelings?

CHAPTER TWELVE

Mary

H IS FINGERS GRAZED HER SOFT LIPS, feeling for the wet center of her mouth as he slammed his penis deep inside of her repeatedly. Mary loved when he put two fingers into her mouth during their relations exercises, which felt more like "sex" to her, as they called it in the Old World. She liked that though; it was like night and day when compared to what she had experienced with other men.

Oh my God, I think I love him...does he know?

She felt his fingers curl over her bottom row of teeth, giving her something to occupy her attention to keep from crying out too loudly. Mary laid on her back, looking up at Jacob, meeting his thrusts. She saw the intensity in his eyes as his heavy panting quickened, and he gave her all she could handle and more. He had both of her legs wrapped around his body, one hand supporting himself on the bed, the other pacifying her moans.

"You like that, don't you?" he said in a winded voice. Mary was not used to men speaking during relations exercises. There was nothing to speak about, only the job of procreation and the benefit of physical exercise in a social setting. It felt more like a duty to her. This though? No, this felt like so much more. It felt like everything.

This position would be their fourth or fifth of the night, she didn't know. She couldn't remember. It all felt like a whirlwind of powerful orgasms, excitement, and being lost in passion so deeply that nothing else mattered in that moment.

The Palace, the teachers, the tenants...her very own moral compass could piss off.

"Yes, yes...Oh yes!" she mumbled as she attempted to answer him from around his fingers creeping over her tongue. Mary could feel him deep, forcefully pulling her into yet another moment of climax as she bit down on those fingers of his.

Jacob never missed a beat, the rhythm of their coupling never breaking stride. Mary could see the fierceness in his eyes intensify and a smile creep over his lips. He loved bringing her to the precipice of an orgasm and watching it play out over her face. The way her eyes shot open, the way she bit down on her lip (or his fingers), and the tremors from her body as she shook and jerked involuntarily. Mary knew he loved all of it, because he had told her as much in bed only days before.

He took both his hands and grabbed both her wrists, lowering himself down to her level, their chests touching, his face on the side of hers. She could feel his breathing calm, almost as if he were holding his breath. She knew he was trying to contain himself and not be too loud as he came finished inside of her. Such was the custom of "sex" or a proper relations exercise.

He removed himself and rolled off her body, and onto his side, and she could feel his seed spill out of her vagina, trickling down onto the bed between her legs. Mary turned onto her side, facing him. His eyes were already closed. She smiled.

She intertwined her legs with Jacob's and felt the hard course hairs of his beard brushing over the soft delicate skin of her forehead. Mary accepted that she was the happiest in these moments. It was wrong though. She should just carry out the act of sex and move on with her day, not get swept up in the act itself and the moments of peace after.

This was a physical relations exercise and nothing more. But telling herself that was a lie when she was with Jacob. It felt different with him. Wrapped in his arms, Mary could feel her heart catch the same rhythm as his, beating in sync with his. The teaching said: "We are all individuals, but we come together to become whole." That was meant within the parameters of humanity, not man and woman individually.

Man gave the woman a child, and the woman bore that child into the world. These were the basics of the man-woman sexual relationship. Somehow in the Old World, things got misconstrued and people came to believe that they owned each other. That was wrong, clearly. Everyone knows what happened twenty years ago. Still...when she was encapsulated in Jacob's arms, she did not feel like just an individual—she felt something more.

Mary took in air through her nose, smelling him, so close. This was her favorite part. The smell that he gave off—it was different from all the others. Mary knew that in the world before the sickness, a woman was not considered old enough for a "proper" sexual relationship until she was eighteen years old. It was never explained what made that age the age of responsibility.

Here in the Palace, you could begin sexual exercises the second you were physically ready to reproduce. This age was different for everyone, but being ready was based on your body, not your mind. At age ten, Palace members were considered old enough and mature enough to make the same decisions as everyone else.

As a child in the Palace, Mary's first memories were that of the child center and her peers. Sure, there were watchers there to make sure everyone had food and drink, had clothes to wear, and got through the day safely, but there was very little coddling from the teachers. Children could interact with each other and learn in that way to gain independence. The idea was that it would teach the children to be self-sufficient and work together to reach common goals. This foundation would hopefully carry over to adulthood.

She could feel Jacob's breath all over her. His body suddenly jerked, but he didn't wake. It was a hypnic jerk, something that happened right before you fell into a deep sleep. Raising her head up to kiss his lips, she helped him relax again so that he might sleep peacefully. He was beautiful to her.

She's stayed in his pod much longer than she should have. She never did this with any of the other men. And even though there were others, Jacob was her favorite. He was different—in so many ways that she could not even begin to understand. This strong feeling that she kept hidden deep inside felt so foreign to her, but at the same time, it felt like home. Maybe because he was not a Palace-born human like all the others she'd had relations with. The desire to be around him all the time was so strong that sometimes she couldn't help but to cry about it when she lay in bed alone in her own pod. She'd never told him that though.

Mary freed one of her arms and placed a hand on the side of his face, caressing his jawline and bringing her fingers though his beard as she stared up at his face. She loved that.

With the other men, she didn't feel a closeness. There was no attachment. It was "Wham bam, thank you ma'am," and she was back to the next thing on her daily agenda. With Jacob, it was something more. Something she couldn't quite put words to. The way he moved, touched her, and looked into her eyes during relations drove her absolutely insane. It left her mind and body whirling out of control like a ribbon swept up in a tornado.

"I really should go back to my own pod now," she said softly, but she didn't move. While she loved the time she got with Jacob, she would often leave totally confused and questioning all that she'd been taught. That was dangerous, because everything here was based on buying into the tenets. The goal was to get into the Greater Understanding Program—to get back out into the world and help with repairing the damage that was created by the sickness. There was so much cleaning, repurposing the earth, and repairing damage to be done that things would not be ready for a full transition from Palace to outside living for another twenty or thirty years. This information was shared with her from Teacher Paul, and she was told not to share it with anyone. Especially the people from the Old World.

The sooner she could get out there to help, the better. This had been her life's goal since she could remember. At only twenty years old, she was as wise and mature as a forty-year-old from the Old World. That wasn't saying much though, considering.

All she could ever think about was getting out in the world to help repair things...until she met Jacob. Then she got the chance to pick his brain about the earth and the people of the Old World. Her desires and values became compromised.

I wonder if he knows how I feel about him when we are together? She considered the idea as she kissed his chest. Of course, he couldn't know. To him, she was a simple Palace girl with stupid questions about the past and someone to have weekly relations exercises with. He was so into their moments together because that's the way they did things in the Old World, not because he felt anything for her.

Mary wriggled free from his slumbering embrace and sat on the edge of the bed as Jacob rolled on his side and continued to sleep.

She sat there, completely naked, her legs as white as milk and her hair as dark as night. She felt a wetness trickling down her inner thigh. Looking down, she noticed more of Jacob's seed exiting her body. Mary wondered: Could this be child number three? That would be amazing. She knew that having children gave her so much more worth in the Palace. Mary had no idea who had fathered the first two, because relations partners could change on a weekly basis. For the most part, you could choose who you wanted to be with for this activity, but if impregnation didn't happen after a designated amount of time, you could be "recommended" to continue relations with someone else.

Of course, once a woman was with child, she would go through the entire child-bearing process on her own. At that point, the male's portion of the process was complete, and the rest was up to the woman. When the child was ready to be delivered, the woman was taken to the infirmary for the procedure. As soon as the child was born, the nurses took the newborn straight to the child center, no stops in between.

Then the job was over, and there were a few months of physical and mental recovery. And just like that, relations exercises started again. While she always had complications getting pregnant, Mary's friend Joline had already given birth to five children, and she was only nineteen.

Something about the whole procreation ordeal seemed off to Mary, but she could never understand why. She knew that she wanted to see her children again. And while she did not own them, she had created them. It mattered to her.

After getting dressed, Mary walked over to Jacob's side of the bed and kissed him on the cheek. She had no idea why she did that. But it felt good, it felt right, and sometimes that was enough of a reason.

CHAPTER THIRTEEN

Trevor

"I KNOW THAT THOSE PARTICULAR MORNING enrichment sessions are hard on you, honey," Trevor said. "Once we get some dinner in us, I'll rub your legs in bed. We can talk about it. I know you enjoy that." He walked over and grabbed a silver tray, which held a plate of food and a drink. He balanced the tray like one of those bears riding a unicycle, but he managed to clumsily make his way to the white couch and coffee table. He set the tray of food down.

"Thank you, dear."

"You don't need to thank me for anything. I love you." Trevor smiled in Amy's direction.

"I just...I just see it all the time. With all the years that have passed, wouldn't you think that I would have healed by now? Sometimes I think that I have, then at other times I'm right back in those rooms. Watching them...you know?" Amy sat down on the couch, wiping a tear from her eye. She hadn't ordered food that evening. Trevor didn't approve of her not eating, but some days were bad days, and the stress of certain topics in morning enrichment would make her lose her appetite.

"Don't get yourself all upset again, Amy. It's hard, I know. The teachers have said that you are making progress in that area though.

Hell, when we first got here, you wouldn't even admit they were gone."
Trevor sat down next to his wife and placed a napkin over his lap. For a
while, no one said anything. They waited.

"Do you ever wonder why, Trevor?"

Trevor didn't look at her. He stared at the TV screen in front of
them. It still read, "Please Wait."

"Do I ever wonder about what, Amy?" But he knew what.

"Why wasn't it us?" Amy looked him in the eye as a tear fell
from hers.

Trevor didn't respond right away. Amy had been fragile since that
day. She was liable to fall off the mental wagon if he didn't pick his
words carefully when speaking about their two children.

Amy had come into the Palace weak and unable to walk on her
own. She couldn't think clearly or put together coherent sentences.
The amount of pain she suffered that day was far too much for her to
take. It was a miracle that she was even a shadow of her former self
today. He thought that he had lost her totally. To hell with the Palace
and everything else if he didn't have her.

There were still times when he could hear Amy mumbling the
names of their children in her sleep. She'd even mimic the motion of
wiping their faces while she dreamed. Scared the hell out of Trevor, but
he would just hold her tighter. Amy taking the death of their children
so hard created a situation in which he didn't get to properly
mourn them.

He needed to be there for her and make sure that she could go on.
Trevor's time in the service in some ways prepared him for dealing
with loss. Numerous friends had died in the war in Iraq. At first it was
hard to deal with, but after a while, it all just began to mesh together,
as harsh as that sounded. The same thing had happened with his children. That was hard to admit, but it was true.

Trevor didn't get the chance to mourn them, and when he noticed
this, he really didn't care to. That fact still made him uneasy; he hoped
that it was just a result of the things that he went through at war and
not a part of his personality. *What kind of man forgets about his children?*
he thought to himself.

Finally, Trevor said, "Maybe it was us." Amy turned to look at him in confusion, but she didn't speak. "Who's better off between the living and the dead?" he continued. Trevor began smoothing out the napkin on his lap while speaking in a low tone.

"They are done with this life. The kids moved on with most of the rest of the world, meanwhile you and I are still straggling behind in this stupid building that we haven't left in over twenty years. I'd say we got the short end of the stick. Try to change your perspective on what happened, Amy. That's all I'm asking," he said as he rubbed her leg.

Trevor turned to look at her, and their eyes met. She leaned in to give him a kiss and palmed the back of his head, just like their first kiss so long ago, back when they were just children with no children of their own. He'd been a young man in the service, and she'd been a young, beautiful stranger working at a retail shop in his town. Since the day he came walking into her store and laid eyes on her, she'd been the only woman for him.

The television screen flashed abruptly with the sound of a familiar voice. There was Sirus, sitting in his office at a big wooden desk, the golden globe of the planet right there in the middle. There was a plate of food in front of him. Looked like chicken, broccoli, and something else Trevor couldn't quite make out. A red drink of some sort was on the right side of his food, and the utensils next to that. The office was dark, the only light illuminating Sirus's face and the desk created by candlelight. The glow cast a dark shadow over his face.

"Hello everyone. We are lucky to have another day with each other to live, love, and prosper. Let us begin with the sacred words, for we are fortunate to be among the few who were chosen to start the world anew. The crimes of man have made it so that we are the chosen to right the world, and that's not to be taken lightly, my family."

Sirus flashed that big but unsettling smile into every Palace pod in every corner of the world. He was being broadcasted to millions, or maybe thousands; no one knew for sure.

Sirus lowered his head and closed his eyes. Trevor and Amy, along with every other soul watching the broadcast, followed his lead. "Thank you for breathing life into every man, woman, child, and life-form that you have deemed fit to walk on your skin, drink of your bosom, and eat of your fruit. We are thankful, and we shall never take your gifts for granted, O Merciful Mother Earth. Amen."

He lifted his head. Now that the words had been said, it was time for the meal to commence. "There is good news to share with everyone before we sup. Mr. Beneford has ascended to the next level and has joined the Greater Understanding Program. With the same work ethic and devotion to the new ways, you too could be promoted to this ascension. Hooray for him, and let that be a testament to how following the process gets you to where you want to be, and that's back out into the world."

Trevor and Amy exchanged a heavy look, but they didn't discuss the news further. It was another difficult topic for them to tackle another day.

Sirus picked up his utensils, placed a napkin over his lap, and began to eat. This signaled to everyone watching that it is now okay to begin dining. Order would be important in the New World; proper traditions would see to that.

CHAPTER FOURTEEN

Dwight

H<small>E COULD REMEMBER IT LIKE IT</small> was yesterday. That Monday morning, Dwight had gone running to his parents' room with the hope of getting some breakfast. They slept in late most mornings because neither of them had jobs. They would stay up all night, playing cards and drinking with another couple across the grass. Their home was in a trailer park in Indiana, and the trailer was owned by his grandmother, who let them live in it after she had moved to Florida with her sister.

Dwight's mother was always using drugs and drinking; even a child could see that. When you were young though, it was neither here nor there as far as your parents' mental or physical ailments. "Where's the food, where's the fun?" At his core, that was all Dwight was really concerned about as a child. He assumed this was why children had to constantly be told not to walk away with strangers, even if they came waving candy from the big white van.

Dwight's father would go out sometimes to do odd jobs with his brothers. Dwight was sure he did the same drugs as his mother, but he seemed to handle it much better than she did. They didn't have much, but they did have each other, and as a child, Dwight didn't really know how bad he had it. There had been nothing to compare it to.

On the morning when everything changed, Dwight had tiptoed to his parents' bedroom door for the third time. He'd tried once around 9:00 a.m. and again about forty-five minutes after that. Sometimes they were slow to wake, so Dwight would check periodically with them to see who would get up and help tend to his childly needs first. He had banged on the door to wake them up. Even harder that third time. He was so hungry, and someone needed to make him a bowl of cereal. It was at least 11:00 a.m. at that point, but no one came to the door.

He banged even harder, turning his hand into a hammer to create a louder sound against the wooden door. Even kicked the bottom of it with his little foot.

Still, no one answered. Walking into the living room, he turned on the television and sat on the brown floral couch that had been gifted to them from a local church upon moving in. The channel was on the local news station. They were talking about people getting sick and how folks should try to make it to a hospital if they could. Adult topics that had no chance of keeping the attention of a ten-year-old boy in need of breakfast and a high-quality cartoon. Dwight sat on the floor with his legs crossed, filthy socks and all, channel-cruising for *Sponge Bob* episodes. He settled for *Teen Titans*.

That week, Dwight was serving a ten-day suspension for getting into a fight with a girl who'd been bullying him. A kid could only be ridiculed for having learning disabilities for so long before the snap occurred. He'd sat in the office with a sense of pride, knowing that he'd worked Olivia Jenner over for a good while before one of the hall monitors was able to pull him off her bleeding body.

After an episode, he thought that maybe his parents weren't home. Sometimes they got up early to do stuff. While rare, it wasn't unheard of. Dwight went back to his room to slide on some pajama pants and then proceeded to walk out on the front porch of the trailer. He could remember how beautiful the day was. Bright and sunny, leaves of autumn doing their jig all over the ground, but it was very quiet. His father's 1998 Honda Civic was still parked on the side there—that meant they were still in the house.

He decided to look through their window from the outside. They didn't have curtains, so he would be able to see them and knock on the glass. That would wake them up, if nothing else.

The window was wide open, and there they were, sprawled across the bed.

"Mom, open the door!" Dwight remembered screaming through the window. He had popped his little head through the window like the Whac-A-Mole game he played at Chuck E. Cheese's whenever they went there for his cousin's birthday parties.

Neither of them made a move. He thought they must have been tired. *Mom was up sick last night, they probably didn't sleep much*, he had thought. A child couldn't begin to fathom the unfathomable at such an early age. After screaming their names a few more times through the window, he decided to climb through and physically wake them. The second his feet landed on the stained brown carpet of their bedroom, the aroma had hit him like a car crash.

The human mind was like a magnificent computer. But it didn't take much for a certain nasty virus to infiltrate the hard drive. Then boom, you are at your local Best Buy, spending the same amount you paid for the computer to get it fixed by Ian and the Geek Squad. Even then, it was never the same again.

The brain processed information much the same way. Dwight was certain that the day he climbed through his parents' window was the same day his brain developed...a glitch. Even though it had all happened so long ago, to him it still felt like last week. The images, smells, and the fear were still so fresh in his memory that he could recall the scent of vomit and feces permeating the room. Sometimes he would randomly smell it, even today. Like it had followed him here.

At night when he lay in bed, he was always fighting sleep because he knew that sleep brought the nightmares that the teachers said should have stopped long ago. He was fighting sleep again tonight, lying naked under the sheets and wondering how they'd react if they found out he was still having those recurring dreams. *Would they think that I was broken?* The ever-present television watched him, watched them all while they slept. The Order maintained that there were no cameras in the pods, but everyone knew that wasn't true. *Nobody speaks on it, but we all know.* Dwight turned over on his side and reached for his penis.

Dwight was given his own pod the day the Palace became home, and since that day, he'd lived alone. The small amount of nurturing and love he received from his mother seemed like tons compared to the rigid figure-it-out-yourself mentality of the Palace. That took a toll after a while. Maybe not for Palace-born children; they knew no difference, but he did, and the disappearance of that love isolated him from everyone.

Sure, he had plenty of food, social time, and clothing. Everyone was super nice, and he could have relations exercises with women. He never wanted to be with a woman in that way though; they didn't turn him on. When it came time to perform, he could never keep his member erect long enough to do the deed, or he would ejaculate prematurely. *Good thing the women here didn't care about stuff like that.*

Dwight began to jerk on himself slowly, so as not to move the covers too much. The TV was watching. If the teachers, the Order, or Sirus caught you doing bad stuff like...pleasing yourself, you could get in trouble.

One thing that did rev Dwight's engine was walking down to the fourth floor and watching them—the little people in the child center. He enjoyed spying on them from the survey area. Only the watchers had access to the kids until age ten. He could never understand why, throughout his time here, he enjoyed watching those kids.

He thought maybe it was because the trauma he suffered the day of the sickness; he was around that age when it all happened. He didn't care enough to mention these feelings to the teachers. They would only judge him and tinker with his brain even more with the questions and counseling, but his hard drive had already been fragmented to no avail. The glitches were here to stay. No amount of talking could make him not become excited by what naturally excited him.

He didn't really want to touch the children; that wasn't even a possibility. He just liked watching them running, playing, smiling. This would always sexually excite him, and he made sure he wore heavy pants like jeans when he watched them. If the teachers or the higher-ups in the Order were to catch him doing this, he would be evaluated and possibly banished. It had been two decades though, and he'd perfected the ways to take his mental pictures when he went to the fourth floor. Times like this, lying in bed and trying to calm himself, were the times when he would go to those mental pictures.

Dwight sped up the tugging and pulling, bringing himself closer to an orgasm. But no, he wanted it to last longer, so he slowed down. Slower motions of his hand moving back and forth ensued as he pictured male children running and jumping. The female brats didn't excite him quite as much as the little boys did. Those were his favorites.

Dwight steadily began to speed up again. "Oh yes...yes," he groaned under his breath, knowing the climax was just around the corner. He froze the visual picture of a young man in his head for masturbation fodder.

Just then, he climaxed hard enough to shake the bed. The whole damn room for all he knew. Dwight laid there, quivering like a solitary leaf on a tree outside of his parents' trailer all those years ago—the last day he had on the outside as a normal child, in a normal world where everything made sense.

Spilling seed was looked down upon in the Palace. There shouldn't be any selfishness involved in any sexual act. What Dwight did in bed every night was terrible. He knew this, but how did one change what couldn't be changed? He was certain no amount of morning enrichments could fix him. Telling someone they were doing something wrong would not, could not, stop the compulsion. There was no Norton AntiVirus for the human brain. *We are what we are.*

Dwight crawled out of bed and stood in the middle of the living room, nude. His right hand was clutched into a fist. Trapping the evidence of his excitement within. He couldn't leave stains on the bed —the cleaning crew would notice and alert Teacher Thomas.

The moonlight from the southern window reflected off his skin. All was silent in the Palace. The buzzing of the television, which read "Please Wait," was the only sound in the room. Dwight went into the bathroom and washed his hands. He stared at himself in the mirror and did not like what he saw, but that was nothing new. He would deal with it though. He had to because there was no other choice. Glitches and all.

CHAPTER FIFTEEN

Mary

"I'D LIKE TO BEGIN BY SAYING that we are all so excited with the progress you've been making. We know it's been challenging to deal with certain emotions you may be experiencing as you age; that's all to be expected. The most important thing is to make sure you bring those feelings to me or another teacher so that we have the opportunity to help you work through them. That's why we're here, after all." Teacher Paul reached across the small wooden table and caressed Mary's hand. "That's why we're *all* here."

They were in a room where mental evaluations took place. This was where members would come to if they needed to speak with Teacher Paul. He would be there if you needed someone to lend you an ear. Selfishness, jealousy, hatred: these were very rare things in the Palace, as everyone owned the same possessions. A culture of independency and helpfulness were in place so that these emotions had little chance of being experienced.

The room was all white, as usual. The only furniture was a small white wooden table and two white chairs on each side. There was one window on the western wall of the room. It was bare, with no curtains to let in the sunlight. Mary felt comfortable in this room; she'd spent more time here than she would ever want to admit to anyone.

She withdrew her hand from Teacher Paul's, smiled, and placed both hands in her lap. "Today I would like to discuss the children I have provided to the center."

Teacher Paul sat back in his seat. "And what about those children would you like to discuss today, Mary?"

"I'm still having dreams about them...why?" She stared Teacher Paul in the face and lost the smile. The time for pleasantries had passed. This wasn't supposed to happen. Those children were not hers, so why did she feel like she'd lost something? Why did she feel like a part of her—no, two pieces of her—had been extracted from her very soul and scattered about?

"Well, that's a difficult question to answer, Mary. First of all, it is known that while the body does experience a certain amount of trauma during child birth, this can also affect chemicals in the brain. I can assure you that it will pass."

"This is the same thing you said with the first child though. The dreams are still happening. I still remember delivering the children like it happened yesterday. I do plan on providing as many babies as my body will allow, but...is this something that I'm going to be dealing with going forward?" Mary's voice began to crack a little. She cleared her throat and waited for his response, pushing the tears deep down.

"Mary, please do not become emotional. That is not necessary. What you are experiencing is a normal occurrence. I'll explain further. Living here in the Palace affords you certain safeties." He paused, adjusting his glasses on the bridge of his nose. "Safeties from both the physical harms and emotional harms that would often come to people in the Old World. Because you have been protected and suffered through very little pain physically or otherwise, when you do encounter a mental shock, and child birth would provide such a shock, it tends to stay with you for some time. Not because it's abnormal for the human body, but because you have gone through so little before now. We have the safety of the Palace to thank for that, amen." His brown eyes sparkled beneath his bifocals, and Mary could see that he was proud of that little explanation.

The look he gave her made Mary feel like she should be happy she was alive and lucky enough to live in this place. "I understand. I'd also like to ask, is it normal that I would like to see how they are doing? How they are growing? To see if I brought healthy children into the world? The second the child comes through the birth canal, they are bundled up and rushed down to the fourth floor. I'm feeling all kinds of things that we have been taught only came with the unclean way of living from before. I've never been outside of this place, so why am I dealing with some of these same issues?"

She adjusted her weight from one side of her body to the other, trying to find a comfortable sitting position or, more likely, to distract herself from the words that were coming out of her mouth. "Please don't confuse my questions for anger, I just want to understand what's going on inside of my body and why. I'm fully devoted to my mission of reaching the Greater Understanding Program. I'm just confused because I don't feel the way I'm told I should. If that makes any sense."

Mary was afraid she could be offending her teacher, and she didn't know how far up these reports went. She knew that honesty was very important here, and she would never tell a lie, but she also didn't want to risk being denied the Greater Understanding Program when she was up for review one day. Certain topics seemed to vex Teacher Paul a bit.

"Let me ask you something, Mary. Why do you believe we keep the mothers away from the children here in the Palace? Why do you believe the Order has decided this is the best course of action to take?" Teacher Paul studied her carefully, like she was an experiment in a biology class. He seemed to be looking inquisitively at her face—no, her eyes—for telltale signs of her true emotions on the matter.

"Well...it's said that the idea of belonging to another caused great strife in the Old World. So many deaths, cheating, hurt feelings, and things of that nature—all based on the idea of 'I Love You.' Whether the feelings were a result of what was called parental-child love or man-woman love, they caused more harm than good. There was nothing inherently beneficial to this thing we called love; the only purpose that it could have served was self-satisfaction, or ownership."

Mary rambled off this information as if she were reading it straight from a workbook. She knew her information on the flaws of the Old World, as anyone living in the Palace did. They did not work jobs.

They did not get married. They did not fill their time with smart phones, video games, or other trivial things of that ilk from the past—those time-consuming tech devices were gone, left behind with the other harmful habits from before. No time was to be wasted doing anything that did not foster personal development.

These things were so loved in the Old World that they took precedence over everything else, the things that truly mattered. In the end, most didn't realize the world was ending because they had their faces glued to a screen playing something called Candy Crush.

Teacher Paul uncrossed his legs and took a drink of water from the glass on the small white table. "Allow me to explain something to you. I think this will give you peace on our reasoning and why you should count yourself and the children you brought into this New World as fortunate." He raised an eyebrow, seemingly asking her to consider what he was about to say.

"You see, Mary, children became ill-developed, traumatized by the things their parents were doing. Some grew up in terrible homes and were scarred throughout that time, making them unable to become contributing members of society by the time they came of age. As you would expect, this left the world in a fractured state for some time. The earth became riddled with humans who loved nothing about the planet except what it could do for them. They loved possessions, which in most cases became other people, but not in a caring way. The 'love' was acted out as dominion over the person as far as their children, family, friends, and love interests.

"We now know, and they even knew toward the end of the Old World, that love was not a thing, it was just a word that became empowered by the media, religions, and word of mouth. The idea of love made people believe that the feelings they had for one another, regardless of how flawed, gave them the right to do as they pleased to each other. It was common for people to think something along the lines of: 'I could take your life, because I love this person and you wronged them,' right? It sounds crazy, but it was very common before the sickness. 'I love and own my child, therefor I will bestow upon him or her all of my own flaws and values, and I'll proudly do so because it is my prerogative to impose upon this individual's life, because I bore him into the world.' It's wrong on so many levels. What works for you may not work for that individual. What you can find peace with, they may not be able to. You understand my gist?"

Mary nodded to show Teacher Paul that she understood the point being made. "So the belief and recorded history of the mother-child relationship proves that inherently the mother would begin to interject her own values and such into the child?"

Teacher Paul nodded and slapped the table with one hand, so hard that the glass of water shook. "Correct, Mary. The thing that was thought to bring us closer was actually pushing us further apart and changing the trajectory of lives. The children you deliver should have every opportunity to become the people they choose to be. You attaching your own life experience and values would only provide a fork in the road that wouldn't otherwise be there.

"Same with interpersonal relationships between adults. The perceived love makes you believe the person should bend to your will and do as you do. It's all linked, so to avoid this, it's best if we keep parents away from the children. The entire thought process on giving life needed to be overhauled. Of course there would be some neurological pushback that surely will be bred out of us in the future. I believe you are feeling the effects of this pushback."

"I want to help, that's my purpose, but I do not want to feel terrible about it. I go to sleep feeling lousy most nights, empty almost. Have any of the other females expressed this to you?" Mary's voice cracked as she gulped down her fears.

"Of course, of course. Listen, it's important that you understand that you and the women of the Palace are helping the earth in such a huge way, and we all appreciate it. I'm going to urge you to stay the course, Mary. You are a very promising member of this Palace."

Hearing those words from him made her feel better. She wasn't alone; other females had these feelings. She would need to learn how to better deal with them. Her hard work was being noticed by the teachers, so maybe it was all worth it.

He reached back across the table, gesturing to Mary to hold his hand again. She complied. "Thank you, sir," she said. "That means a lot to me, as do these talks."

"That's what I'm here for. Contact me anytime to discuss things that may be bothering you or things that don't make sense within your body chemistry." Holding her hand in his and caressing the top with his other hand, he smiled again and released Mary back to her floor.

CHAPTER SIXTEEN

Sirus

S IRUS'S VISITOR SAT AT THE MASSIVE desk by himself, nervous, picking at his fingernails anxiously. Andre had been sitting for a few minutes, and Sirus hadn't spoken a word to him other than "Have a seat, my friend." He stood next to the grandfather clock and measured Andre's attitude, trying to figure out what he would like to say to him. The tension in the room was thick, the atmosphere not conducive to having a two-sided conversation. Sirus preferred that though. There wasn't much this gentleman had to say that would tickle his fancy.

Right when the unease of the room reached its heaviest and most awkward peak, Sirus decided to speak. "I know this must feel odd to you, Andre. I'm quiet because it's important to choose your words correctly when addressing a peer. I see you as such, so I will give you the respect that is due. May I speak freely, Andre?" Sirus didn't budge from his spot in the darkness of the room, but he smiled at Andre. The clock provided the background music for his words.

"P-Please do, Sirus sir, please do." Andre stuttered over his words.

Sirus began to move toward Andre, almost prowling across the mahogany-brown carpet. There was a reason his office was decorated in color rather than white. It gave the room a different kind of feel, like it had been plucked straight from the Old World. Everything here would be recognizable to Andre, but only because of what he had seen in books or magazines. Andre would feel strangely at home somehow, and at the same time fearful of the unknown. That was the whole purpose.

"In the Old World, there was a wealth of different religions. You have learned what a religion is, correct?" Sirus started walking laps around the room, staring at Andre.

"Yes, sir."

"Good, good. Now, I am going to give you some information on an important tool of one very special religion during the end of the Old World. There was a religious sect that went by the name of Christianity. I won't get into the origin or how it came to be, the Council of Nicaea, Rome, or that whole mess of circumstances that put it all together. You wouldn't understand anyway. You only need to understand the purpose of religion and whom it served to follow this particular tale."

Andre ran his hands over the tight curly kinks of his hair. Sirus could see he was getting warm. Maybe even starting to sweat.

"In any case, Christianity's main figures were good and evil, light and dark, or God and Satan. Satan, ironically, was a creation of the God figure in this story. You may ask yourself: Why would a god, who was said to be perfect, go and create his own opposition? Apart from becoming insanely bored with your mindless followers and wanting to have some fun, I'm not sure why anyone would do such a thing.

"Doesn't make any practical sense, but not much did in those days, so it was allowed to prosper for thousands of years. This idea that the world was ruled by both a perfect God and an evil entity called Satan, or the devil, still flourished. Are you still with me, Andre?" Sirus stopped pacing and raised an eyebrow at him, checking his response.

"If I'm understanding you, there was a religious group that ruled the world prior to the sickness, and the key figures were the good and evil avatars that are present in virtually every religious idea. This follows the same path of what we have been taught about belief systems in morning enrichments." Andre had a hopeful gleam in his eyes, trying to appease Sirus with his answer.

Now standing behind his chair, which was pushed into the desk, Sirus grabbed the back of the chair and leaned in. "Bingo, young Andre. Very good. I'm impressed."

Sirus pulled the chair from the desk and took a seat. He balled his fist and covered it with his other hand, placing them on the desk in front of him and leaning forward casually. Sitting like a proper young lad, not the way you would expect a man of his rank or stature to sit. It was almost playful.

"This Satan figure was an angel in God's army of angel friends that he created for himself. If you haven't noticed yet, this is a very lonely God. He goes around creating all kinds of issues for himself. This angel, Satan, was special in many ways among all the others.

"Satan became jealous of God, gathers some friends, and attempts to overthrow the big guy or some nonsense like that. God finds out about the coup and banishes the bad angels, including Satan, from Heaven."

Andre blinked, his eyes questioning.

"Oh, sorry. Heaven is the magical, all-loving place where they all lived together. Satan and his merry band of evil angels are banished to Earth, which so happens to be where God also created man. Hell, what a place to send the evilest creation ever concocted, right? Talk about not giving men a fair shot at this thing called life, right?"

Sirus winked at him, and he was suddenly attacked with a fit of laughter that lasted for a minute or so. The whole time, Andre sat in his seat on the other side of the desk, grasping the arms of the chair.

It was clear by the look on Andre's face that he thought Sirus was crazy.

"I'm sorry, please forgive me. Foresight is the gift of the aged, I know. Allow me to continue. Satan is now on Earth with man, and he notices they are doing pretty good for themselves. Well, there are only two humans, Adam and Eve. Male and female, of course. They run and frolic throughout the Garden of Eden, and God has one caveat for these two perfect bastards living in happiness forever. Just don't eat from a certain tree in the garden!"

Andre laughed. Sirus could hear the forced enthusiasm, but the fear was present in his eyes; the eyes told no lies.

"That was it. They could eat of everything else in the garden, just not the fruit from one specific tree. This tree had fruit that would give the humans knowledge of all things good and evil. They would become aware of their nudity, and everything outside of their blissful ignorance. Satan, the evil one, somehow becomes a snake, and talks Eve into eating the forbidden fruit. She then talks Adam into doing it with her. Women have always had the power of persuasion, gotta watch 'em!"

Sirus pounded his fist against the desk with a laugh, making Andre jump nearly a foot in the air. "The foolish humans eat the fruit, God gets angry...imagine that. God then declares that all men will pay for that sin with their souls in hell, which is run by his old running mate, Satan. Ahh, you see, you see? Tricky, right? Admit it—this story is crazy in all the right ways, huh?" Sirus glared from across the desk and spun the golden globe once, awaiting Andre's response.

Andre seemed to relax a bit at seeing Sirus's playful smile. He finally gave Sirus a smile back. "It's all nonsensical, in my opinion. I follow the story, but do you mean to tell me that people ever believed in such rubbish?" Andre sank into his chair in relative comfort.

"I do, young Andre, I do. In fact, lots of the people in this very Palace were Christians in the Old World. All that stuff is now outlawed, so you wouldn't hear them speaking about it. I'd even wager your parents or grandparents were Christians. You were only six or seven years old when you were found in your aunt's rundown apartment and brought here during the sickness. It's not odd that you wouldn't remember any of this." Again rising from his seat, Sirus glided over to Andre's side of the desk and sat on the edge, right next to him.

With one leg dangling and the other firmly planted on the ground, he looked down at the young man and saw the fear twinkling in his eyes beneath the soft brown irises. Hazel was the name of that color.

This troubled Sirus. He didn't want fear—he preferred understanding and for the lesson to be known.

"I'll wrap up my story for you, Andre. So...the Satan character seduces Adam and Eve to bite the forbidden fruit, and this condemns all of man to hellfire and brimstone. God later allows cooler heads to prevail and creates himself in human form by impregnating the wife of another man. God in human form, which was known as the savior Jesus Christ, becomes a prophet and performs miracles and such, but he is later killed by the government. Three days later, he rises back into the clouds to be with the 'real' God, and BOOM!"

Sirus again smacked the desk hard, right in front of Andre's face, shaking the globe statue in the center. He couldn't resist spooking Andre further. It was just too easy.

"The terrible thing that Adam and Eve did was forgiven...kinda. I mean, in the Old World, they still believed you could go to hell if you didn't accept the baby Jesus character as your lord and savior. For the most part though, you could do whatever the fuck you wanted to do to the planet and still wind up in Heaven with that joke of a creator."

Sirus stood and walked back over to the clock with his hands in his pockets, returning to the darkness as he leaned against the wall. The wallpaper there was printed with the image of the Sistine Chapel in the Vatican. That was stuff from a different world though.

"Andre, all Satan wanted to do was give the humans knowledge about the world, the true world. And because he did just that, the God of this religion threw a tantrum and cursed everyone to hell. Sure, he cleaned it up with Jesus, but still, ya know? Why do you believe God was so angered that Satan gave the humans the power of knowledge? Since when is knowledge a terrible thing? It's, not right?"

Sirus began tapping on the clock's glass in rhythm with the tick-tocks. He was not smiling, but made sure not to look too serious either. Indifference was the perfectly structured emotion on his face, shrouded in the darkness of this part of the office.

Andre cleared his throat and straightened up in his seat. Here it was. Now was the time he would show Sirus that he had been listening to the story and not the sound of that ancient clock in the corner.

"I think that the God of the Old World was angry at Satan because he told the humans something he did not want them to know. I see no other reason why."

Sirus grinned and began a slow clap. Slow at first, then faster, until it was a full applause. "Goooood boy, Andre. You have been listening! I ask you now, why would he not want them to have the knowledge? It's a good thing, correct?"

Andre appeared to become more upbeat. He seemed to forget who he was speaking to. Sirus's left eye twitched—he was not a man to got cocky with. "Because he was a cruel God, and selfish. He clearly wanted to keep certain things to himself and only give the humans the info he deemed necessary for their happiness. That shouldn't be his decision to make though."

"NO!" Sirus screamed. "You are wrong, sir. As asinine as this entire religion and story is, the bottom line of the issue is that the humans were tricked into finding out things that would eventually lead to thousands of years of suffering. Both in the book, and in real life, through holy wars like the crusades, and witch hunts like the Inquisition. The basic idea of information existing does not mean that the knowledge is beneficial to everyone. In this case, it was not."

Sirus walked back to the desk and sat down once more. The happy grin was long gone. "Which brings me to the reason I wanted to speak to you. I've been alerted by one of the Palace-born individuals that you have been talking to some of them about different things that you remember from the very little time that you spent outside before coming here. No matter how small and trivial you may believe them to be, you do understand it could create a setting in which that information disrupts the fundamental morality and individuality we are cultivating here. Furthermore, you had the brain of a child at the time, so your memories are not up to par. You are not the man to be giving historical lessons to Palace-born individuals."

Andre's mouth fell open, his eyes darting from side to side. Sirus could see the machine in his eyes that was his brain working, trying to come up with an excuse. He had nothing though. He sat there in pure terror, unable to verbalize any of the thoughts in his mind.

"You have been told many times to forget about the Old World. That talk doesn't belong in these walls. You see, in many ways, you are like Satan, moving around and sneakily whispering things into the ears of the innocent." Sirus squinted one eye at Andre and cocked his head to the side. "You wouldn't be trying to start some kind of mutiny, would you?"

Andre got up out of his seat so fast it all but fell over. He caught the chair and steadied it back into place. "Sirus, that was not my intention! I appreciate everything the Order is doing for all of us, and I've only tried to be as helpful as I can be. You have to believe me."

Sirus raised a hand, and the young man halted his rambling.

"No need to explain, my friend. As I said, it's not a huge deal and of no consequence, because you are being promoted." Sirus raised both eyebrows and offered a wide smile, showing all of his beautiful white teeth. Just like that, he was able to morph his somber face into the mug of Andre's best buddy. He could see how his rapidly changing moods confused Andre, and toying with the kid made him giddy inside. It wasn't every day that Sirus got a chance to talk face to face with Palace members, so when he did...he relished it.

"Wait a minute," Andre began. "Are you saying that I've been chosen to go into the Greater Understanding Program?" He took his time sitting down again. "I thought I was in trouble, Sirus. Are you being serious right now?"

"I'm serious as a heart attack, young fellow. I was joshing ya about the Satan comparison, but that is serious business. You know that you can't just say whatever comes to your mind here. Do not let that occur again, do you understand?"

Andre nodded, still looking unsure.

"Well, great. That's all I needed to hear. Easy peasy, lemon squeezy." Sirus rose from the chair and leaned across the desk to extend his hand and shake Andre's. "Congratulations. You have amazing references from all of the teachers on your floor, and your peers seem to love you. I'll also have you know that you are one of the younger members to get into the Greater Understanding Program. The time you have spent here has been amazing, and this Palace is all the better for your hard work and commitment to gaining knowledge about the Old World and the new."

The young man couldn't seem to erase his look of half excitement, half bewilderment off his face. "Thank you so much, Sirus, and thanks to all of the teachers and the Order. I don't know what to say other than thank you. I had no idea I was even being considered."

Tears began to fall from Andre's eyes, his hands grabbing the top of his head in that *oh my god, I can't believe this* gesture.

"Trust me, you earned this, young man. Not everyone is accepted into the Greater Understanding Program, so we are sure to pick care-fully. This is no gift to you, Andre. You deserve this." Sirus clasped both hands together in front of himself and gave a slight bow.

Wiping tears from his eyes, Andre thanked him again and walked toward the door, sniffing and clearing his throat the whole way.

"Teacher Simon is outside of this room with your belongings and a protective suit for you. He will fill you in on what you will need to know. Off you go, Andre, before I decide that we can't part with you, and I have you stay for another twenty years." Sirus smiled and nodded his head toward the door. Andre left the office on the nineteenth floor with Teacher Simon, and Sirus watched them head down the corridor, making their exit from the secret area of the Palace.

OLD HABITS DIE HARD

CHAPTER SEVENTEEN

Jacob

J ACOB STOOD IN A GRAND ELEVATOR, slowly moving down to the fourth floor with a portion of his ME class. The other half were taking a different elevator down. He stared up at the weight limit panel on the elevator, because that's what people did when they got in an elevator with more than four or five people—and there were about thirteen people on this one right now.

Teacher Luke was taking them down to the child center to check up on the children from the survey area. No one was allowed inside of the center; there was to be no contact from anyone but the watchers until age ten. Jacob couldn't possibly count the amount of times he'd been there to watch the kids grow up, but it was one of the more interesting morning enrichments in the Palace.

He enjoyed the lectures and things, but you could only listen to how much you sucked in your past life before it all started to sound like mumbling nonsense. No matter how different they tried to make the subjects or how many different teachers they got to oversee them, it all ended up being a repeat of the same topics and ideas. Like church in the Old World, you could only talk about the same Bible before it got old. *Well, to anyone with a brain at least,* he thought. The teachers and the Order meant well; they only wanted what was best for those who survived, and much had been given in the way of keeping everyone alive.

He thought about how he'd watched Mary and a bunch of the other Palace members grow into adults from this very survey room as he stepped off the elevator and into a long hallway.

Moving to the right to let everyone else get out into the hallway from the elevator, Jacob noticed that Trevor wasn't present for today's morning enrichment. Child center visits weren't something he missed. Trevor said seeing the children made him think of his children, and that gave him some happiness. He was a troubled soul if there ever was one. Must be something important if he didn't show up for this today.

To get to the actual survey room, they had to walk all the way down a long hallway and through a security door, which could only be opened with keycards that the teachers kept clipped to their belts or waistbands. Then around a few corners, until they came to the stairs that led down to the big white room with clear glass walls that served as windows. They were two-way mirrors, like the kind in police stations.

Essentially, the child center surrounded the survey area, so regardless of which way Jacob looked, he could see the children playing and taking part in activities all around him. The children only saw a big square-shaped structure made with mirrors for them to see themselves and each other as they played.

Once arriving in the observation room, Teacher Luke got everyone in a circle so that they could all have portions of the child center to study.

"Okay guys, great to be back down here with you to check out the future of this planet and see how they are maturing," Teacher Luke said, standing in the middle of the group.

"A few of you are just moving up to this level, so I'll give some need-to-know information on what's going on here. Feel free to move around and survey. Please don't tap on the windows, we don't want to disrupt them. We are here to watch, that is all."

The rule was to move around clockwise, but only when the person to your right was done watching. Though the teachers didn't care if you just moved around freely; the room was big enough to support that. And many Palace members had favorite activities they liked to watch the children engage in, like games, reading, climbing—different things like that.

Teacher Luke continued on, repeating the same things that Jacob had been hearing over and over throughout his time in the Palace, so he ignored the speech and watched the children instead.

Jacob leaned against one wall/window and viewed a little boy pushing another child. The aggressor was a redheaded chubby little bastard, and he had just shoved a small Hispanic-looking child to the ground. There were no teachers to be found in the area; they wouldn't intervene anyway.

Jacob thought it would be interesting to see how that situation played out, so he continued to watch. The best way to check the validity of the Palace ideas about human nature was to watch the children. They always did what came naturally to them, and what was natural for humankind was to hurt each other for their own satisfaction. It was all Jacob had ever seen on the outside world—and inside the Palace.

The big kid stood up over the small one and nudged him with his foot in the stomach—not a kick, but close to it. He snickered at him and looked around to see if anyone was watching. Knowing he was doing something wrong, he pretended to help the other child up. But when the smaller kid went to grab his hand, the bully pulled it back and laughed even harder, then walked away.

The most telling thing in the incident was how sneaky the fat kid was. He knew exactly what he was doing, knew that it would be looked down upon, so before he became the number one dickhead, he made sure none of the watchers were observing. Jacob thought to himself, *Ain't that the truth of it all right there?* People did what they thought they could get away with when no one was watching. In this microcosm, the small run-in with two children gave a good look into the psyche of man as a whole.

Jacob wasn't shocked to see this type of behavior. For the most part, there were lots of good things going on in the child center. But from time to time, he would see the children become violent with each other for little to no reason at all.

The teachers explained this was because the kids didn't have relations exercises to help them blow off steam, or defuse, and it would
need to come out in some way. A small amount of violence would be
permitted for the sake of them learning to deal with their emotions as
well as cause and effect. Cause and effect were on the menu today, and
the fat ginger kid was about to get an adult-sized helping.

Like a natural reaction, the smaller child made it to his feet, still
clutching his stomach. He looked over and spotted a toy truck about
the size of a football from a nearby toy box. He grabbed the toy and
went running for the redhead, who at this point was so high on his
own self-satisfaction that he didn't hear the pitter-patter of shoes
behind him.

The small Hispanic kid stretched his arm back as far as it could
possibly go, and that little arm fired back out with violent speed,
leaving the toy truck falling from the sky in his small hand like a comet
aimed at the other child's skull. The force of the strike was so hard
that one of the wheels on the toy truck went spinning toward another
group of children.

Jacob never budged, and neither did the other kids who were
watching. He'd been down here many times and had seen similar
things. He knew that in no time the watchers would magically show up
to stop things from going too far. *But what was too far here in the child
center?*

The blow knocked the fat kid out cold, and his lifeless body fell to
the rainbow-colored carpet as if his limbs were made of spaghetti.
Blood poured from his already red hair as he lay there on the floor,
alone. No one came to his aid. There was no need for that though,
because the smaller child dropped the truck and walked over to a
watcher on the other side of the room. He grabbed her hand and
mouthed something to her.

They walked together over to the body of the other child. The
watcher, who was gorgeous (they all were), got down on one knee and
said something to the Hispanic kid. He smiled, picked up the truck,
and skipped over to another group of children to continue playing, as
if nothing at all had happened. The female watcher woke the bleeding

child up, whispered something to him, and then walked him into a bathroom.

Jacob looked around to see if anyone else had noticed the ordeal, but there was no one in this particular section of the room but him and one other guy. He noticed it was Dwight, a guy who had always weirded him out. The dude was nice enough, very polite and quiet. But there was just something about him that was odd, and he'd always been that way.

Jacob remembered that Dwight was just a small kid when they all got to the Palace. He was given his own pod and had a few wild outbursts in the following years and spent a lot of time being evaluated for odd behavior and screaming fits. There had been nothing like that in recent years though. When there was free time to socialize, go to Palace events, listen to appropriate music (nothing violent or with cursing), or just shoot the shit in the auditorium and watch old movies...he was never present. Nothing wrong with staying to yourself, Jacob could appreciate that. He was often the same way. But Dwight was different. Trevor always called him a fruit; he hated the guy.

Is the guy hard right now? Jacob wondered as he watched Dwight in the opposite corner with his hand in his pocket. He seemed to be touching himself through his jeans. Partly because Jacob was disgusted, and partly due to pure boredom, he decided to walk closer to Dwight to verify the creepiness, hoping that he was wrong.

Dwight noticed Jacob getting closer and turned his body to the right, like he was trying to hide something. He then readjusted his pants from the back.

"Did you just see that fight with those kids?" Jacob tried to make conversation with Dwight, hoping that he wouldn't feel accused of anything. While waiting for a reply, he tried to circle around the man. He was too late though. The weirdo had clearly seen him coming. But Jacob knew what he saw.

"Yeah, yeah man, I saw it. Kid kinda got what was coming to him, huh?" A nervous grin appeared on Dwight's face, small yellow teeth showing through his thin dry lips. He had a big nose with a high bridge. It reminded Jacob of that actor with the long, slim nose from that movie about the piano.

Dwight had stringy blond hair, which gave the impression that he didn't seem to keep up with daily showers. He must not have gotten the memo that they were a requirement. He had big brown eyes, very bright, with a hidden intelligence behind them. He looked at Jacob then back to the kids, disregarding him as unimportant.

"I don't know about that, man, but you seemed to be moving weird over here. Are you okay? Should I get Teacher Luke to check you out if you aren't feeling well?" Jacob nodded at the teacher and then looked Dwight up and down.

"Naw man, I'm good actually. I don't know what you think you saw, maybe my legs got tired from standing or something." Dwight looked away from the child center and glanced at Jacob once more, noticeably annoyed. "Thanks for asking though, Jacob."

Dwight walked away, moving closer to a different group of Palace members who were watching a game of kickball between groups of children on the other side of the survey room. "He is so damn weird."

Jacob remembered a time a little over five years ago, when Dwight and another guy almost came to blows in a Palace celebration for humanity's fifteen years of survival. Dwight had said something to the other guy (who later ended up getting the Greater Understanding promotion) that really pissed him off. Dwight had to be rushed to the infirmary to treat his broken nose. Jacob remembered because the fight was the talk of the town for months. That type of stuff didn't occur often here.

Jacob went back to the spot where he'd watched the kids fight; it seemed to be reasonably quiet in that area of the room. Seeing the children play made him think about the times when he was a kid, running around with friends, climbing trees, and going down to the creek to catch frogs and other creepy-crawlies. Weekend sleepovers, Little League baseball games in the summer, and football games in the fall. These children here would never know the happiness of being a kid before the world went away.

They were safe from the sickness though, that was something. Jacob wondered if the tradeoff was worth it as he watched the children play.

CHAPTER EIGHTEEN

Trevor

TREVOR ENJOYED SITTING ALONE IN THE courtyard while Amy did her thing. It made him feel like he was back home at Oak Park. He had loved that park; he and some buddies would go there, drink some cold ones, and do a little hunting or fishing. Many summers were spent there with the family as well. Grilling out, throwing the ball around, just spending time together.

Sometimes he missed that the most, spending time with those he loved. Of course, the Palace courtyard wasn't the same as Oak Park, but he could always play pretend. It made him feel like he wasn't in a plush prison for a little while. For all the Palace had going for it, it was still a place they could not leave, at least not without being accepted into the Greater Understanding Program.

And who knew if that was even a real thing. He had his doubts. Whether it was because of the sickness outside or some other reason, this place still felt like a prison to him.

Amy loved to walk around out here with her friends, and Trevor thought it was important for her to have those friends. Her mind being idle was good for no one, especially herself. She would get to thinking about the kids and had a tendency to lose sight of reality. With all the help that she'd received here in the Palace, she still needed more. Or maybe there wasn't enough help for her. Something in her mind had become unhinged that day, and he knew it would never reconnect the same way again.

A part of himself didn't care about that. That was hard for Trevor to admit, but as long as she was here, in any capacity, that would do. He thought it interesting the measures his mind would go to heal itself.

Trevor noticed Malcom Patton walking over in his direction. Malcom was close to his age, more likely in his late fifties—an old guy by Palace standards. Here, you were either a Palace-born idiot, a semi-young person from the outside, or a relic of the Old World, and that was anyone who was around the age of thirty to forty when the sickness wiped out the entire planet. All but them. *Lucky us*, Trevor thought while extending his hand for Malcom to shake.

"Hey there, buddy. How's the Big House here treating you?" Trevor asked. "Another repetitive morning enrichment and some forced sex today?" He coughed up some laughter while looking around to make sure he hadn't been heard by anyone.

Malcom grabbed a seat next to Trevor on the stone bench in the beautiful courtyard. He let out a relaxed sigh once he settled into the bench and put a hand on Trevor's shoulder. "Buddy...I'm fifty-six. I'm not having much sex these days, forced or not." He laughed and looked around to see if anyone was paying attention. Then he lowered his voice. "Unless you smuggled some of those magic beans in here, you know, to help get the soldier standing at attention. You a serviceman, you know what I mean." Malcom laughed.

They had been great friends for some time now. Most of the Old World people were stuck with each other. The Palace-born were different—overly helpful and indoctrinated to be honest. They meant well, but they just didn't get along like Old World humans did with each other.

"We better keep it down, old friend, or we'll end up in a small room with Teacher Lobotomy, uhh I mean, Teacher Paul," Malcom whispered. He gave Trevor a wink.

Trevor laid a finger over his lips and returned the wink to Malcom, and they both cracked up laughing. It was nice having folks from the

Old World here with him, made him feel like he was able be himself, if even for a little.

"How are ya moving today, old man?" Malcom wiped tears of laughter from his eyes.

"I'm still kicking, my friend." Trevor looked over to see Amy still walking laps with her friends and enjoying the conversations they were having.

"That's all we can ask for in here, huh?" Malcom unwrapped a piece of pound cake from a paper towel and broke a few pieces off to eat. He offered Trevor a piece, but Trevor declined, shaking his head as he stared up into the sky. Malcom pulled his hand back and ate the piece of cake himself. He looked up and spotted birds flying in and out of the quarantine zone "What are you looking at, Trevor? You okay?"

They both sat there in the courtyard of the Palace, staring at the sky, Trevor looked at Malcom, raising an eyebrow. "How do you think they know that past the red flags is the cutoff? I've never seen anyone out here with any type of equipment. In all of twenty years, nothing. You think they may be lying to us all about that? Wouldn't be the first time, right?" Trevor bumped Malcom's arm with his own in a joking away.

"Hmm, I couldn't tell you. Maybe, maybe not. Shit, I don't know. I do know that you saw what happened during the sickness, just like I did. That really happened. Now, while I don't know much about the quarantine zone or any of that stuff, I would give the Order the benefit of the doubt." Malcom shrugged and went back to picking off pieces of his pound cake and popping them into his mouth.

"You know," he went on, "you gotta be careful with that stuff, Trevor. I mean, why would they lie about something so stupid? From what I've understood, we are being kept safe. I seen what's out there, and I don't want any part of it. I just don't see why they would lie. How does the government benefit?"

"Why wouldn't they? You'd be surprised about the things people will lie about when it's getting them what they want." Trevor giggled and bent down to tie his shoe. "You'd be surprised for sure. They can get over on some folks, but I've seen their lies. I was a part of those lies when I was in the service. I know better."

"Well I hear that." Malcom paused for a few seconds and continued. "But we got what we got, ya know? They've always done right, and still doing right by us. Without the Order, we wouldn't even be alive. I say as long as they keep feeding, clothing, and protecting us from that sickness, then I don't care a lick what they lie about." He popped another piece of cake into his mouth and waved at a Palace member walking by.

"Yeah, yeah, yeah, that's what everyone here thinks." Trevor finished tying up his white walking shoes, sat with his back on the bench, and looked at Malcom with skepticism in his eyes. "That's the type of thing they were saying to us over there in Iraq. They had us thinking stuff was one way when it was actually the other. The old government had us over in fuckin' sand country, killing more civilians than anything else. We thought we were gonna be bringing the pain to the people that blew up the towers over here, ended up not being the case, or at least not the way a lot of us saw it after a few years.

"I don't recall seeing no Iraq uniform for the armed forces; most those folks were people just trying to protect their homes. We did what we had to do, and we took care of business. I'm just saying...it wasn't what we thought it was gonna be."

Trevor spit on the ground next to the bench and offered his hand for a piece of the pound cake from Malcom's paper towel. Malcom broke off a piece into Trevor's hand, ate the rest, and balled up the paper. He got up and looked around the beautiful courtyard, taking in all the gorgeous flowers, trees, and amazing landscaping. Sticking the balled-up paper into the back pocket of his tan slacks, he looked at Trevor and pointed at him.

"Let me tell you something, sir. You been a good friend to me since we been here, and Lord knows that's something I needed. I lost my entire family. I was barely holding on, and even thought about killing myself a few times. Folks like you and a few others kept me on the wagon, and you will always be my friend for that...but I think you are wrong about this place. Honestly, I think you should be a bit more appreciative to what the Order does for us. They could have left us all out there to die.

"The United States government, hell, all the governments of the world, were destroyed. They got together all they could muster and put together something new to provide some type of stability, and we got that here. No, they haven't done everything perfectly, but would you expect 'em to?"

The volume of Malcom's voice rose steadily. He was visibly angry and starting to cause a scene. Trevor raised his hands and tried to motion for Malcom to calm down, but it didn't seem to do anything.

"You got your life, dontcha? Yeah, you do. That alone should be enough for you to just be happy." Malcom was shaking at that point and burning a hole through Trevor with his stare. Trevor looked around and noticed a few people looking their way. Malcom saw it too. He lowered his voice and placed his hands on his narrow hips.

"You get to see the Old World become the new world. They say that ninety to ninety-five percent of the folks in the world are dead and will never get a chance to bitch about what someone else did to help others, like you are doing right now. Don't you dare complain. You hear me? Don't you dare." Malcom turned away from Trevor and stormed back into the Palace.

Trevor looked around to see if he still had a small audience. The people outside had turned away after Malcom went into the building. Palace members did not handle conflict well; they would rather not see it whenever it reared its ugly head. Trevor was happy about that. The last thing he needed was for a teacher to have witnessed what happened and begin the constant questions about the issue.

He paid no attention to Malcom's outburst; his friend was prone to those for little to no reason. The man was kindhearted, but he had a bit of a short fuse and was emotional to say the least. Trevor knew he was lucky to have Amy here with him. Malcom was right about the fact that many didn't get to see this new world, or whatever it was becoming. His children were among the many. But Amy got to see it, and for that, Trevor was happy.

He got up from the bench and walked over to a bush of roses and picked one. He put the rose up to his nose and inhaled the aroma. It smelled just like the roses on his grandma's farm. She had the most beautiful flowers that bloomed every spring, and she would bring hell and its horses if you got anywhere near them. He would always find a way to smell the roses though. That was so long ago, it could have been a different life altogether. Things got hazy when he thought about the past; the concept of then and now was confusing for him in most cases. Maybe it was his age.

He picked a few more roses and bundled them together. Hiding his hand behind his back, he headed in Amy's direction. She always loved roses.

CHAPTER NINETEEN

Mary

WHENEVER AN INDIVIDUAL WAS STRUGGLING WITH a high amount of stress and needed intervention, there were different counseling methods or activities one could do in the Palace to better deal with it all. Both the stress relief activities and the counseling sessions were handled on the eighth floor of the Palace. Mary and a handful of others took full advantage of these options when they began to feel the pressure of the responsibilities they had. Mental stability was of the utmost importance here, and was not to be taken for granted.

There was no harm in using what was available to feel better about herself, which would help her stay focused on the task at hand. And for Mary, that was doing all she could to get into the Greater Understand Program. Talks with Teacher Paul helped tremendously. There was a gym on the first floor that was open to everyone in the Palace; she ran there and did boxing routines daily. And Mary was not a stranger to the eighth floor and the offerings of stress-relief activities there. At only age nineteen, Mary had been through a lot, and she needed time to unwind, to think, and to recommit to the mission.

Lying naked inside of the long rectangular box filled Mary with relief. The softness of the surrounding linens and fabrics felt so smooth on her skin, like wearing silk all over her body. The smell of the fresh dirt surrounding her outside of the box reminded her of the courtyard and how she enjoyed spending time walking the trail there and picking flowers to bring into her pod. The smell was comforting.

Death had been a common fear of all human life since the beginning of time. It was the reason humans had been creating gods since the moment they could scribble suns, moons, and stick figures on cave walls. Moving from those caves into the most luxurious buildings of the world, mankind had one constant for thousands of years: people could not deal with life without their impending death looming somewhere in the background, as if they could remember not existing before sliding out of their mother's birth canal. Time as a construct served to measure that very thing. From the moment humans took their first breath until the time their pyre burned in the night, sending their matter floating around as ashes through the atmosphere to eventually land on the earth, they constantly worried about the "after."

This fear of death carried a bigger effect on life than anyone realized in the Old World. The worry of dying kept many from going after their dreams, instead staying in their homes and only socializing through cell phone apps. Instead of going out to buy goods they needed, many would purchase them online and have them delivered, all to avoid danger and a slight possibility of death. Becoming obsessed with living a long life served to make sure they never lived at all.

O Merciful Mother of Earth, I'm thankful to be one of a small group you have entrusted to remain here. I do not believe myself to be special in any way, shape, or form. So many men and women who were pure of heart and mind perished during the sickness, the same as the unfavorable. I do believe that I'm here today, in this moment, because I can and will do what's necessary to make—

Mary heard a loud thud dropping just over her face. She paid the sound no mind, she'd been here a hundred times before. She laid there, arms at her sides, feet pointing straight up. Her body was covered with goosebumps, and her nipples hardened to a pink point over the soft flesh of her breasts. The feeling of being exposed allowed her to think more clearly.

I will not repeat the mistakes of the past, nor will I allow others to take advantage of you, themselves, or any others, for we are one. I will not allow your resources to be pillaged and capitalized upon by the wicked. We have offended in the past, and for that we paid dearly with human lives. This was deserved, I know that. It is not my place to judge your ways of dealing with the crimes of men, but it is my job to learn from them and heed your ways...and I do. We all do now.

Mary felt a warm tear trickle down her cold cheek. The tears fell down her face, making a wet trail that passed her ears and found a home in her silky dark hair. Another thud dropped on the wood above her face.

Nothing will stop my stride. I will reach my goals, and surpass them. Life will not scare me out of the position that you have placed me in. The memories of child birth, the fears of my children's future or lack thereof, the strange feelings I'm beginning to experience with Jacob, not even death itself could evoke enough fear inside of me to stop this momentum.

Mary wanted to wipe her face, but there wasn't enough room to move her arms. The sound of dirt hitting the top of the casket quickened and became steady. The whole time she remained calm, opened her eyes, and thought about the fact that she was buried six feet down.

It was a common stress-release exercise offered on the eighth floor of the Palace. The simulation of death and the ritual of being buried was helpful to some. The teachers believed that a big part of the human experience was the fear of the unknown, and the biggest unknown was death and how that would feel. While the burial activity didn't provide the full experience of death, it did offer portions of that "after" experience. You were buried in a casket, which, for obvious reasons, had air circulation, so there was no true fear of dying from loss of breath. There was a lot to be said about the constricting feeling of being inside of a casket though, about the feeling of the pressure bearing down on the wood from the dirt and rocks.

After the casket was fully covered with dirt, the subject was meant to stay in the ground and meditate. To think about life and death, and all that entailed. It was a time to reflect on loving the life you had and accepting the amount of time you were given on this planet; knowing that you used every minute to better yourself and take care of the planet should always be enough. After an hour, the casket was dug up and the subject retrieved. After so many sessions, it was said that subjects would come to terms with things like their mortality; they would be better able to accept control of the things that could be controlled, and let go of the things that couldn't. Mary had been coming to the eighth floor for mock burial sessions for over five years, and every night she dreamed about the children she'd created.

CHAPTER TWENTY

Dwight

ELSEWHERE IN THE PALACE, A MAN sat inside of his shower, fully clothed. The showerhead dripped just enough to provide a steady drop, drop, drop on his forehead. Kind of like the Japanese water torture from World War II. For some it could feel like torture, but for Dwight it was...relaxing, calming even. Dwight Patterson sat just beneath the showerhead with his back against the wall. He looked up at the ceiling and allowed the dripping of the showerhead to tap, tap, tap on his forehead. He'd been doing this for so long, he didn't know when he figured out that it made him feel better. One day while sitting in the shower, pleasing himself to his mental Rolodex of the things that get him hot, he discovered this little trick that made him think better. Normally his mind raced and he couldn't focus on one thing for more than a few seconds. The tapping helped with that.

"What's the point of even being here?" he said to no one as he counted the cracks on the ceiling (another calming method he'd figured out while living in the Palace). Dwight had come up with a lot of things to do in the bathroom except actually taking a shower. That television was a camera, peeping into his pod. Watching him, measuring him, and hoping to catch him doing something wrong so that he could never get out of there. But for Dwight, there was no such thing as "out of here." They only let the goody-goodies out. He couldn't be "normal" long enough to be noticed by the teachers or Sirus, so why even try?

Dwight smacked the shower tiles next to his leg and cursed. *Fuck this place.* He thought about the constant idea always looming at the surface of his mind. That the government had done all of this to them. He just knew they'd somehow made everyone sick for their own purposes, and he was going to find out why.

Dwight's father had been a full-blown aluminum-foil-cap-wearing conspiracy theorist who believed every video he watched on YouTube. Always watching conspiracy videos on the living room computer that was donated to them by a well-off cousin to help his mother find a job. *Infowars* was his favorite website to get his information.

Unlike a lot of the people who had forgotten most of their old lives, Dwight remembered his prior life more vividly every day. It was the only thing that kept him going in this place. Of course, he could put on the good-boy mask when need be, but the truth was he hated the Palace and everyone inside of it. His father would watch and often quote this fat idiot from the website who was always screaming until his face turned red. Dwight's mom had hated the screaming fat idiot. FEMA camps, underground bunkers, and vaccinations meant to wipe out the entire planet were common ideas expressed in Dwight's household. *Turns out you were right, Dad.* Another drop of water thumped his forehead, sending trickles down his face.

After a few more minutes, he stood up in the shower and walked out of the bathroom, over to his perfectly made bed. He sat down on the side of it, wiping the water off his face with the back of his sleeve. He didn't want the camera in the television to pick up on what he was doing. They were tricky in this place. He lay back on the bed with his feet still flat on the floor and put his hands behind his head.

It's time I break out of this place. He was already thirty years old, or something close to it. There seemed to be no days, weeks, or months in this monotonous place, so it was hard to keep track. They were all just waiting for something to happen—something that might never happen for some. He'd never be on the teacher's-pet list to get into the

Greater Understanding Program. He saw the way everyone looked at him, like he was crazy or something.

Dwight turned his head to the left to look at the television, expecting to find the "Please Wait" message on the screen. Only this time it didn't say "Please Wait." It was time for Sirus to say the prayer and eat supper with everyone. Dwight knew better though. He was betting that on the other end somewhere, there was a room of teachers watching him, watching them all.

He was going to have to find a way to get his hands on one of those protective suits the supplies teachers wore when they came in from outside of the safe radius. It couldn't be too hard to beat up one of those guys and get his suit. Then he could leave. Dwight had no idea what he'd do once he was away from this place, but anything was better than being here, learning the same shit over and over. He'd have to plan before he could make a move, but it was a necessary action he needed to take. He would soon be driven insane by these walls, the pods, the stupid courtyard. He had to go.

Dwight popped up from the bed and made his way to the door of his pod. He touched the knob, then paused. He walked over to the television and touched the screen with a finger. Looking directly into the screen, he stuck his long dirty tongue out. "Fuck...you," he said to the screen. *No need to play nice anymore,* he thought as he walked out of his pod, slamming the door behind him. Enough was enough.

CHAPTER TWENTY-ONE

Nicholas

NICHOLAS JOHNSON SAT ON THE WHITE couch that mirrored the same exact couch of every pod in the Palace. A silver tray of breakfast sat on the table before him. A banana, apple, pancakes, and sausage. Same thing he ate every morning. Not because there weren't other options, but because it was the last breakfast Wendy had made for him the day before he lost her. Before he lost everyone. *Everything is fine...just fine.* That's what he'd been telling himself for the last twenty years. More mornings than not, his mind went back to that day twenty years ago.

They had eaten breakfast before taking their twelve-year-old daughter, Stephanie, to get a sports physical for basketball season. They had also stopped at a sporting goods store to buy her some new basketball shoes. Stephanie had conned him into getting her the new Michael Jordan shoes by promising she would rake up all the new leaves in the front yard. The deal was made, and they shook on it.

Nicholas peeled his breakfast banana, and the beginnings of a smile appeared on the left corner of his lips. He'd been doing a lot of reminiscing about the past lately, and it made him feel excited about his future plans.

Wendy had made pork ribs in the oven that night along with his favorite sides: string beans and macaroni and cheese. She knew he liked his mac and cheese the way his mother made it for him, in the oven with melted cheese on the top. She was amazing like that, and she had never missed out on a moment to show him exactly how much she loved him, and that made him love her that much more. After dinner, Stephanie went upstairs to watch a movie in her room and get some sleep. Wendy cleaned up the kitchen and living room while he went upstairs to their room to find a movie for them to watch before hopping in the shower. He had been careful not to use up all the warm water. Wendy would bite his entire head off if he did that.

This thought brought a full smile to his face as he bit into the banana and washed it down with a cup of coffee. In these times, all you had were your memories. And the memories you chose to remember had everything to do with how you regarded the past. This morning he would choose to remember them in the best of lights. That last day they had together felt as normal as any other day: mundane errands and the taken-for-granted times when he should have asked for another hug, an extra kiss from Wendy. Or maybe told Stephanie how proud of her he was. Hindsight had the vision of a powerful telescope though, and it worked to the advantage of no one.

He and Wendy had taken a shower together that night. And after, when they were both smelling fresh and clean and lying on the soft sheets, they had sex. Not just the normal routine sex they had twice a week. They had *amazing* sex, with the same passion that they had for each other as seventeen-year-olds over twenty years before that night. He brought Wendy to an orgasm three times, even had to put a hand over her mouth to stop the loud moans from disturbing their daughter. When they had finished, Wendy collapsed on his chest, legs still shaking while she struggled to catch her breath. That wasn't the end though. She then got up and used a warm washcloth to clean the sex from their bodies. She even went back downstairs to make Nicholas a bowl of ice-cream for dessert.

The thought of that last night with Wendy excited Nicholas even today, but there was no time for that. Masturbation was not allowed in the Palace anyway, so he hadn't done it in years. Instead he grabbed a sausage link and placed it in the middle of a pancake, then curved the pancake around the sausage, poured syrup over the makeshift corndog, and took half of it into his mouth at once. He and his daughter Stephanie always ate their pancakes like that. It was their thing.

Nicholas had sex once more with his wife that night, and then they fell asleep watching a movie. In the middle of the night, Nicholas woke up to use the bathroom. On his way back to the bed, he heard Stephanie in her room coughing up a storm. An hour later, Wendy woke him up with the burning touch of her skin. Her leg grazed his in the middle of the night, and he remembered it being so hot that it scared him. Not long after that, the coughing began, along with the running back and forth to the toilet to spit up what sounded like huge amounts of mucus. Then came the constant vomiting.

From 3:00 a.m. until 11:00 a.m. that morning, he had tried to help the two most important people in his life. Running ice to one room, a bucket to the other room, all the while calling nine-one-one as he checked on his wife and child. The phone line was busy all night. There was no help for them, and he would later find out there was no hope for anyone. His night was a carbon copy of millions of nights for millions of people. The few who lived through the sickness would suffer the memories of it all. Nicholas didn't count himself as lucky. Lucky would have been dying in bed with his wife.

What the united governments of the world have done is amazing. I've told the teachers and anyone who would listen as much, Nicholas thought as he ate the remainder of his pancakes and sausage. He then drank the rest of the coffee.

After they both had stopped breathing that day, Nicholas ran out of the house, finally breaking down to his knees in the front yard. It was one of the most beautiful days he had ever seen, so bright, perfect weather, and yet there had not been a soul in sight. No one to help him. He went to both neighbors' houses. The cars were parked out front, but there were no answers when he knocked on the doors. He pounded and screamed at the top of his lungs for someone, but no one came. It was as if the entire neighborhood vanished.

He had gone back to his own home and sat on the porch steps, trying to call the police, the ambulance, the attorney general—hell, anyone that would answer. After ten minutes of non-stop calls with no answer, he pulled up the news apps on his phone.

Nicholas had spent the next hour sobbing and reading about how the world was literally ending. His own world had already ended when he couldn't save his wife and child. He knew there would be no cavalry, at least not one that would come to save lives. The orders from the president of the United States were to get to a hospital, government building, or the closest sporting arena.

At 3:00 p.m. that day, Nicholas accepted the fact that at age twenty-seven, his life was over. He stripped his wife naked and washed her body clean, like she had done for him hours ago after sex. Crying like an infant the whole time, hardly able to contain himself, he had cleaned his wife and daughter. They deserved that. After stripping the comforter and dirty sheets off his marriage bed, he laid both bodies on the clean mattress, kissed them both on the forehead, and left the bedroom. But not before getting the 9 mm pistol from beneath his side of the mattress. Nicholas went into the living room and sat on the couch, cried a bit more, then inserted the gun into his mouth. He closed his eyes, and then it happened.

He heard a vehicle on the street. The big white van...

IN THE LAST TWENTY YEARS, Nicholas had done his best to work through what happened to him, to his family, to the world. He had been successful at accepting what was to come, and he had lived a decent life since the events that took place back then...when the world was different. Some kinds of hurt would never go away though. It wasn't even a matter of getting over it; he was over it. He didn't cry about Wendy or Stephanie anymore. But he was tired of living without them, and for him, that was enough to do now what he should have done on the couch of his family's home twenty years ago.

Nicholas abruptly grabbed the knife meant to spread butter on his pancakes and plunged it into the right side of his throat. It didn't go in so deep that it came out the other side of his neck, but it was in deep enough. Blood squirted out of the puncture like a water sprinkler, pumping from his neck, covering his shirt and the white couch in blood.

Nicholas did not cry out for help; he didn't cry at all. There would be no help for him, just like there had been none for his loved ones. He grabbed the arm of the couch to steady himself as his legs bucked out like an angry bull. They were involuntary movements from the trauma and pain, but in his brain, he was as calm as a sleeping child. It was time, and he wanted nothing more than to be with his girls again. So much blood came spurting from the right side of his throat that his entire shirt and jeans were now red, and half of the couch looked the same. As the pain began to subside and his heartrate slowed down, he laid down on the couch and let death take him off to wherever it was that death took men. Today he didn't care where that was, as long as it was out of here. Hopefully he would end up back in the arms of Wendy and Stephanie. That would be just amazing.

THE ROOM WAS NOW QUIET. There were no sounds of any kind. Nicholas Johnson decided to check out of the Palace suites early. He laid there with his left hand dangling off the couch, both legs curled beneath him, and a smile on his face. No one could be happier to be dead. The television watched, "Please Wait" plastered across the screen, as usual. Two teachers later walked into the pod and closed the door behind them. They carried Nicholas into the bathroom and washed his body clean. Disinfected and replaced the now crimson furniture. His items were removed from the pod, and the room was prepared for someone new. No one saw or heard from Nicholas again, and no excuse was given. The only authority of the land owed excuses to no one.

CHAPTER TWENTY-TWO

Jacob

J ACOB LAID IN BED WITH BEADS of sweat peppering his face. He'd been tossing and turning, fluffing and re-fluffing the pillows, kicking the sheets off, then grabbing them for comfort a second later. The dreams were back. These particular dreams had become a regular thing for Jacob, to the point that he tried to stay up as late as possible to avoid sleep.

Ordering coffee all day and night, drinking and thinking until he crashed in the a.m., the dark circles under his eyes had become heavier and more pronounced. He looked as though he had an iron deficiency, and the late nights caused him to lose focus in the waking hours of the day. Last week he'd missed out on an exercise activity in the gym with some friends (excitement here was few and far between) because he forgot the time. The dreams came in spurts. For a few months he had them on a nightly basis, and then for the next month or two, there would be nothing; he'd just sleep through the night and dream of nothing at all. These weren't nightmares or anything that would scare a normal man or even a child for that matter, they were just dreams. For him though, he would prefer nightmares about vampires, swamp monsters, or falling into a bottomless hole. He would prefer that over the memories of his life...before.

As much as he tried to fight it, Jacob felt himself drifting off.

While driving home from the Little League Championship after a big win, Jacob and his family stopped at McDonald's to get something to eat. His friend Logan, who was also the team's umpire, rode in the back seat with Jacob. Logan was a bit bigger than Jacob even though he was a few months younger. His honey-mustard blond hair was cut short into a buzz cut. Logan's father was in the navy, and they both kept their hair that way. His small pig nose and beady eyes made him look angrier than he actually was. Logan was a sweetheart and had been Jacob's best friend up until the end of his life.

The smiles on their faces were seemingly laminated on. Their cheeks were humming with pain from smiling, but they couldn't stop. They examined each other's trophies as if they were different, switching them back and forth.

"Let me see yours!"

"Wow, this is so awesome."

Jacob's father, Mathew, watched them through the rearview mirror, and Jacob could see himself through his father's eyes. He could feel what his father felt. Mathew enjoyed watching them in their element, in their childlike, carefree state that all adults watched in secret jealousy. To be young again with the entire world at your feet, that would be the best. Mathew held Valerie's hand as they drove into the McDonalds drive-thru. He rubbed the top of her knuckles with his fingers, and when she turned to look at him, he wrinkled his nose a bit, making a funny face that would always get a giggle out of her.

Both boys in the back wanted happy meals. Jacob's parents got sweet teas, and apple pies for later. They always got the same thing when they went there. Mathew said that McDonald's was made of rubbish and pig innards. Jacob said, "I don't care what's in it, Dad, it tastes so good." His tongue came shooting out of his mouth with mushed chicken nuggets covering it, and he ducked the swinging hand coming from his father. Jacob loved his mother a lot, but the connection that he shared with his father was unmatched.

After dropping Logan off at home, Jacob's father dropped his mother off at the house and told him to get in the front seat. Mathew told his wife that he would be taking Jacob to get a surprise gift for winning the championship game today.

His father told him on the way to Walmart that he was very proud of him, and that his mother was as well. They both knew just how hard he had been working at hitting and fielding as a first baseman. Hard work paid off, and they wanted to do something nice for him. Jacob felt like he had the best parents in the world that day. Away went thoughts of all the punishments for fighting outside with neighborhood kids, getting a C in science class, and being a bit too lippy with his mother. None of that mattered today. He was loved.

They got to Walmart and walked up the electronics aisle. Jacob's father stopped in front of the game systems and called over an employee to get one out of the cage for him. The employee waddled over to them like a giant pear with feet, looking angry about having to do work. Imagine that.

"I'd like to get the PS4 if you have any available. Thank you," Mathew said to the Walmart employee while tousling Jacob's chestnut hair so that it got in his eyes. Jacob smiled from ear to ear and brushed the hair away.

On the ride home, Jacob stared out the window, replaying the baseball game in his head. Mathew looked over at him and pushed his shoulder a bit.

"Hey kid, you happy about the video game thing? I kind of expected you to be a little more excited. Everything okay?"

"Yeah, I'm happy. I'm gonna hook it up as soon as I get home. I was just thinking about the baseball game today. Thanks for buying it for me. I said that when we were in the store."

Jacob reached in the back seat and grabbed the big box. He looked on the back at the unique features and other doodads included—faking interest to show his dad he appreciated it.

"Okay, well that's good. Took a pretty penny out of the savings account to get that for you. If there is something different you would rather have, we could return this, you know. Just making sure you're happy with it, Jake."

Mathew stared out at the road as he drove. He turned the AC on in the car, touching the vents to make sure it was coming out cold.

"There is a quote, Jacob. I can't think of it exactly, but it goes something like, 'We want things until we get them, then we aren't excited about it anymore.' I've never been accused of being a scholar, especially as far as quotes. You get the idea though, right kid?"

Mathew looked over at Jacob to make sure he was following.

"Yeah...I think I do, Dad. I want the PS4, I do. I'm happy to have it. Maybe I'm not as excited as you thought I would be, but I've been playing it over at Davey's house after school, so maybe that's part of it. I really appreciate it though, and I don't want to take it back and get anything else. What's the big deal? Did you expect me to drop tears about it?" Jacob said it with an attitude in *his voice and demeanor, turning to look out the window again and mumbling under his breath.*

"I didn't say that, Jacob. I was just making sure it was something you still wanted. As long as you are happy with it, then I'm happy too. Sorry I asked."

Jacob woke up dripping sweat, his blanket on the floor next to the bed. His tossing and turning had caused him to knock his glass from the nightstand, the water now soaking through the blanket. He sat up in the bed, reached down to grab the corner of the blanket, and wiped his face off with a dry portion of it before throwing it across the bed behind him.

Jacob hated those dreams; they reminded him of a life that felt more like a movie than anything he could fathom today. He knew those memories were real, they were things that he had experienced, but twenty years of a different reality could lead your mind to play tricks on you.

He got out of bed and walked into the dark bathroom. The only light was the moon reflecting off of the bathroom mirror and the glass shower, which gave the entire bathroom a dark blue hue. Jacob stood over the toilet and began to relieve himself.

How long will my life be a flash of MEs, lectures, sexual exercises, and dreams reminding me of what can never be again? he thought while shaking his penis dry and flushing the toilet.

Walking over to the mirror above the sink, he looked at himself and didn't recognize the person in the mirror. He hadn't for some time now. There were remnants of the young college man taking courses at Xavier University glaring back at him, but he was different. The once young man was now staring into the eyes of a scared old man, and he was ashamed of himself for so many reasons.

He had become a man who was so satisfied with the *chance* to live that he didn't care that he hadn't actually lived a day since he walked through those Palace doors. He touched the mirror and traced the shape of his face, realizing that for him, "living" had stopped the day he came here.

Sure, he was alive as far as a heartbeat, but he hadn't accomplished anything. There was a world out there still, and yes, it was all messed up now, but how long would he continue to wait to get into the Greater Understanding Program to see it?

For the first few years, everyone was happy just to be safe, and at the same time wondering if they would get sick. Things were uneasy, and no one had trusted anyone here. The teachers did all they could to bring a bunch of mentally disturbed strangers to begin seeing each other as brothers and sisters. There was so much fear in the beginning, so much confusion.

They were all picked up in big white vans and taken to US Bank Arena, where they were put in lines for processing. The US Army was running the whole operation. After completing forms with their names, addresses, birthdates, and things like that, they were given a vaccination shot of some kind to suppress the flu bug. There had to be at least a thousand people at the arena being processed and vaccinated. Only three hundred of them made it to this Palace. Sadly though, none of those people were Leanne, Logan, Mikey, or anyone else that he knew. Jacob was totally alone, so he didn't care where they were being taken. He had mentally checked out, still in a state of shock.

There were people at the arena who must have been taken to different Palaces, but no one knew where, and the teachers never talked about other Palaces beyond the fact that they existed.

Jacob went back to his bed to lie down. He stared at the television facing him at the opposite end of the room. "Please Wait" was all there was to see. The constant message had been so very strange for Jacob in the beginning. It was weird having a TV for nothing more than Palace messages and the evening words from Sirus. No TV shows, no new movies, no football games to sit back and watch with a beer. But after a while, even the abnormal could become the norm. He eventually got accustomed to things that would have had him crying insanity or listing his rights in the Old World. He had to if he wanted to survive. And he did.

CHAPTER TWENTY-THREE

Trevor

LYING IN BED NEXT TO THE love of his life, Trevor thought about the thing that had come to consume his mind every night since getting out of that van and running inside the Palace. Time was a funny thing here; the consensus was that it had been twenty years, but time in the Palace was like time in any casino from the Old World. There were no clocks, calendars, or anything that would allow you to get caught up in the concept of time at all. Did it really matter how much time had passed anyway? It all meshed together like one big continuous day.

It had been a long time since coming to the Palace, and since the very day he stepped through those metal doors and walked upon the ice-white marble floors, he knew something was off about all of it. They all thought it, but when you were "saved" from the jaws of death, you didn't ask questions. Furthermore, if you wished to stay safe, you didn't ask questions. Trevor saw it as running into the witch's house for fear of the big bad wolf outside. And that witch wanted to cook Hansel and Gretel.

Everyone knew that the government had "plans" in place for situations that could arise: nuclear war, tornado, hurricanes, pandemics, etc. Trevor thought that the precise planning of the Palaces was too calculated. The huge structures seemed to be made specifically for this type of thing, even for this amount of people. It felt like they were all children showing up to summer camp that was already set for them to assimilate.

Trevor wasn't new to the tricks and vile ways of the United States government. He was a member of the Marine Corps and had heard all about the false flag events of the past from friends while in the service. Nothing official of course.

But would you expect something like that to be official? Trevor thought while rubbing his wife's back with his right hand. He was lying flat on his own back, staring at the ceiling of their pod. His hand glided over the pale lavender silk nightgown she wore. He could feel every curve and arch in her back, every twitch in her sleep. She was dreaming.

Trevor thought about the false flag with World War II. We wanted Pearl Harbor to be attacked so that we could enter that world. His own father mentioned that to him once. There was another with the first World Trade Center bombing in 1993, and the obvious second World Trade Center attack in 2001, which brought the towers down, killing thousands. There were other bullshit events like Sandy Hook, the Boston Marathon bombing, and a few other weird things that seemed to be executed by the government at the time. His belief in these questionable events made him wary of anything that happened in the United States.

There is no more United States. Trevor moved his hand up to Amy's hair and began playing with it, weaving the dark chocolate strands into a tangled and frayed rope with his fingers.

He had always thought that the sickness was created by the United States government. There was no way that he or anyone else could even know for sure if the rest of the world was truly as bad off as the Order said they were. For all they knew, it was just America that was going through this.

Who did one go to in this situation to report possible foul play? The teachers? Higher-ups in the Order who never showed their faces, other than that weird Sirus who wanted you to watch him eat…While you ate your own food, which is odd on a totally different level. There was no one. He should just be happy to have a place to sleep, eat, have sex, and learn the same information in a hundred new ways. Trevor thought that it all became overly redundant a few years in, and now they were waiting on a chance to get out.

Why would they construct the Palace in such a way? No public kitchens, so many activity rooms and areas for lectures? It made no sense—unless it was meant to happen. And if that was the case, then he'd been right all along. Trevor sneezed, shooting a hand up to his face to cover his nose and muffle the sound. He didn't want to wake Amy.

Lying there, listening to the constant humming that made up the sound of nothingness, he wondered if it even mattered. Being right wouldn't change anything; they were still there, and all they had was each other. Trevor could be in the depths of Hades, and as long as he had Amy, it would be enough. The not knowing had become an itching on the inside of his skull over the years. He wanted to scratch it, but all he had were ideas and rumors. This place was safe, and it was good for his wife. He knew that.

He untangled her hair and rubbed it flat against the back of her skull. Amy tried to find comfort in her sleep, moving and mumbling something that didn't come out clearly. Trevor knew what she was saying; he knew what she was dreaming about. The dream came for her every night when she finally found sleep. That was okay though, he would always be there for her when she woke. When she was disheveled and desperate for a familiar face, he would be there.

Trevor had these suspicions about the Palace from the very beginning, and the longer they were here, the more apparent it became that the Greater Understanding Program was close to impossible to get into. At least for an old man like him. And since he and Amy were not getting any younger, maybe they would never get in, never be able to leave here. So, the question in his head became: could he stay here for the rest of his life, never knowing what was going on past the quarantine area? The answer to that question was a resounding *yes*, as long as Amy was there. Trevor rolled over on his right side, put his left arm over his wife, and held her throughout the night, shielding her from the nightmares of a world past.

CHAPTER TWENTY-FOUR

Michelle

Y ESTERDAY, ANOTHER ONE DIED. IT WAS a common thing in the child center, nothing to be alarmed about, but still...another one died. She had been around children her entire life, seeing them, playing with them, sometimes feeding them from a bottle. It was very painful to watch a child lie in a baby bed and die...alone. The idea was for the children to learn to thrive on their own, but in some cases, there were the unfortunate souls who couldn't find the will to live.

For Michelle, it was easy to handpick the infants that would become candidates to pass away in the first few revolutions of life. They were frequently undersized, had issues latching on to bottle nipples, and had very little going on in their brains.

Not that you could see inside of their brains, but it was all in the eyes for Michelle. She could see the cogs moving through the eyes— excitement for life, a hunger to make a connection. The strong ones in infancy powered through that lack of connection. They were told the babies passed away for other reasons. Complications during birth, or some type of syndrome they wouldn't understand because they were just children themselves, but she thought there was more to it than that. She thought they were being rushed through a crucial point of any human's life. She had no idea how she made it this far without a decent amount of human interaction. She was not without her issues though.

There were watchers that stayed in the nursery at all times, coordinating schedules every few hours to fill any holes. For the most part they were there to flip the children from their backs to their bellies periodically through the day, make sure their feeding tubes were connected, change diapers, and perform any kind of resuscitation if needed. All too often it was needed. The nursery was always loud for the first few months of an infant's life; they cried, reached out for love—then eventually they stopped crying, almost as if they accepted that no one was coming.

Michelle couldn't remember how many times she woke up to a child being wrapped in a black plastic bag and taken out of the child center. They were taught not to regard the passing of human life as a negative, something about their energy returning back from whence it came. It was sad though, and sometimes she would cry at night about it. In the Old World, a mother would breastfeed her babies, but now they had other ways, more sufficient and safer ways, to nourish infants. Each baby bed had a device that carried a tube from the wall. Michelle assumed the milk was some type of formula. Breastfeeding was said to become an issue for infants because it promoted reliance on the mother, and it was unsafe in the way that the adult female could pass off diseases post-birth to the child.

This she would not miss so much about the child center. She would miss her friends though, her family, all that she had ever known. She would now have the chance to move into a pod and begin learning about the world outside of the Palace, but she wasn't sure she was ready for that. The thought of leaving still saddened her, so she made sure that none of the watchers knew she was apprehensive about moving on to the next level. She got the feeling, they all got the intense feeling, that they were expected to be happy to leave here at age ten, running into adulthood with no fears or inhibitions.

Watchers were like teachers for the child center. Unlike teachers though, watchers did not interfere unless there was a chance of serious injury (though Michelle wondered about that sometimes). They brought food and clean clothes, collected the dirty clothes, and provided some teachings a few times a week, but it was all very fast and to the point. The children understood that the watchers were there to make sure things didn't go wrong, and to keep them on the desired path.

This was a far cry from how children were lorded over in the Old World. The approach in the child center was to withdraw the coddling and allow children to figure things out by themselves or together. Like all things, this could go left—and it sometimes did—but even this was to be expected. Watchers often said to the children: "The biggest lie ever told is that everyone has a right to live. Those with the will and the know-how will inherit the earth."

Michelle sat in a small bed, in a room of identical beds that looked exactly the same as her own. Same size, same bedding, even the colors. About seven beds per room was how the sleeping areas were set up in the child center. The carpet was a plush cherry red, the walls canary yellow. The ceiling was blue, with glow-in-the-dark decals either drawn or pasted onto it. She didn't know which, but all the children seemed to enjoy it at night.

Michelle had emotionally and mentally outgrown this place. She knew that, but it was all she knew nonetheless. There was a difference between aging out of an institution (for all intents and purposes, this was a learning institution) and being mentally ready to take the next challenge. She felt that she needed more time in this stage before moving on. The Order had government officials in roles that made the rules, and they knew human nature much better than she did, so she followed the rules. Michelle often felt like an oddball for not being ready to move on. That was her secret though. And if the watchers didn't know this, all would be fine.

Her age group was in the community area of the center this morning. The ten-year-olds spent most waking hours there, learning to delegate tasks and work together. No one decided anything alone; everybody was in on every decision, and that was the way the watchers wanted things. They were taught that everyone is important and has a voice. Being nonviolent and instead using logic and hard work to accomplish things was the goal. Repeating the ways of people before the sickness was a sure way to repeat the events of the sickness in the future. They were given a second chance to try this all over again, and the governments of the world would make sure they did things right this time around. Most times, they fell short of this goal, but that was to be expected. A certain amount of fighting human nature went into the team building and distribution of labor portions. To Michelle, it almost felt natural for some of the kids to be confrontational, or to want to be the leader.

Michelle stood up and straightened the wrinkles on her perfectly made bed. She had been in a nervous repetition of making the bed, sitting on it, smoothing it back out, and sitting on it again. She was nervous and unsure about the meeting.

What if I don't end up on a floor with anyone I know from the child center? She scared herself with thoughts of being alone up there. She should not care though; she should simply move to the next level and begin learning. But she did care. How could she not?

The person she had connected with the most here was Morgan. Morgan had moved into the pods about half a year ago, and it had been hard for Michelle to deal with. You go ten straight years of seeing someone daily, learning with them, building with them, coming to rely on them both emotionally and mentally, then BOOM, they are gone, and you don't speak anymore. Michelle was old enough to know there was an observation structure in the middle of the child center, and Michelle often wondered if Morgan had come down to see her and the others. Mostly her though.

She hoped that she ended up on the same floor as Morgan. Michelle missed her. Missed her smile, her touch, and the way she was always there when Michelle got scared or lonely. She enjoyed memories of her best friend, but at the same time, thinking of Morgan made her feel uneasy, unclean even. She liked many of the kids she grew up with, but with Morgan...she liked her differently. The thought of the way she actually cared for Morgan was troubling because it was a big mistake made by the people from before, and not to be repeated. Every time a decision came up in the child center, it was compared to similar decisions of the ones who brought upon the sickness.

What time did the watcher say Teacher Paul would come down to talk? Was it 10 a.m. or 11 a.m.? She looked into the mirror on the side of her bed and brushed her hair straight. Knots of blonde kinks came undone with every brush stroke. The quiet snapping sounds turned into silky brushing movements, transforming her hair from a pale blonde nest into a blanket of long beautiful hair that reached down to her shoulders. The freckles on her nose and cheekbones had always bothered her, but she had learned to accept it. "One must accept who they are, because we are all special." No matter how many times she repeated that saying, it didn't change the fact that she hated her freckles.

Michelle set the pink brush on her white nightstand and looked back into the mirror to make sure she looked presentable for Teacher Paul. She was as pleased as she could be with her appearance. Brown speckles danced in the forest-green irises of the eyes she used to survey herself. She was ready, but she wasn't. On the outside, yes, she could put on the pretty face and the smile that went along with it. She could say the words that provided a source of commitment and confidence, but did she feel that deep in her being? No. She knew that none of the ten-year-olds felt that. It was all a farce, but what was the alternative? The floor was not open to opinions or recommendations. Her time in the child center was over. It was best to accept that and play the game.

As if on cue, a watcher arrived then to take her to the meeting. He had a cleanly shaven bald head, no facial hair, and a stare that made him look bothered, like the task of retrieving Michelle was not at the top of his list. She had to walk fast to keep up with him. They passed by the nursery window, and she looked at the babies for what could be the last time. How many would make it to the pods in the next ten years? She would be twenty years old, and they would be the same age as she was today. That thought alone hurt her stomach; it felt as though her heart fell into her feet. She mentally grabbed those tears and stuffed them back into her tear ducts. *Be strong, Michelle*, she told herself, and the forced pleasant look on her face came shining through as she followed the watcher.

Michelle was shown to a small room, the same room that watchers came and went from. She had never been inside. Upon entering the small room, she noticed there was only a table and two chairs, along with another door on the other side of the room, which she thought led to the rest of the Palace. An older white man sat on one side with a big inviting smile on his face. He had one hand extended out, palm flat, inviting Michelle to have a seat on the other side of the table.

"Hello Michelle, I'm Teacher Paul, and I'm here to help you with your level ascension. We are very happy to have you moving into a pod and ready to commence with MEs, lectures, and getting you accustomed to the way we do things in the adult portion of the Palace. You can have a seat." Teacher Paul nodded his head toward the chair in front of her.

Michelle reluctantly pulled out her chair. The watcher closed the door on his way out, leaving them alone to conduct their business. She had never seen a man dressed this way, or one who acted so friendly. The watchers wore white pants, white button-up shirts, and white shoes. Teacher Paul was wearing a black jacket with a white-collared shirt beneath and black pants. He was smiling and talking differently... like she was a friend or something. The watchers weren't like that. They weren't mean either, they were just different. It was hard to explain. His disposition and kind face made her feel better about everything. Still not happy, but better, and that was a good thing.

Michelle clumsily got into her seat, almost tripping on one of the legs of the chair. She couldn't take her eyes off the older man and the softness of his face. So foreign to her.

"Thank you, sir, I'm happy to be getting the chance to move up to the pods. It's exciting to begin my adult learning and come into adulthood. I can't express how happy I am." Just like the teachers rehearsed with her. *I wonder if he believes me?* Michelle thought to herself as she gave the fake smile she had been perfecting since she'd had a memory of anything. Teeth exposed, lips peeled back, eyes fixed upon those of the person she was talking to. What she felt on the inside though was fear, a feeling of being exposed, and ill prepared for what was to come.

"That's a good thing, right?" Teacher Paul reached down into a plastic carrying bag on the side of his chair and fetched a manila folder. He opened the folder and pulled out a few papers before laying them on the table.

"Your pod is ready for you. Remember the latest member to move on to the Greater Understanding Program? Andre? He used to occupy that pod since the very beginning. Andre was able to keep up on all of his learning and be a great role model for everyone around him. Now he is out in the world, helping to make it better for all of us. We are getting much closer to being able to leave these Palaces and get back to living the way we were meant to, amen. I thought you would get a kick out of the information regarding the prior resident of the pod."

Michelle abruptly burst with excitement, throwing both hands in the air and letting out a small yelp of happiness. Her cheeks became flushed, providing a rosy backdrop for her assorted freckles.

"That's so amazing! That has to mean wonderful things for me as well. I'll keep the tradition of the pod going by being someone you and the other teachers can be proud of. I'm ready to start learning and being an outstanding member of the Palace. Anything asked of me, I'll be sure to perform that task to the best of my abilities." *Wow, why did I do that?* She wondered if he was able to read just how disingenuous that was. But the smile never left Michelle's face. She held the eye contact with Teacher Paul the whole way through the exchange. *Nailed it.*

Teacher Paul gave a quick smile and looked back down at the papers in front of him. He licked a finger and peeled through them individually. Reading over a few lines, he nodded his head in agreement with what he saw.

"Looks like you have been a model child in this sector. All great recommendations from the watchers, and your peers see you as a helpful and delightful friend. That's great, and it's something we look for in the adults we accept into the Greater Understanding Program."

Teacher Paul slid the papers back into the folder and put it back into the bag on the floor by his side. She was nervous and wanted to go back to the child center and be with her friends. She wanted to go back and watch the babies, to still be a child. With all of her being, she did not want to be an adult. She didn't feel ready. She didn't feel like a big person.

Even still, Michelle went on raving about how happy she was. She even cried a bit while listening to Teacher Paul explain a day in the life of a pod member. Michelle could tell that he was happy to see such emotion out of a youngster coming into her own. The tears were real, they just weren't for the reason he assumed.

"They are doing a great job with you all here in the child center. It's nice to see this amount of enthusiasm for what's to come," Teacher Paul said as he got up and grabbed his bag. He walked over to her side of the table, shook her hand, and explained that a different teacher would be back to retrieve her in a few hours. She would have time to say goodbye to the people in the child center and collect any small belongings she had.

Even after the door shut behind him, Michelle cried.

Like the infants who died because they lacked acknowledgment and human touch, Michelle was being thrust into an adult world before she was ready. She felt like no one would be there for her when she left the child center. Immediately, she felt alone...again. A part of her died in that small room. To grin and bear the idea of walking away from every friend she had, and then to be put into a situation she was not ready for—it was heartbreaking. In that moment, she understood why some of the babies...just died.

As she wiped her face clean, she put away the sadness and pulled the happy mask over her face once again. Michelle left the small room and ran over to the other ten-year-olds to tell them how happy she was about leaving, making sure not to look in the direction of the nursery. She would not cry saying goodbye to her friends.

CHAPTER TWENTY-FIVE

Mary

L YING ON HER BACK IN JACOB'S bed, panting like an excited dog, Mary struggled to catch her breath. Her mind was spinning out of control as she tried to maneuver around the wet spot she'd created. Mary's thighs were burning, and her lower back was yelling for her to stop the madness. She was spent, but she loved it. Her legs were hidden beneath the soft cotton of the white sheets, one big tangle of trembling flesh and bedding. Her upper body was exposed to the cool AC, which had her nipples standing at attention. Aroused and ready to be stimulated, she could go for another round.

She sat up in the bed with her back straight against the headboard. Reaching for the water on the nightstand, she almost knocked it over, nudging the glass with her index and middle finger and leaving it slightly tipping to the side. Mary managed to catch the glass, and she brought it to her dry lips, letting the cool water bathe her tongue. She could feel the cold liquid move from her mouth all the way down her chest. She needed it.

Watching Jacob from the bed was her favorite part of the relations exercise meetings. This impromptu meeting was unscheduled and solely for their pleasure, and she enjoyed watching his older but still fit body go about its work of showering and putting on lotions and hair gel. She sometimes wondered if he even noticed she was tracking his every move in those moments. Measuring every stretch of the muscles in his back when he reached for the shampoo in the shower, every ripple that appeared in his biceps and triceps when he washed his hair. She even noticed that he was afraid of the shampoo getting in his eyes, and so he washed his hair with his head down and eyes tightly shut. This tickled her every time she spied it. Even though he was so strong and manly to her, she liked how he could be such a baby sometimes.

Mary had never lingered like this with any man she had sex with (she was ready to just call it what it was—it was *sex*). The enjoyment she felt with Jacob was otherworldly, and it went against everything she'd been taught in the child center about pod living. There was not supposed to be more to this sex thing than reproduction and basic health benefits. Sure, it felt good (in some cases), but there was much more to her attraction to Jacob than just the sex.

Jacob stepped out of the shower, dripping water and placing his feet heel first so as not to trip on the slick bathroom tile. He grabbed a towel and dried his face and hair first. Jacob wrapped the towel around his waist and winked at her before moving to an area of the bathroom she could not see. This scene had played out a few times though, so she knew he was putting on deodorant first, then hair gel. His hair had begun to thin on the top recently, and she knew he thought the gel helped to hide that fact. Truth was, he couldn't hide a new mole on his body; she had studied every part of him from head to toe.

Mary decided that the time of appreciating had come to an end, and it was now time to get up and get dressed. She couldn't stay in Jacob's room the entire day, after all. She freed her legs from the sheets and stood up on the left side of the bed. It was a struggle, but she managed. Yawning, Mary reached up to the ceiling as far as she could. Her back thanked her for this with a slight cracking sound. Jacob walked out of the bathroom, still nude, but dry, and walked toward the nutrition dispensary, no doubt to grab a drink for himself. Mary bent over, knees straight, and touched her toes, stretching a bit more (and giving Jacob a little show). While touching her toes, she looked from behind her legs to see if Jacob had noticed. He hadn't.

He had a way about him that almost made her want him even

more. As of late, she'd been thinking about him more than she wanted to admit, and she didn't even know if he thought about her at all. He didn't talk a lot, but when they were with each other sexually or the few times when they were discussing things that were real, the bond was powerful. A man short of words, but passionate about the things he cared about. The thought of her being one of said things brought the hint of a smile to her lips.

After going into the bathroom and cleaning herself up, removing the smell of him from her skin, she pulled her blue jeans back on and put on her *Cheers* tee shirt. She loved this shirt; it was her favorite, even though she had no idea what *Cheers* was. Jacob tried to explain to her that it was a television show from a long time ago. There was a lot lost in translation when people from the Old World tried to explain things to Palace-born folks. Mary slid into her shoes and sat on the bed next to Jacob, who was now in his boxers, drinking a glass of water.

"Are you going to get dressed?" she asked. "The day is still early, and I know you have some lectures or activities you could do for the rest of the day. Did you get a chance to see the two new babies in the child center?" Mary rubbed Jacob's knee and displayed a beautiful smile full of bright white teeth. She'd learned that trick as a kid in the child center, the smile of champions.

"Yeah, when you leave I'll put some clothes on. Don't feel real motivated to do much of anything today." Jacob sat at the foot of the bed with her, staring into his glass of water, swirling it around in circles. "I was down there the other day, didn't notice any new babies though. I don't really care, honestly."

"Ouch, big meanie." Mary clutched her stomach as if she'd taken a shot to the gut. "That's our future down their, sir." She rubbed his shoulder gently. They both laughed.

Jacob got up and took the glass of water back to the silver tray next to the food dispensary. "Yeah, that's what I keep hearing from everyone here." He walked over to the closet area of the pod, opposite of the bed and bathroom. Mary watched him pull a pair of pants off a hanger and lift a navy blue sweatshirt off the top shelf of the closet. *Patriots* was printed across the front of the shirt.

Mary stood and walked toward Jacob. "I know you are starting to get more and more discouraged about the progress being made here, but I can assure you—"

"Please do not lecture me about what's going on here," Jacob cut her off, pants in one hand, sweatshirt in the other. "I have the teachers and everyone else to do that. Not you, please. This is all that you know, Mary. With all due respect, I'll feel the way that I choose to on matters concerning the Order. I'm just saying I don't buy the whole 'child center is the future' nonsense. No offense to you, but drop it." He began putting on his pants.

"I respect your right to feel that way, Jacob, I was just saying it's not so bad here, and you are among one of the top authorities on the Old World. I know that myself and a lot of the other members here highly respect you for sharing all of your knowledge and point of view. You will be getting into the Greater Understanding Program in no time." The thought of Jacob leaving her here alone almost made her want to cry mid-sentence.

"And I've been hearing that since the first year I got here. It's the same thing year after year. 'We are getting closer to leaving the Palace. You are valued here, and the Greater Understanding Program is gonna be lucky to have you.' Yet nothing ever happens. I've learned the same things over and over, counseled so many Palace-born people, and still nothing." Jacob's anger was showing now, his brow furrowed and lips pressed together tightly. Mary watched him visibly struggle to get his temper under control. He exhaled and calmed down.

She was trying to have a heartfelt dialogue with Jacob, but couldn't stop looking at his body. She snapped out of her trance and moved closer to him, touching his chest and smiling at him, hoping to help calm the situation. She put both hands on the sides of his face, feeling the fuzz of his beard rub between her fingers.

"It's going to happen, Jacob, I know so. For both of us. We will both get into the Greater Understanding Program and leave this place forever. You have to believe that." Mary attempted to move her hands to his head and play with his hair like she did when he was asleep.

"Stop, Mary." He knocked her hand down.

"Jacob! What's wrong with you?"

"You know what's wrong with me. Same thing that's wrong with everyone here. None of this is okay. It's not normal, and maybe you don't feel it, but I think you do. I'm just getting sick of the bullshit. For me, this was never supposed to be a long-term thing. It was meant to be a year or two and then back out into the world." He looked at her, and for the first time, he looked vulnerable. Like a child almost.

"I don't know what the plan is here, but it doesn't seem to be getting back to living outside of this building." Frustrated, he punched the closet door and slammed it shut. "Listen Mary, you are more likely to get into that program before me, and that would be great for you. You have this grand plan about what it's gonna be like to get out there and heal the world, and that's admirable. Facts are though, you don't know what's awaiting you or anyone else outside of the quarantine area. None of us do. We know what they tell us, and that's it. You need to open your eyes to some of the shady things that are happening in here. Nothing adds up, Mary."

"Would you like for me to leave here without you? Would that make you happy if I got into the program and you didn't? You are saying all these terrible things about the Palace—what if I got into the program and had to go without you. Then what?"

Jacob looked confused and amused at the same time. He giggled and began to put his belt through the loops of his pants. He mumbled something under his breath and then looked up at her.

"What do you mean? Why would that even matter? Remember, no one belongs to anyone in this new world, so it doesn't matter. The Order has made sure to deprogram you all from feeling anything. Are you telling me that you care if we leave here together or not? I'm an old man; you are a young, beautiful person with a lot ahead of you, I'm sure of it." Jacob walked past Mary to sit on the messy bed again, bending down to get his shoes from beneath the bed. As he put his shoes on, she realized he was using getting dressed to avoid getting close to her.

She stood there with her back to him, not knowing what to say. There was no ME for this situation, no lecture that could have prepared her for a talk about personal feelings for another human *romantically*. She was lost and befuddled as to what was going on inside of her. Mary turned to face him.

"Well, I care about you, Jacob, same way as I care about everyone here and everyone out in the world." She knew she wasn't being truthful with him. Or with herself. There was no one else alive that she felt this strongly for.

Jacob read her face for a second or two without speaking, neither one willing to break the silence. They both cared for each other. Mary knew this to be true, even if they weren't willing to say it.

For a flash of a second, she observed what looked like hurt on his face. He morphed the expression into indifference an instant later. Mary took a step toward him, but Jacob raised a hand to stop her in her place.

"That's what I thought. So, it doesn't matter if you went and I stayed here. None of it really matters. You feel the same for me as you do everyone else here, right?"

"It does matter, Jacob. I care."

"You care about what, Mary? Mankind? O Merciful Mother Earth? Yeah, we know, that's all you Palace people care about." He wore a smug look on his face. Pain was beneath it though, Mary could see that. It made her feel terrible, because that wasn't how she felt at all. When she was around Jacob, she couldn't care less about Mother Earth or anyone living on this entire planet. Just him. But he didn't believe that. How could he? She couldn't vocalize it. And really, she didn't understand it herself.

"Okay Jacob, I understand how you feel. I've never been outside of this place, and I know that's the backdrop of why I can't relate to your feelings. For that I'm sorry...I'll just leave." Mary could feel a tear go streaking down her cheek as she turned away before he could see her crying.

"Mary, stop. Come back," Jacob yelled to her when she was almost at the door. He began to run toward her, but the door swung open before she was able to grab the knob. She jumped back in fear and held her hands up to her face as the door came close to hitting her. Jacob grabbed her arm and pulled her back, protecting her.

There stood Teacher Luke in the doorway, shaggy black hair falling over his forehead and big brown surprised eyes. He was caught off guard just as much as they were. Clearly, he meant to enter the room but didn't realize they were so close to the door.

"Hey...guys, I was just walking by, and I heard a bit of arguing coming from this room? In no way do I want to get in the middle of a relations exercise or even a difference of opinion, but I would ask you both to keep the noise down. If I could hear it, others can too." He stepped inside of the room, staring at them both with a friendly face. He closed the door behind him, but not before Mary saw a few members walking past.

"We are so sorry, Teacher Luke. It was nothing. We just got excited talking about Mother Earth and the amazing things we could do when we get into the Greater Understanding Program." Mary gave a lopsided smile and what could only be considered an awkward attempt at a polite curtsy.

Jacob rolled his eyes and waved his hand at both of them in a dismissive manner. He turned around and walked toward the bed.

"This is fucking stupid," he said under his breath. Mary gasped—she knew that because she could hear it, Teacher Luke could too.

Teacher Luke took a fast step toward Jacob, still wearing a grin on his face, but his eyes were serious.

"Excuse me, Jacob, there is no reason to be disrespectful. I'm telling you that you could be heard outside of your door." His eyes sparkled as he winked at Jacob. "I'm not sure what's causing this attitude from you, but I'm available to talk about it with you if that's something you would like to discuss further. This is not something that you would be reprimanded for, but being disrespectful to a teacher could change things exponentially. Correct yourself right this second and take my advice, for that's all I'm offering at this point."

Jacob made a move toward the teacher. "Hold on, who do yo—"

"We are sorry, Teacher Luke!" Mary practically yelled as she grabbed the teacher's hand and directed his attention to her, spinning him around to face her and cutting Jacob off short.

"We will be sure to keep the noise down. I will leave with you now actually, as I'm on my way to my pod to get lunch. Would you escort me there?" He turned his head and continued to look at Jacob with what appeared to be enjoyment...excitement even. Jacob turned away and sat on a chair near the bed, and Teacher Luke looked at Mary, allowing the pleasant smile to return to his face.

"Of course I'll escort you to your pod, Mary." Teacher Luke paused and turned back to Jacob, who sat on the small white chair, brooding like a child and trying to keep his cool.

"But first, why are you two together today, anyway? This is not a relations exercise day, and there was no clearance in the books for you to have a visitor in your pod today, Jacob." He walked to the foot of the bed and picked up the sheet, rolling it up into a tight ball, all the while never taking his eyes from Jacob. Mary was scared; she didn't want to get a referral, and she didn't want Jacob to get one either, especially by saying something that could get them into more trouble.

Mary looked over to Jacob, shaking her head no, hoping that he would not let his pride take over and cause them more trouble. The teacher was still looking at Jacob, so he could not see her gesture.

Teacher Luke lifted the balled-up sheet to his face and buried his nose within it, still holding eye contact with Jacob. He inhaled deeply, taking in the full scent of the sex that had just occurred a few minutes prior. He exhaled and dropped the sheet on the floor.

"You may want to put this on the floor next to the exit, Mr. Cole. It seems to have been used for...relations." Teacher Luke said the word with a slippery drawl and a smirk. Mary could tell he sounded different, like he was using a joking voice. He sounded so oddly animated, his tone turned Mary's skin into gooseflesh. A chill traveled down her spine, moving down to her legs, making them weak enough to nearly buckle beneath her weight.

"I'll remind you both that relations exercises are only on scheduled days. Now, I'm not saying that this is what I've seen here today with my own eyes...but I have other senses that give me a hunch this was the case." He touched a finger to his nose and glided toward Mary, moving past her and opening the door.

"Let's get to your pod, Mary. Jacob, I can imagine you have things to do today as well. I'd urge you to stay out of trouble, and in the future, keep things quiet. Especially if you are going to break the rules. Wouldn't want to get a referral, or worse." He grabbed Mary's hand and exited the room, leaving Jacob behind in his pod.

They moved down the long corridor with Teacher Luke leading the way at least five paces in front of her. Mary followed behind, not sure what to say, if there was anything to say at all. She hoped this didn't get back to the higher-ups in the Order. She knew she shouldn't have had relations exercises with Jacob today, that she shouldn't even be in his pod without authorized permission from a teacher.

Why would I even risk this trouble to do something like that? She walked up the hallway, ashamed of herself, ashamed that she even put herself in the position to backslide. Even though she was worried about moving further from the Greater Understanding Program, she was more worried about how Jacob was feeling right now. At that moment, she had answered her own question...*That's why you risked it.* Despite her fears, an enormous smile appeared on her face.

CHAPTER TWENTY-SIX

Sirus

H E STOOD IN THE LIGHT OF the window, blocking the beams from fully coming into the office. But the light that had escaped his obstruction managed to brighten the room up. He held a wine glass filled with a well-aged Chateau Lafite—that was his favorite. It helped Sirus get in the mood to speak to Palace members. There was so much they didn't understand about the world, or themselves for that matter. Someone had to do the hard work, and he was charged with that duty.

Sirus lifted the glass to his face, not drinking, just catching the scent of the wine. The smell was almost as invigorating as the taste. He inhaled, letting the smell linger in his nostrils before exhaling and letting it escape.

The sunlight was strong, the heat warming his face. He liked that. For early summer, it was very hot today. Sirus took a small sip from the wine glass, staring out into the courtyard. He'd been watching someone from the window for the last week or so. This individual had become of interest. His behavior was odd. At some point, they would need to speak, but not today. Today he had a meeting with a special someone.

Sirus set the glass on the desk behind him without turning around.

He grabbed the curtain and closed it forcefully, then turned around to regard his newest visitor. Tilting his glasses down on his nose, he presented a warm, inviting smile.

"Today is a wonderful day, is it not, Diane?" Sirus pulled his seat out and finally sat down to talk. "Forgive me for not getting to you sooner, I did not mean to be rude. I was in deep thought when you were shown into my space here. I'm hoping I did not offend." He plastered sincerity all over his handsome face.

Diane's complexion flushed with red, from her neck all the way up to her hairline, her bronzed skin turning crimson in real time. She ogled Sirus and seemingly struggled to form the words to reply. "No not at all, take as long as you need, sir. I feel fortunate for the chance to get to speak to you. I can wait. Sir."

The woman had no idea what she was saying. She could not stop gawking at him. Sirus was fully aware that by most women's standards, everything she saw was utterly magnificent. His perfect white teeth, his thick hair with not a strand out of place. His eyes were magnets, pulling her in, and that was exactly his intention. By the way she bit her soft bottom lip, he could tell that she wanted to book a future relations exercise with him. Obviously, that wouldn't be possible. No one who left Sirus's office went back to the Palace.

"I'm ashamed, my dear, but I do thank you for sparing me the embarrassment." Sirus reached for her hand across the desk. Diane met his gesture and gave her hand over without hesitation. He rubbed it, letting his fingers glide over the veins in her hand while giving an apologetic bow. He noticed the subtle movement in her chair as the woman clutched her legs together tight. She looked away from him and locked her gaze on the big clock in the dark corner. He could just bet she was getting warm and moist between those legs. The thought amused him to no end.

"I have a long day ahead, and I've already had a drink, so let me get on with the business at hand before I render myself no good to anyone." Sirus let out a hearty laugh, his shoulders bouncing while he removed his glasses and laid them on the table, just on top of a file that read *Diane Tanahill*.

"Please sir, you don't have to apologize to me. I'm no one. You are...Sirus. I'm overjoyed to be here. Is there anything, anything at all I can do for you, sir?" She slowly spread her legs in front of the desk. Her hands rested on her knees, creeping closer to her inner thighs.

Sirus knew this was her default; she'd learned how to play men, how to get them to go against their...better judgment and sully their names and morale to please her carnal needs. She thought him a basic male. Sirus didn't know if this offended him or excited him, but he would play her game for a bit.

"I wanted to ask you a question, Diane. What do you remember of the Old World? I know you were around fifteen years old when the government reps found you and delivered you to us. That would make you roughly...thirty-five now?" He tilted the palm of his hand up and down in a give-or-take gesture.

Diane's eyes narrowed a bit. "Yeah, somewhere around there, I'd say. Time is a funny thing here, as you know. But everyone agrees it's been twenty years, so yes, thirty-five."

"Okay, so you may have seen or heard of some of this stuff. In the Old World, humans were careless, selfish things. They didn't mean to be this way, it was just the way the world was, for better or worse right?" Sirus sat back in his seat and removed his black suit jacket, laying it on the right corner of the desk. He began rolling up the sleeves of his white dress shirt.

Diane swallowed and scooted her chair closer to her side of the desk, as though she were so interested in what he was saying that she wanted to hear better. Her legs were now beneath the desk, her lower half out of his view. He raised a pointed eyebrow.

"Can you imagine that there were practices amongst pregnant women in the Old World that allowed a poor excuse for a doctor to suck the living child out of their wombs?" Scooting his chair closer to the desk as well, Sirus placed both elbows on the surface, resting his bearded face in his hands, making him look like a pouty twelve-year-old.

It was easy to see she was not actually paying attention to his words. Not because his banter was not interesting, of course it was. But the flexing in her right arm gave him a clue as to the business going on beneath his beautiful desk. *She is touching herself beneath my desk —how fascinating she was.*

"Yes, a woman could pay a doctor to remove the baby from her abdomen, maybe even take a pill to kill the child, or get the little guy, or girl, sucked right out of her soft, supple, vagina." Sirus delivered the last words in the most sensual of ways, allowing his lips to annunciate every syllable.

"It's said that on this continent alone, women were willingly terminating millions upon millions of their offspring." His face hardened as he got up from his chair and went back to the window. Moving the curtain to the side just a little, he looked out to check on his latest subject. He could multitask.

In the reflection of the glass, Sirus could clearly see her in the chair. He had no idea if she knew, but he was guessing not. It was possible that she knew and simply didn't care. Her legs were open beneath the desk now, she was going at it as if he was not there at all. It was clear to him that she was trying to be sly, but the plan was failing in a big way. Sirus thought he could hear her hand's movements beneath the air conditioner in his office. She was quite excited. He smiled.

"I hope you are following me here, Mrs. Tanahill."

"Yes, yes sir, I am. I'm confused and hurt just thinking about why the women of the Old World would take the option to do any of that."

"I know, right? Unthinkable, I say." He continued to look out at the courtyard; his mark seemed to have moved out of his vision. Sirus looked upward at the sky as he addressed the woman behind him.

"I ask myself the same thing though: Why would women terminate the unborn children? That's not something that a loving parent would do. What reason could there possibly be to destroy life before it ever got a chance at life? None that I can think of, and neither can you, it seems." Sirus removed his hand from the curtain and let it fall closed again, covering the room in darkness once more. He began his march around the desk, playing his pacing game.

His abrupt turn away from the window caused her to jump. Her closed eyes were now aware, and her hand shot from beneath the desk to her side. Her legs slammed shut, and he was tickled knowing that she had likely orgasmed multiple times.

"No sir, no reason I could think. I've given the Palace eight children since the time I've arrived here, and I will give more, until I cannot anymore. I think those women were not appreciative of the gifts Mother Earth bestowed upon them. There is no wonder why the sickness came, right?"

Sirus froze in place and pointed a finger at her like a gun. "Right you are, beautiful young lady. Not appreciating the gifts Mother Earth bestowed upon them!" He almost hopped off the ground with excitement as he flashed her a grin and a wink. Then he continued his trek around the office with background music from the clock. *Tick-tock.*

"The females back then were not getting pregnant or having children because they wanted them, or because they wanted to give the gift of the earth to her offspring. They were becoming pregnant to hold on to men who were not men at all. They had children to get handouts from the government of that time. I know, I was old enough to remember these times, and it's true. Very unfortunate, but true all the same."

Sirus stopped again, right there behind Diane. He put his hand on her shoulders and rubbed them deeply. Moving his face closer to hers, he let his trim beard rub against her cheek as he spoke into her ear. "You do believe my words, don't you, Diane?" Sirus whispered.

"Of course, you understand me, Diane, because you would never do anything like that, right? No, no, not you. "He was amused by how far her own sexual appetite would allow her to let things go. She was weak...weak for him. He could sense the bones in her body turn into spaghetti as she slumped further into the seat.

Sirus released her shoulders allowing her to have control of her body back again. He wanted her to know that he knew what had been taking place beneath the desk. But would she even care? Likely not.

Sirus grabbed his suit jacket from the desk, put it on, and walked to where the clock was. He began tapping on the glass of the clock face in the rhythm of the ticking.

"Women forgot what they were created for, Diane. They began to give in to the same carnal nature that rules man. Women were meant to be better. When the standard of the creator falters, everything collapses shortly after. And I mean creator of life in the physical sense. Your creator is Mother Earth.

"You see, when a woman stops caring to hold her man to a standard, she repeats the same message to her son, then her daughter. Everything gets out of whack. After a while you end up with chaos and ruin. Prior to the sickness, everything was in disarray. There were wars all over the world, crime was a common thing, education was not a priority, and I've just finished telling you about how mothers no longer wanted to be mothers.

"I'm going to ask you a question, Mrs. Tanahill, and I want you to be honest with me, okay? You know that honesty is very important here."

The woman's panic was clear in the way her eyes shot all around the room. Perhaps she thought he would call security to take her away. That idea was funny to him. When she finally locked eyes with him once more, she nodded.

"How many abortions have you given yourself in the last five years?"

"I haven't——"

Sirus raised a hand to stop her. "Lying would cause me to get upset. We have been having a good talk thus far; please don't sully it with impure things like lies. If I meant to have you punished, that would be happening right now. I'm just trying to understand. We offer everything here that you could possibly want. Food, drink, clothing, sexual companionship within reason, safety, education, and a lot of other things. Why would you do it?"

"I don't know what you are talking about, sir. I would never do a thing like that. I've gotten older, and maybe things aren't working like they did when I was younger. I've carried and delivered eight children to the child center. I don't believe my body can handle it anymore." All sexual desire had vacated the look in her eyes.

"I've given you a chance to level with me, Diane. It saddens me that I have to do so much in order to get the truth out of you. Maybe you do understand the women of the past a bit more than you lead on. Did your mother have a good number of male friends? Did she leave you alone in your room while she entertained company in the other room? Or maybe she gave you a new step-father every few months."

Sirus walked to his chair, pulled out the seat, and sat down. He grabbed the manila folder with her name on it and opened it up to rifle through a few of the papers. "I do not say that to be cruel. You must believe that's not my way. I do think it is important that you understand yourself in order for you to take the next step that we have in store for you."

He slid Diane's folder across the desk. She opened it and looked through some of the pictures and papers. After a few seconds, she closed the folder and was silent, staring at the desk, not able to look Sirus in the face.

"I know you can't find the words, dear, so don't worry about it. I'll do the talking. We have evidence of over seven self-administered abortions that you have managed by way of slamming your abdomen against objects in your pod. This was initially figured out by the people in the infirmary...and we do have other means of finding out things."

"I'm so sorry, Sirus, I have just had so many children, and it's taken a terrible toll on my bod—"

"Shhh." He cut her off with a hand in the air. "I said I would do the talking now. You had your opportunity to give me the truth, and you opted to be dishonest. That's something you will have to live with, Diane.

"As I was saying, you have given yourself seven abortions, you have been found to masturbate every free moment you have in your pod, and you have been having sex with many of the men on your floor. You had to know this was a bad idea. This is not the Old World, Mrs. Tanahill. You cannot behave that way here," Sirus said while giving her his best concerned face.

"I do understand, Sirus. I've messed up a lot. I've tried so hard to be the way I'm expected to be. The urges, I can't fight them sometimes. I've let you down, the Order, the teachers, and myself. I'll accept whatever punishment may be waiting for me." Diane slumped into her seat and went back to staring at the desk.

"On the contrary, Mrs. Tanahill. You are not here to be punished, I've told you that. You are here to be promoted. We are going to put you into the Greater Understanding Program. You have been with us for quite some time, and we appreciate all the long, hard years you have endured inside of this place."

Diane's eyes widened, threatening to pop out of her head. She sat up straight in the chair as she looked up at him, eyes welling with tears.

"But...but...why would you? I don't deserve it," she cried.

"It's my job to decide who deserves and who does not. The Order has appointed me to that position, and I take all things into consideration when making these decisions. While the things you did were not becoming of you or the values we teach here, I do understand what you have gone through. I think you need a new setting and new responsibilities. You have accomplished all you can here in the Palace. It's time you move on to the next level."

Sirus allowed her time to dry her face, make amends with him, apologize, cry, dry her face again, and eventually go with Teacher Simon, who was waiting on the outside of the door to take her to the next destination.

Once she was out of the room, Sirus pulled a white handkerchief out of his back pocket and spit on it. He walked over to where she'd been sitting and proceeded to wipe the seat clean. He felt the sides of his mouth quirk upwards in an amused grin. He tossed the handkerchief into the waste basket next to the exit door, picked up his glasses from the desk, and made his way back to the window facing the courtyard.

Sirus opened the curtain as wide as he could and looked out into the world. He took it all in and was happy with what he saw. Order, happiness, and friendly faces. He would make sure that those things remained in place. That was his job, after all.

CHAPTER TWENTY-SEVEN

Jacob

JACOB SAT IN A CHAIR, HOLDING onto a book. But instead of reading its pages, he was staring at a magnificent view of the main entrance. The book was not important. Today it was a prop for a bigger plan. On the first floor of the Palace was the center plaza area, which housed the main entrance into the Palace. The area was mostly used for socializing because of course, they couldn't actually use this exit to leave. At least, no one ever had before.

The entrance doors were made of glass and stood about fifteen feet tall. The first-floor walls of the lobby were also glass. Most everyone there thought that this enormous building was once a five-star hotel before it was remodeled to function as a Palace. The way the pods were set up made it hard for Jacob to believe this idea. Everything about this place seemed deliberate to him.

Coming down here was an activity Jacob had enjoyed since the very beginning. It was less about reading to him and more about keeping his eye on the prize. In the beginning, they were supposed to be released in a year or two. The Palace was never meant to be a long-term deal, at least that's not how it was explained. Going back out into the world to lick their wounds, return home, and get back to living as they had lived before was on the agenda after a short period of time.

Soon that year or two turned into three to five years, then eventually everyone got accustomed to living here. The safety and certainty that the Palace provided made it comfortable. People stopped asking when they were leaving and seemed to accept their fate. It wasn't a bad deal, and most of all, it allowed everyone who had lost so much to forget that reality and grasp onto a new one. But for Jacob, this was not a utopia. And he believed there were others who felt the same way. He would test that theory today.

He didn't even know the title of the book he was pretending to flip the pages of. He had picked it up from the community area on his way here. For him, the time of asking was done, the answers irrelevant at this point. He wanted to leave, and his mind was set on doing just that.

But would Mary come with him? He had been thinking about this for a few weeks now. Over the last month, their bond had gotten much stronger, and he was not sure that he could leave without her.

Something was not right here, and he didn't want to stick around to see what happened. Friends, or family as *they* liked to call them, came up missing out of thin air. Then the other Palace members were later told through pre-meal announcements that the individual had suddenly ascended to the Greater Understanding Program. Never seemed to be any of the Palace-born folks, only the people that came from the outside twenty years ago. Jacob wasn't an old man just yet, and he most definitely wasn't born yesterday.

Oddities had been occurring since the very beginning, but at that time, no one cared to consider things. Twenty years of being cooped up, a series of letdowns, and his own personal struggles had made Jacob have a change of heart. He knew Mary wanted to leave as well. *Through the Greater Understanding Program though*. He wondered if she cared how she got out of this place. If anyone cared.

There was always the chance that they would drop dead the second they stepped past the red flags in the grass. That's what they had been told, and based on what happened to the world, that story wasn't out of the question. He had seen the sickness at work, and it still haunted his dreams at night.

These years sleeping alone and being in solitude with his thoughts had given him much time to think about who he was, what he was willing to deal with, and what he was willing to do to get out of here. Jacob hadn't gotten a chance to talk to Trevor about his plan, but he would as soon as they saw each other again. He would need at least one friend on his side when he decided to leave. At the very least, he could rely on Trevor not ratting him out to the teachers, even if he didn't want to leave.

Jacob turned a few pages all at once while watching the security guards at the door. He was trying to build up the confidence to get up and put his plan into motion. Eight to ten guards were stationed there every day, seven days a week. They switched shifts, so the doors were never left unattended. At any given time, there were multiple guards inside and outside of the main doors.

The soldiers wore black uniforms and carried handguns. Jacob could never figure out the reason for the guns. The assumption was that the weapons were for protection if a Palace member became violent. This very rarely happened, and when it did, no one was shot. He had never seen the security guards pull a gun out of the holster. *Would I need a weapon?* What if he was caught and they tried to hurt him or keep him here?

Jacob set the book on the table and finally got up. Shuffling toward the security guards, toward the doors, he felt sick. So much could go wrong, but he had thought about this for years. For years he had tossed and turned at night and asked himself, *What if?* Today was the day he would find out.

There were other Palace members in the plaza center. Some were reading or talking to each other, having drinks, eating fine foods and laughing about nothing. They were lost in their own self-importance, but this was a regular thing here and part of the reason he needed to go, or at least find out if that option was even available.

The sun was streaming through the glass of the first floor, filling the central plaza with the brightness of the afternoon. The day was truly beautiful; was there a better day to give himself some clarity? He thought not as he felt the corner of his mouth rise into a grin.

Two women sitting near the entrance stared at him as he walked past their table. "Hello," they both said at the same time with a wave. He never made eye-contact or took the time to respond to them. He continued walking toward the entrance. Others were beginning to notice him as he crossed the red line that Palace members were not allowed to cross, which was about six feet from the double doors and the security guards.

A guard near the entrance didn't notice Jacob coming in his direction. The man was busy speaking to one of the suppliers. The suppliers were the ones who brought boxes of goods to the Palace via helicopter, landing within the quarantine zone. They were never seen on the upper level floors of the Palace, just here at the main entrance dropping things off, or near the courtyard outside, speaking to security there. They wore black jackets with black billed caps and black shades. A few of them wore yellow raincoats, regardless of the weather, and they always wore a yellow hat. These yellow raincoat individuals never carried containers; they gave directions and did all the talking.

One of the men was talking to the security guard as Jacob walked past them both, or tried to. The security guard grabbed his arm, scowling at Jacob. The look on his face was confused and angry.

"What are you doing, sir? Why are you over the line?" he said, pushing Jacob a few feet back. The guard put his hand on the gun hanging by his side from a belt clip. "You need to back up, sir."

Jacob began to move backwards as the man in the yellow jacket walked out into the warm weather, letting the breeze of the day come flowing into the Palace. He never looked at or regarded Jacob's presence at all. Three other security guards nearby were watching, expecting Jacob to comply and get back behind the red line.

He stood there staring at the security guard, wondering how far the man was willing to go to keep him from leaving through the main entrance. The guard was fully prepared to begin shooting at him it seemed. "I'm sorry, I must have gotten mixed up. Am I not able to get to the courtyard from this exit?" Jacob said to the guard. A crowd had begun to form as other Palace members came walking up to watch. Not much excitement happened in the Palace, so even marginal tension was liable to catch everyone's attention. And when the gossip started, it would later be exaggerated. Jacob was counting on that.

"You are a man of age in this Palace, you know that you are not to use this exit. I'll ask you once more to return behind that red line."

The guard stepped into an offensive stance, keeping his hand on the weapon as he nodded to the line behind Jacob. Additional security entered the Palace through the main doors. They must have been stationed outside. The newly arriving guards stood at the entrance with their hands behind their backs and their feet in a wide stance.

Jacob smiled at the security guards and took three steps back. He was now back in place, and there was nothing more for people to see. "I'm sorry, sir, I got confused. No need for things to escalate. Please don't hurt me...I'll be going now." Jacob turned to see a crowd of fifteen or twenty people watching. With any luck, every last one of them would tell others about what they saw today. Jacob wore a cunning smile as he walked back to his table, picked up the book, and headed toward the elevators.

The crowd stayed where they were, staring at the wound-up security guards. Jacob could hear lots of chattering, outrage, accusations, and gossip. The confrontation between the middle-aged man and one of the security guards at the entrance would be the talk of the Palace, and that's exactly what Jacob wanted.

CHAPTER TWENTY-EIGHT

Dwight

D WIGHT SAT IN THE PLAZA AREA of the Palace on the first floor, doing some people watching. Deposits for the spank bank, he liked to call it. While sitting at a four-person table, he thought about the old guy who'd gotten hassled by the security near the entrance. It was the same guy who'd butted into his secret session when they were down in the survey area of the child center.

Dwight remembered how excited he was that day, almost to the point of exploding in his jeans before that guy started bothering him. "Jacob," he muttered under his breath, snapping his fingers when he suddenly remembered the name. Dwight didn't like him. He didn't like much of anyone in this place, and he was tempted to take off and run out those double doors just to see what happened.

According to the Palace gossip, Jacob had only stepped over the line...well, he also got close to the door, but that was no reason for the security guards to behave the way that they did, getting everyone in the area all in a fuss.

Dwight only caught the tail end of the big drama, arriving to the plaza just as Jacob was leaving. Lots of people were whispering about it though. When Dwight had joined the back of the crowd, a woman eagerly told him that one of the security guards actually threatened to *shoot* Jacob where he stood. "*Now why would the guards get so uptight just because an old dude gets close to the door?*" Dwight pondered as he got up from his spot at the table. It didn't make any sense at all to him. Unless...his theories were correct.

What if the government was only keeping them in the Palace to do testing on them in their sleep? When he was sleeping at night, he sometimes heard steps in his pod. He never got up to check though, because he was afraid they would kill him or make him sick with their testing. Dwight remembered the time he woke up with a weird bump on his right side shoulder blade. He just knew they'd put some kind of implant inside of his arm.

His father once showed him a conspiracy about microchips and how the government was planning to put microchips in the bodies of citizens in order to track them or even control them. Dwight had spent that entire morning trying to dig the microchip out of his arm. It must have gotten deep in his back though; he couldn't find it after cutting and digging for a good two hours. *They are good at what they do,* he thought as he walked over to a kiosk to get a bag of chips. His favorite kind, barbecue.

Chomping on the chips, Dwight leaned against the wall, watching Palace members come and go from the gym, dressed in their small shorts, tight shirts, and running shoes. If he were able to get some concrete evidence to show what was really going on here, maybe he could convince some people to help him get ahold of those protective suits and take back the country.

He waved at a guy walking past in small biker shorts and a sleeveless blue shirt. "Saved in the spank bank. Thanks for your service, sir," he said, low enough so that no one could hear.

Dwight wasn't sure what Jacob was doing. The guy wasn't crazy, and even if he was, he would try his best to pretend not to be, just so he wouldn't have to deal with a million mental evaluations. The main doors were off-limits to them; everyone knew that. They were only allowed to use the east exit leading out to the courtyard. Pulling a gun or threatening with a gun seemed pretty over the top.

He hated the courtyard and all of the stupid flowers and shrubbery.

There was always a bunch of old people out there. Dwight called it the old folks home.

A beautiful woman walked past him then with a magazine in her hand. Her long auburn hair blew behind her like a cape on Superman. Full lips, a nice figure, and the cutest little nose you could ever see. She didn't even register on the spank bank meter. *Doesn't hurt to be polite*, he thought as he waved to her.

Dwight decided it was time to vacate the first floor and make his way back to the pod. He had enough mental images to masturbate to in his brain. He tossed the empty chip bag in a garbage bin and started down the hallway that led to the elevator. He hit the button and waited for what seemed like five minutes. Always took a long time to get back up to the higher floors of the Palace once you were on the first floor. He hoped that no one came to wait with him. Dwight hated to be around people to begin with; being in an enclosed area like an elevator with someone was the worst. He was lucky though; no one came before he heard the bing of the elevator arriving.

The fourth floor was Dwight's stop. He had lived on that floor since he came into the Palace. You were not able to switch rooms for any reason, so the people that lived on your floor were the people you got to know the most. Of course, he had a few acquaintances on some of the other floors, but the majority were from the fourth floor. No one seemed to care for Dwight's floor, and the fake smiles had run their course years ago. After handling his personal business in his pod, he was going to start working on a plan. *They have everyone here fooled about who they are, but not me*, he thought as the elevator moved up the floors.

Dwight felt the elevator begin to slow at the third floor. It trudged to a full stop, then came another bing sound. The elevator doors opened, and there was Teacher Paul. Dwight couldn't stand Teacher Paul. He was always trying to be nice and get people to like him. Dwight moved to the side and looked down at the corner nearest him. Being so close to people always made him uncomfortable.

Teacher Paul stepped into the elevator, holding a folder in one hand. "Hello Dwight, have you been behaving yourself?"

Dwight looked at the teacher out of the corner of his eye. Eye contact was not his strong suit. "Yes sir, always. I'm great actually, just going to my pod to relax before dinner with Sirus." His mumbled response was nearly inaudible. Raising his head slightly, he noticed movement and spied someone else lagging behind. She stepped into the elevator with a big box of belongings, and he noticed she was young. Very young.

She had to be fresh from the child center. Dwight felt himself becoming immediately aroused. She wasn't all that cute, but she was young, and for him, that was what mattered. The girl stared down at the floor, never looking up to meet his gaze. She moved to stand between himself and Teacher Paul. He knew this was likely her first time on an elevator, and her first day out of the child center. She looked terrified. Something about her fear turned Dwight on even more.

If there was a god, he would put this freckle-faced brat on the fourth floor with him. He was mentally drooling at the thought of it. Just as the elevator began to move up, Teacher Paul looked over the girl's head at Dwight.

"Michelle, this is Dwight. Dwight, this is Michelle. You two will hopefully see a lot of each other." The girl nodded but still didn't look up at him. She was staring at the box in her hands, clearly nervous. "Don't hesitate to reach out for guidance from older Palace members like this gentleman," Teacher Paul said. Dwight was certainly hoping she would come to him for help. She could come to his pod for anything. There hadn't been a youngster on his floor for some years now, and the reality of it was very appealing to him.

Stealing glances of her out of the corner of his eye, he desperately hoped to see them both get out of the elevator on the next floor with him. He wanted to cross his fingers for it to happen. The elevator came to a stop, and neither Teacher Paul nor the little girl moved. The teacher looked at Dwight and motioned for him to go on ahead.

"Have a good day to both of you, and may Mother Earth grant you all that you desire in this life and the next," Dwight said, taking one last look at the plain-looking blonde girl. He didn't spare Teacher Paul a single glance as he took a mental snapshot of her face before stepping out of the elevator.

Just as he got to his pod door and turned the lock with his key, he heard footsteps from down the hall. It was Teacher Paul and the little girl, walking in the opposite direction of the elevator! The sheer possibilities of what this meant for him almost made Dwight faint at the thought. "Oh my God," he said quietly as he continued watching them walk a mere fifteen doors down from his own. *Could this day get any better?* He felt his penis stiffen and throb in his pants.

Dwight watched as Teacher Paul unlocked her pod door with a key from his right-side pocket. Michelle looked down the hallway in his direction (or maybe past him), and Dwight waved, extending each finger, moving them all individually. The wave almost said *come to me*, or at least that was his intent. Dwight couldn't be sure, but it looked like she waved back at him with just the slightest twitch of her hand. He thought she resembled the bully who used to tease him at school, Olivia Jenner. That made him feel angry for a slight second, then he quickly let the excitement take over his mood once more.

Dwight walked into his pod with a pep in his step that he hadn't felt since he was a kid, running around the trailer park with friends. They'd been carefree then, not knowing they were playing in the final days of the Old World. He felt revitalized, excited, and on top of the world.

That afternoon, Dwight masturbated in his shower nine times in a row. That was a personal record for him. Afterwards, he laid down in his bed, got beneath the covers, and wondered if Michelle liked him. "She waved back, and I think I saw a smile," he said to himself. For the rest of that afternoon and night, Dwight laid in bed, rubbing his penis raw and thinking about her. He didn't bother to eat dinner with Sirus that night. Instead, he put a sheet over the television and came up with a plan.

CHAPTER TWENTY-NINE

Trevor

W ALKING INTO HIS HOME, TREVOR KNEW *something was wrong. The scent of death hung heavy in the air, crawling up his nostrils and breeding in his brain. The smell couldn't be mistaken for anything else in the world.*

He spotted blood all over the stairs, so much blood he could have slipped in it. As he climbed, his boots left prints on the carpet. Whose blood is this? *he thought to himself while grabbing the banister to keep his footing. The steps were soddened and mushy, the sound of squishing filling the room with each of his movements. Trevor was afraid. Not afraid for his wife and children, but afraid for himself.* What had happened here? And why did there seem to be no one home?

Trevor stopped on the stairs and waited, listening for signs of anyone in the house. To the right of the staircase, the wall displayed a child's bloody handprint. His heart dropped a level, and he came close to vomiting where he stood. He prayed it wasn't the handprint of one of his children. Which child are you more afraid for though? *he asked himself.* Which one do you want to still be among the living?

One step at a time. Trevor lifted one boot after the other, blood dripping from the soles, the blood of one of his children or maybe both. Could be Amy's blood as well, he supposed. That didn't sound right though. It wasn't Amy. Never Amy.

No matter how many gruesome steps he took, there always seemed to be ten more steps to go. The climb was maddening. Crimson-colored fingerprints led up each side of the stairwell, some seeming to spell out the names of his children. Michael and Tricia, every few steps.

He finally reached the top of the steps, tired and out of breath. Trevor bent over with his hands on his knees, panting and coughing. After catching his breath, he stood up straight and looked around, noticing that all the rooms had closed doors. He knew that if he went into Michael's room, he would find both his son and Amy inside. Trevor knew this because he'd had this dream time and time again. He touched the door, wanting to run inside and save them both, but that never happened in this dream.

Instead, Trevor turned around and began walking toward Tricia's room, which was across from Michael's. Taking this route may provide a different ending to the nightmare that never seemed to go away. He grabbed the doorknob and found it slick with blood. He wiped his hand off on his pants and opened the door.

Trevor walked into the room. Even though it was no later than 11 a.m., it was pitch black. He flipped the light switch, but it didn't work. Just as he began to walk toward where he knew her bed was, the television to his left snapped on. Trevor nearly jumped out of his skin, it scared him so bad.

The words "Please Wait" flashed across the screen. The light from the TV illuminated the bed. Turning toward the bed, he could now make out multiple figures. He stepped closer reluctantly. Seeing your children die once was enough to make a man go mad...having to see this in subsequent nightmares for the last twenty years was enough to make reality and hell merge together.

The bodies were tangled together like a blood-soaked human spider. It was hard for Trevor to make out which limbs belonged to which body. The heads were distinguishable though, and they belonged to each of his children. Trevor covered his eyes with one hand and his mouth with the other hand, the same hand that was just covered in blood from the doorknob moments before. Trevor spit blood onto the floor and turned around, and was again facing the television. The screen was now blinking "Please Wait," "Please Wait." He no longer wanted the light; it was a terrible light that could only show him the grotesque and twisted bodies of his children. He went to turn it off, but nothing happened. Click...click...nothing. No matter how many times he pressed the button, the TV would not go off.

Trevor was crying now, slapping, punching, and clawing at the TV. He couldn't get it to turn off, and he couldn't knock it over because it was bolted to the floor. Tiring himself out once again, Trevor fell onto the floor, desperate to catch his breath. On his hands and knees, he looked up to see the television mocking him. "Please Wait" flashed more rapidly, creating a strobe light effect in the room.

He got to his feet, knowing he would have to face his children in order for this nightmare to come to its conclusion. This was the way of dreams. Trevor stepped forward and looked at the misshapen form lying tangled in the bed, twisted and pulsating.

The eyes of each of his children appeared to be gouged out. Maroon-colored sockets had taken the place of beautiful blue eyes. Blood streamed down their faces like running eyeliner. It took every ounce of his strength to not run screaming out of the room. Wouldn't work anyway, Trevor had tried that in other nightmares exactly like this one, and the door was always locked.

"Daddy...why are you here now?" the thing that was once his son said. His mouth, which was once filled with small white teeth, was now a dark toothless clam, opening and slamming shut with each word. The dark bloody holes were staring at Trevor. Even though there were no pupils, somehow, they still managed to stare in accusation. "You were not here when I needed you...I died alone," Michael said.

"No, no you didn't, son. Don't say that, please don't say that. I didn't know you were so sick...I tried, Michael." A broken squealing sound left Trevor's throat as he tried to walk closer to the twisted monstrosity on the bed, but his legs wouldn't move. He felt like he was stuck in quicksand. Tricia's eyes were still closed, blood running down her eyelids, past her nose, and into her hysterically laughing mouth, also void of any teeth.

She laughed nonstop, a gargling, tortured laugh. There was no pleasure in the laugh; it almost seemed to hurt her, but she did not stop.

"Shut up! Stop laughing at me!" Trevor screamed while trying to get his legs out of the invisible quicksand.

"Even though you left us to die, Father, we will never leave you. Family stays together forever, in life and in death. That's what you said, Dad...you said that," Michael spewed, regarding Trevor with his sad, nonexistent eyes.

"I'd never leave you, son, you have to believe me. Please Michael, Tricia,

please believe me," he begged the horrific monsters residing in his daughter's old bed.

Tricia continued to laugh at him. Laughing and choking on blood and bile the entire time. Trevor wanted to shut them both up. They were lying to him, saying things that weren't true. He loved them, he would give his life for theirs.

Because he couldn't move forward, Trevor put his hands over his ears and turned to run out of the room. As he turned around, he came face to face with Amy. Her face was as hideous as the things in the bed behind him. Her once magical eyes were but mangled pits with skin dangling onto her cheeks. Amy's lips were smiling as she screamed at him. At first, he couldn't make out any words, but the screaming continued, and he finally managed to hear her. "WAKE UP, WAKE UP, WAKE UP!" she shrieked.

Trevor was pulled back into reality by his wife.

Amy, the real Amy, not the Amy of his nightmares, was above him, out of breath and beating on the side of his arm. "Wake up, Trevor," she said in a harsh-sounding whisper. Fear was written all over her face, her eyes darting back and forth as she struggled to wake Trevor up.

"I'm awake, Amy. What's wrong, baby? I'm awake. What's going on?" Trevor grabbed both of her hands and held them close to her chest.

"Trevor, something is going on. We have to get out of here. Something strange is happening. I saw it." Amy ripped her arms away from him and stood up. She walked over to the closet and back to the bed, pacing and mumbling. "I saw it," she repeated over and over.

Trevor sat up in bed, wiping sleep from his eyes. He remembered that whatever he said, he needed to speak to her in a very calm voice. The teachers warned him that when Amy had these...spells, not to get angry with her and to be very calm. The harsher his response to her behavior, the worse her outburst would become.

"Amy, come over here and sit with me, baby. Tell me about it." Trevor slapped a spot on the bed next to him.

"No, Trevor, I'm serious. I saw it. They have all been lying to us. It's not what they say it is." The look on her face was pure terror. "You have to believe me," she said. "They didn't think I saw them, but I did." She walked up to the bed and looked deep into Trevor's eyes. Her face was beautiful in the night, the light from the moon shining against her pale creamy skin. He wanted to kiss her right then and tell her everything was going to be okay. He wanted to lay her down, rub her back, and hold her tight until she forgot about what she thought she saw.

From time to time, Amy would have slips in reality. She had made much progress in the way of getting back to who she was before the kids had died, but with the trauma and the effects of old age creeping up on them both, the episodes would still happen. Lately it had been happening a lot more, and really she just needed to be heard, then comforted. After a nap, she would no longer mention the thing she was raving about before.

"Trevor, will you believe me, honey? I know I get off balance sometimes, but please, I need you to believe me tonight. I saw it, I swear I did." A tear rolled down her face. In the dark with the shadow of the moon, it looked like a diamond falling down her cheek. Hopelessness clouded Amy's face, but she calmed herself and sat next to him on the bed. Trevor could feel her entire body shaking the mattress. He put an arm over her shoulders to still the trembles.

"Just tell me what happened, I'm here for you. I want to hear about what you saw, darling. Talk to me."

"Are you going to believe me?" she said calmly. She was taking deep breaths and exhaling just as deeply.

"Yes, I always believe you, honey. Talk to me." Trevor pulled her closer. He wanted to make her feel safe; it made him feel good to do so.

"Okay, listen to me. Do not interrupt, and please, do not coddle me like a child or someone who is not aware of what they are saying." She gave him a stern look.

"I promise I won't interrupt. Tell me." Trevor pulled his arm from around her shoulder and sat back on the bed to give her some space. Amy got ahold of her breathing.

"Okay. When I was coming back inside from walking with the girls, I went down to the central plaza to get a drink and grab a magazine. Well, I didn't know that they were closing the area off for construction for the night. You know how they're building a track for running on the other side of the gym?" Amy said, gradually speeding up as she talked.

"Take your time, Amy. No reason to rush. Yes, I know they're doing some construction at night down there. They've been telling us in morning enrichment classes for a few weeks now." Trevor rubbed her knee and gave her his full attention. He knew that he only needed to hear her out and then get her to bed.

"Right, well I guess no one noticed me come into the area. I was the only Palace member there, and that's when I saw it. A chopper came down from the sky, just outside of the main doors. It was so loud, and so close to the building."

Trevor grabbed her hand. "Amy, you know that they bring in the supplies via chopper. That's normal, baby."

"Is it normal for the suppliers to get off the chopper with no protective suit on?" She looked at Trevor gravely. "They are coming from out in the world, from areas that are not quarantined. I've watched men get out of those choppers time and time again, and they are always wearing the suits. They have to because the air from Palace to Palace is not clean. Why would they get out of the chopper with no suits now, when they never did before? That doesn't make sense, Trevor."

"What do you mean? You mean they took them off at the door, right? They don't wear those things into the building out of fear of contamination." Trevor was confused, but a part of his mind told him to not pay her any attention. *Don't let her get you all worked up.*

"No Trevor, I'm not stupid. I've been here with you for the last twenty years. I know how the contamination process works. I was close. I could see that they got off the chopper with no protective suits on. Two of them had on black security guard uniforms, and one had on the yellow raincoat with the stupid hat." Amy put up one finger, signaling for him to wait. Then she got up and went over to the door, put her face against it, and cupped a hand over here ear, listening to see if anyone was walking past. She came back to the bed and sat down calmly.

"Please believe me," she whispered to him. "The three men walked into the building, and I panicked, thinking they would see me, so I took off. One of the men did see me run down the hallway to the elevators. He called after me, but I was too afraid to turn around. I wasn't supposed to see that. I was able to get into the elevator and get here to our pod, but I'm so scared. I think one of them saw my face. What if they did, Trevor?"

Trevor didn't know if he should take this story seriously, or if he should just pay lip service to the conversation and get her to sleep, where she would likely forget all about it. "I'm sure they didn't see you, Amy. If they had, they would have knocked on the door by now. Are you sure you saw the men get off the chopper with no protective suits? You do know what that would mean, don't you?" He looked into the eyes that he had drowned inside of for so many years.

"I'm positive, and yes, I know what that means. That's why I'm so scared. We should try to get out of here. I'm scared they are going to find out it was me and do something to me." She grabbed Trevor and hugged him tightly, beginning to cry again. Her frail and skinny body fit inside of his clutches like that of a child. Trevor rolled over with her in his arms and laid on his side, spooning her. He rubbed her shoulder with his free arm, comforting her.

"Okay, I do believe you. No one is coming tonight, and if someone does, they have to deal with me first. There is a lot I don't think is right with this place, but it is safe. Don't worry about anything. Try to get some rest, and let's go over this again in the morning. We can talk about leaving or trying to leave if you still feel that way. Is that okay, Amy?" Trevor kissed the back of her neck.

"Are you sure?" she asked him.

"I'm positive. If you want to leave, we will leave. Just try to sleep for now."

She did not return a reply; she was already falling asleep, and by morning, she would not remember a thing about tonight. Trevor kissed the back of her neck once more, grabbed the blanket, and covered them both with it. Eventually sleep found him again. And thankfully, he didn't dream.

CHAPTER THIRTY

Mary

IT HAD BEEN ABOUT A WEEK since she and Jacob got busted by Teacher Luke. Mary hadn't been able to work up the courage to speak to Jacob since then, but today would be the day. Walking down to his pod was nerve-racking for her, but coming to see him had always been that way. She felt things when they were together that she'd never felt before.

What would she say when she saw him? She had no idea. The hope was that when she saw his face, the right words would pour out of her mouth and all would be great again. They could become closer, get on the same path to reaching the Greater Understanding Program.

Even though Jacob was a lot older than Mary, they had a connection that could not be denied. She no longer wanted to be with anyone else for relations exercises; for some reason, she now felt like sex should only be between Jacob and herself. This went against everything she had ever been taught. *Is he rubbing off on me? His ways are different, and I'm becoming different...*

Walking along the third floor, she hoped she wouldn't run into Teacher Luke again. He was usually walking the hallways of this floor, being creepy as usual. Mary was naturally apprehensive and shy—she didn't like attracting attention—but Teacher Luke always made her feel like he was noticing her...in all the wrong ways. A few of the other girls in the Palace had said as much, even claiming that he had cornered them before. According to these girls, Luke had never actually done anything physical, but he did make them feel afraid and uncomfortable.

As Mary got closer to Jacob's door, she was relieved that she hadn't seen Teacher Luke, but the anxiety of the conversation about to take place came rushing back to the top of her mind. *Maybe he won't be in his pod. He likes to go to the gym at this time*, she thought while raising a hand to knock on the pod door she had visited so many times, both with and without approval. Mary swallowed, then knocked. Then she waited...knocked again.

She felt a rush of relief when he still didn't answer. She spun around and took a few shaky steps down the hall before Jacob's door swung open behind her. She turned to find him looking at her.

They both gave a little smirk, and he looked the opposite way down the hallway, making sure Teacher Luke wasn't coming. They were in the clear, and Jacob waved her into his pod. She complied.

Mary walked into the pod and sat on the bed, waiting for Jacob to sit next to her like he always did. Normally they would have already begun relations exercises. There would be passionate kissing, hair pulling, heavy breathing, and cuddling if this was any other day. But it was not any other day. It was today, and she could clearly see that Jacob was in no mood for sex.

Mary noticed that Jacob stopped short of the love seat. He stood there looking at her, waiting for her to say something. She did come to his room, after all. His face looked so calm, filled with indifference. Jacob had his hands in the pockets of his blue jeans. Today he was wearing a grey button-down shirt with the sleeves rolled up to his forearms. That look always made Mary so hot below the waist, and today was no different. *Fight the urge, Mary, and talk to him*, she told herself. Mary stood up and walked over to him, glaring at him, knowing that she needed to say something fast or he was liable to throw her out of the pod.

Jacob began to speak. Mary placed one finger over his lips, then touched his arm with her free hand.

"Jacob, please let me speak. I do not wish to get into a verbal confrontation with you. I want to let you know how I feel in the best way that I know how. All of these feelings I'm experiencing are very new to me, and I don't know how to process it all. If I allow it to continue to stress me out, I'll end up on the eighth floor, burying myself alive for days at a time." Mary removed her finger from his lip and pulled his arm to lead him over to the bed. Jacob said nothing, but he followed and sat down beside her.

"I'm just going to come out and say it because I don't know how this is supposed to go, and I don't want you to think I'm some immature idiot," Mary said, looking down at the floor.

"I don't think you're—"

Mary cut him off by placing a firm hand on his leg. He abruptly ceased speaking.

"I don't know what love is, Jacob. From what I know, it was a tool used for control in the Old World. Men and women would say that word, and it would somehow give them dominion over the person they had this 'love' for." Mary looked up, into Jacob's eyes.

"While I know on a scientific level that love is just lust, selfishness, oxytocin, and other chemical changes happening in the body...I feel in my heart that there is more to it than that. I've been spiraling out of control since I began having talks with you a few years back, and as of late, the feelings have gotten so strong that I can't think of anything else. I'm beginning to make myself look like a fool to everyone around." Mary wiped her eye, stopping a tear from dropping.

"It doesn't matter to me at all," she went on when Jacob didn't respond. "I'll continue to be a fool if it means I get to be around you more and we get to spend more time together. I have no desire to be with another man here, or anywhere out in the world. That became clear to me when Teacher Luke caught us in here. It was obvious what we were doing, and we could have gotten into so much trouble. I cared more about how you were feeling than anything. I just wanted him to leave your pod."

Jacob moved in and kissed her cheekbone, stopping another tear in its tracks. Their foreheads met, noses touching; the electricity between them almost made Mary want to collapse.

"I know what you are feeling, Mary, and honestly, I feel the same way. I'm not good at showing it; most of the things that happen between us on my end are a habit of how we—we as in the people from the Old World—behave naturally to 'loving' someone.

"There was a woman from the Old World that I was coupled with. She passed away when the sickness came for everyone. I took that hard, right along with the deaths of my parents and close friends, but her...Leanne dying hurt me in a unique way. I closed myself off to everyone, everyone except you. I can't close myself off from you. I've had relations exercises with different women here, but I've never felt anything at all for them. With you it feels...different."

He kissed Mary's lips and ran both hands through her hair, caressing her scalp.

"I can't stop crying, Jacob." Mary's face contorted into the biggest smile, exposing every tooth in her mouth. She couldn't stop smiling either. She didn't even know what this meant, but it made her happier than she had ever been. Never knowing a feeling like this was criminal, and she thought everyone should be able to experience it.

"Listen, Mary, I have something I want to talk to you about. I'm happy that you came over; honestly, I was gonna come find you anyway." Jacob grabbed both of her hands in his own and placed them in her lap, speaking closely to her face. She could tell he was being careful so as not to be overheard. They could never be sure if Teacher Luke or someone else was listening at the door again. For most, whispering was like a second language in the Palace.

"I've come up with a plan, Mary, and I want you to come with me," Jacob said.

"Go where, Jacob? Where are you going?" Bewilderment transformed her face. "There's only one way to leave the Palace, and that's through the Greater Understanding Program. We couldn't get farther than a hundred yards without dying from the sickness that ended the Old World; how else could we leave but through that program?" Was he going crazy?

"Now it's time for you to listen to me, Mary, just hear me out. Try to hear me through all the things you have been taught. Please. I know that it won't make a lot of sense to you, but listen to what I have to say

—because I do not want to do this without you." Mary just nodded her head. Jacob stood from the bed and began pacing the floor while speaking.

"Stuff around here is not what you think it is—it's not what any of us believe it to be. Since we got here, things have been off, but because there was no other choice, no one cared to mention it. We got here over two decades ago, and it was only supposed to be a year or so until the quarantine area was expanded to the cities, then we could all leave and begin helping to fix the carnage and death that took over the planet."

Mary fixed her eyes on him and really tried to understand what he was saying to her. Keeping up with topics on things from before her time was always a struggle, and Jacob spoke so quickly when he was excited about something. She thought he sometimes forgot she was not from the Old World. Like he mistook her for someone from his past. Leanne, perhaps.

"After a while, only certain people were being released back into the world, and it didn't seem to have any rhyme or reason as to why. This was through the Greater Understanding Program. There wasn't always a level of 'knowledge' you had to reach before getting the chance to enter the program. At one point, there was nothing in particular you had to do; it seemed to be a random choosing.

"The years went by, and we all became complacent about weird things we all noticed with the newborn children—they were not allowed to be raised by their birth parents. I don't need to tell you about the child center, you grew up there. To you, this all seems normal, but to us folks from the Old World, it's foreign and not the way things used to be. I know you could argue that we needed to do things differently, that undeniably, the old ways brought us here. I agree to an extent, but that brings me to my point."

Jacob stopped his pacing and laid his hands on her shoulders. He bent down and kissed her lips again. "Stay with me, Mary. I know it's hard to deal with."

"Jacob, I'm listening. Just get it all out so I can process. Please." Jacob stepped back and sat on the back of the sofa. He continued to tell his truth to Mary.

"Myself and others believe that things are not exactly what we think they are. Honestly, I don't know what's happening here, but I think we can find out. I wanted to see what would happen if I got close to the main doors or pretended to walk outside. The guard was ready to pull his gun on me to get me back behind the red line." Jacob whispered to Mary from the sofa, "He didn't actually do it, as some are saying, but I know he would have if I had walked through the door."

"Red line?" Mary was confused.

"Yes, the red line near the main entrance. You might not have noticed it because no one ever gets that close to those doors, but there is a red line there that we are not allowed to pass. It's there. I walked past it and near the main door, where the security is stationed. The guy would have killed me before allowing me to go outside. I had no intentions of doing so, but I just wanted to see how he would react," Jacob said, eyes flickering the whole time.

"Wait, but that doesn't make sense to me. Why would they react that way when we can go out into the courtyard from the east exit, and there is no security there at all? Clearly, they aren't trying to keep us inside the Palace. We can leave whenever we want to." Mary wanted to be right about this.

Jacob walked back to the bed and sat beside her again.

"But think about it. You can't get to the grassy area beyond those red flags from the courtyard, so why would there be security there? The only exit in the Palace that we know of where you can go beyond the flags would be the main entrance." Jacob's eyebrows went up a level. The look he gave her said, *This didn't occur to you?*

"Jacob, why would you want to leave? You witnessed firsthand what the sickness did to the planet, and it's still out there. Why would you want to throw your life away?" Mary was getting visibly upset, her voice rising an octave. Tears filled her eyes. She knew one hard blink would break the levee and the waterworks would begin.

Jacob cupped the side of her young soft face with his wide aging hand. The contrast showed the difference in age and size between them more than ever. He rubbed her face and squashed the tear that began to fall with his large thumb.

"Mary...what if the sickness went away long ago?" Jacob said, staring into Mary's eyes. She watched the fear, anguish, and reluctance animate his pupils. "What if it's actually safe to be on the outside, and they are keeping us here for other reasons? I don't know what those reasons would be, but at this point, I don't know if we can believe anything they say or have said. What if the rest of the world was not wiped out? What if there are others still out there? I need to know, Mary, and I want you to go with me. I know it's a lot to ask, and I'm turning your entire understanding of the world on its head, but I want you by my side. If you can't come with me, I'd appr—"

"I'll go," Mary said swiftly and with confidence, cutting him off before he could finish the sentence. "If you are going, I'm going. I don't know what's going on in the Palace, and at this point, I don't care. But what I do care about is being with you regardless of how things turn out."

"I love you, Mary..."

CHAPTER THIRTY-ONE

Michelle

ICHELLE SAT ON HER BRAND-NEW PERFECTLY made bed, picking through items from the box she brought with her from the child center. Alone for the first time in her entire life, she didn't know how to feel about it. She didn't feel as scared now, but she was also not excited about the new life she had before her. It was all so new and different from what she was accustomed to, it would take some adjusting. To her, this pod was worlds away from her life in the child center.

While there were rainbows and colorful teddy bears in her old home, now there was only white paint in abundance. Her eyes would have to adjust to the lack of color, but she assumed there was a reason for all the white. She would enter this new level ascension with an open heart and with great confidence in the Order and teachers alike. She had never had a reason to doubt them before, and she wouldn't do it now. The time had arrived to grow up. It didn't make things any easier, but she knew, in theory, she was at the right age and education level to be on her own.

Michelle was intimidated coming from a situation in which she was the oldest and wisest to now being the youngest and most in need of guidance. This was the case for all Palace-born children, and some were now as old as twenty and could help her adjust. Teacher Paul even said he would check in with her this week for introductions to other Palace-born individuals. For that she was grateful.

Rifling through the box of items, she pulled out a deck of cards and dropped it into the open drawer of her nightstand along with the hairbrush and book from her old life. She didn't have much; no one here had much though, so that was normal.

What they all lacked in personal items, they made up for in logic and caring for themselves and everything around them. That was the whole point of the Palace; that, and of course to house human life until they could get back out into the world. She would be a part of that transition. The thought brought a sideways smile to her face.

Michelle crossed her arms over her small chest and began giving herself the tour. Teacher Paul had a meeting to attend, so he had let her in the pod and said, "Make yourself at home," before delivering an excited smile and moving on with his day. She thought he had a kind face.

There was not much to discover here, however. There was one room—one big room, but still, one room. The bathroom did have a door. This was a plus, she supposed. Couldn't do your business in front of company, after all. The child center was much bigger, but the many new places she could now visit were more than what she had access to down there.

Michelle spotted the table with three chairs surrounding it. She figured that area was for hosting company. The sofa with a coffee table in front of it was for dinner; she understood Sirus would come on the television each night before the evening meal. Right now, the screen displayed the "Please Wait" message. She knew that was normal.

Making her way over to the nutrition dispensary, which she learned about in the child center, she touched the keypad and looked over the menu of things that could be ordered. Michelle gave a greedy grin while scrolling through the options. This was definitely an upgrade.

In the child center, they were to eat what the watchers brought for them to eat. The food and drinks were always good; the children just lacked being able to make their own choice. Maybe things would not be as daunting as she thought. There were advantages to being considered an adult.

After inputting her dinner for the night and the meals for the next day, she decided to finish unpacking things from her box. The central plaza, she was told, was a place she could meet people, and there was a Palace liaison there to show her all of the amenities of the Palace Program. After unpacking, she could make her way to the first floor to do some adventuring until dinner.

As Michelle reached the bed and sat down, a loud knock came from across the room. *Bang. Bang. Bang.* The sound scared her, and she jumped up fast and stared at the door, puzzled at who could be knocking and for what reason. The sound came once more, but softer this time. *Bang. Bang.*

Michelle walked over to the door and stared through the peephole. She didn't recognize the person on the other side. *Maybe it's someone sent by one of the teachers, like a guide.* She decided she was being cautious for no reason at all. Michelle twisted the lock on the door counterclockwise and turned the knob to greet the small man with dirty blonde hair, emphasis on dirty.

The man's head was tilted toward the ground, but he was gazing up at her with big brown focused eyes. The stranger raised one hand to wave hello, though he didn't speak. Michelle opened the door fully and stepped back, allowing the man to walk inside. She assumed he was a teacher. *Who else could it be?* she thought to herself while stepping back to let him inside. She closed the door behind him and came back around to face him.

"Hello. Are you one of the teachers? No offense to you, sir, I'm new here in the pods. I haven't really had the chance to socialize yet." Michelle smiled, hoping to make a good impression.

"Yeah, uh, yes...I'm a teacher. What are you—I mean, are you liking your pod?"

Michelle noticed the teacher lock the door behind his back. She was confused about why he would do it in that way, like he was trying to hide it from her.

"I'm just now getting settled, but it's a beautiful pod. I'm thankful Mother Earth has provided, and I'm lucky to be here. Thank you, sir."

She put her hand out to shake his. He hesitantly gripped her small hand with a weak wrist, almost as if he didn't want to touch her. "Would you like to have a seat, sir? I could order us something to drink if that pleases you. I'll just do that."

Michelle noticed that her voice sounded small and intimidated, the nervousness apparent in her words. She approached the nutrition dispensary in hopes of breaking the odd tension in the room that had suddenly become the backdrop of the brief conversation. She touched the keypad to order something, not because she was thirsty or because the teacher asked, but because she was jittery and didn't know what else to do with her body.

Before she could get a chance to scroll through the drink options, a powerful force slammed against her back, smashing her face against the dispenser. A blitz of pain came rushing to Michelle's brain by way of a cracked eye socket. She could feel warm liquid pouring down the side of her face like water from a faucet. The stars were appearing and disappearing in her mind—she couldn't see or think straight. Before she could react to what was happening, she was being held up against the nutrition dispensary, the man's hand wrapped around her freshly brushed wheat-blonde hair.

He reached under her skirt with his other hand, trying to touch her vagina, scratching and digging at her while using his body to pin her against the wall. Michelle's legs were spaghetti. If not for his weight against her, she would have fallen to the ground. He got close to her ear, his breath hot and rancid against her cheek.

"Listen to me, you little bitch. Don't look at my face...don't ask me who I am. And do not, whatever you do, little girl, do *not* scream. Do everything that I tell you to do, or I'll kill you here and now. They won't find your body for weeks." The man licked her ear afterwards and inhaled deeply, trapping her scent within his nostrils. His breathing was rampant and heavy, his excitement obvious and terrifying.

As Michelle's confusion dimmed, she became clear on what the situation was. Why would a teacher be doing this? Her mind was spinning out of control, searching for answers. Why was this happening to her? She woke up this morning in the child center, surrounded by friends and loved ones. Now she was experiencing this nightmare.

The man kept her hair balled up in his hand and rushed her to the bathroom, taking his hand from beneath her skirt and covering her mouth just in case she decided to scream. Michelle had no intentions of screaming; she would comply and do what he said. If this was a test or something that the adults did, then she would need to get used to it. She could only see out of one eye at this point, and blood was still streaming down her face, painting her yellow shirt with brownish red streaks.

Upon reaching the bathroom, the man pushed her onto the floor. She collapsed to the ground, hair sticking to the blood all over her face. She did not look up at him; he'd told her not to do so, and she would not disobey. He sat on her back, putting all his weight on her to stop her from moving, and pulled her panties down around her ankles. He started to touch her...and to do whatever he desired. Still, she did not move. If this was a part of what the Palace Program was about, then she would not cause problems. As she understood things, relations exercises would not begin until around age twelve, depending on body development. Maybe she had that wrong.

Michelle's head lay on the once white linoleum, a puddle of rosy wetness creating a silhouette of the side of her face while the man did what he'd come to do with the bottom half of her body. It all lasted at least an hour or two. At one point, he even pulled something sharp out of his pocket and began cutting her hair. Her long, golden hair was splayed all over the floor. She had no idea why, but she was young and inexperienced. Maybe this would be explained later.

At first, the pain she felt during the ordeal was enormous. She had never experienced agony like this, like any of this. Eventually, she stopped feeling the pain at all other than a smashing headache; everything below her waist went numb. Michelle only wanted the situation to be over.

He talked through much of it, calling her awful names she'd never heard before and warning her not to scream. She tried to tune it out, but there was something in his voice. Something familiar. It clicked then—she had seen this man before, on the elevator. Teacher Paul had introduced him to her not even four hours ago. She remembered looking down the hall as he'd waved to her. She was too far away to get a good look at his face then, and she had avoided eye contact with him in the elevator, keeping her head down the whole time.

It was him though; she knew that now. This was not a teacher or anyone who should be in her room at all. Fear set in, and her heart began to speed up as she realized this was *not* something that was normal for adults. She understood that now.

Michelle began to mumble. The man didn't notice, or he didn't care to notice, as she struggled to get the words out. Finally, she was able to take a deep breath and find her voice.

CHAPTER THIRTY-TWO

Dwight

"I REMEMBER YOU! YOU'RE DWIGHT! WHY are you doing this, Dwight? Please stop! I want you to just stop..."

He had ignored the girl's initial attempts to speak out, but this got Dwight's attention. He stopped his tiresome pumping, got to his feet, and went to retrieve a pillow from the bed. When he returned a few seconds later, he didn't say a word as he grabbed the brat by the arm, making her flip from her belly to her back. He grimaced at the mess that was now her face. No beautiful smile, no adorable freckles, no long flowing hair or magical green eyes. All the magic was gone from the one eye that could still open. The rest of her face was a mask of surrealistic carnage.

The girl tried to smile. She tried to put on that fake smile he saw all the Palace-born folk wearing every day. A tooth was missing, but she didn't seem to notice. Blood spilled out of her mouth with the smile.

"Please, Dwight, let's just stop. I'm so—"

Dwight interrupted Michelle's final plea by slamming the pillow over her face. He placed his hands on either side of it to make sure she could not turn her head left or right. Then he sat down on her stomach and applied more pressure. Her arms swung wildly at first, her legs kicking like she was riding a bicycle beneath him.

"You shouldn't have said my name…How dumb are you Palace-idiot kids?" Dwight said, keeping his voice low. "This is best for both of us." Michelle's body was so small underneath his own, she couldn't move. Eventually she stopped trying. The legs stopped wheeling and the arms went limp. Her body deflated beneath his weight, all the wind and life escaping her. He felt like it should have taken longer to suffocate a person, like there should have been more fight in her. *Oh well*, he thought.

Dwight didn't want to look at her again. He left the pillow over her face and got to his feet. He'd made sure he didn't get too loud during the entire ordeal, so there was no rush in cleaning himself up and making it back to his pod. Stepping over her body, he turned the sink on and washed his hands clean. He made sure his face was presentable, scrubbed a few small blood stains off his Steelers sweatshirt, and closed the bathroom door as he walked out into the living area of the pod.

Walking past the bed, Dwight saw that the nightstand drawer was open and noticed a pretty pink brush inside. He reached in and grabbed the brush, stuck it in the back pocket of his khaki pants, and started toward the door. "Please Wait" was plastered on the TV screen. It was mocking him. Did the people inside see him? At this point, did he care?

The people in the television know what I did, he said to himself. Dwight stopped in front of the troublesome device and thought for a second or two. He then raised his right leg and kicked the screen to pieces. Sparks and smoke hissed and popped from the hole where the screen once was. "Fuck you," he mumbled. Dwight opened the door, looked both ways for any teachers, and exited the pod of Michelle, newest member of the Palace Program, now deceased. It was the first time in the twenty-year history of the program that a Palace member had committed murder.

CHAPTER THIRTY-THREE

Trevor

TREVOR WALKED OUT OF THE EIGHTH-FLOOR relaxation room, which he visited at least once a week to get a full-body massage and some words of encouragement. That was all he needed to relieve stress. He didn't really believe in the stupid de-stressing nonsense anyway. *Ya problems are still problems when ya get done bullshitting around.* His father always said that. But a massage, was a massage, regardless of the reasoning.

He rounded the corner of the spotless white hallway, making his way to the elevators. Lunch was calling his name, and he knew he had a delicious turkey club waiting for him in the nutrition dispensary. The walks throughout the Palace tended to be long and cumbersome. The elevators led up to the eighteenth floor, which was the top floor. Problem was though, there was only one set of elevators, so over the years, as the Palace grew and new additions were built, the walks from elevator to lectures, morning enrichments, and other activities had become quite the trek.

Far up the corridor, Trevor heard the elevator bing and saw a teacher step out. They locked eyes as the teacher began jogging toward him. It caught Trevor off guard because the teachers never ran inside the Palace, no one did. He stopped moving and waited for the man to approach.

Teacher Thomas was rarely seen. He monitored the floor that Trevor lived on and could be found there more times than not. They would talk from time to time about Thomas's wife from the Old World, who didn't make it to the Palace. Thomas would also listen to Trevor's stories about Amy and how she was adjusting. He was one of the only teachers Trevor actually enjoyed speaking to.

Once the teacher got to Trevor, he grabbed his arm, struggling to catch his breath as he bent over and put his other hand on his knee. Something was wrong, Trevor could see that.

"Trevor, you have to get down to your pod. There is a message for you on the television. It's Sirus." Teacher Thomas struggled to get the words out while standing up straight and exhaling deeply.

Trevor's face transformed into puzzled bewilderment. He couldn't understand why the coordinator of the Palace Program would want to talk to him.

"Wait a minute...Sirus wants to speak to me? Why? We have no business with each other. I've been in this place for this long, and now he wants to talk to me? Are we getting out of here?" *Are we being considered for the Greater Understanding Program?* For a fleeting moment, he pictured finally being able to leave this place with Amy.

"I believe it's about your wife, sir. Please don't be angry with me for telling you this. Just go down to your pod, and Sirus will come on the television to give you the information. Go now. Please, Trevor." His face was distraught as he begged Trevor to go.

For a man of his age, Trevor moved well. He took off running as fast as he could to the elevator, hoping to catch it before it moved on to another floor. Teacher Thomas said nothing else. He just waited back in the corridor as Trevor caught the elevator before it answered the call of a different Palace member. He jammed on the fifth-floor button at least ten times, not stopping until the door closed.

When Trevor finally burst into his pod door, he threw the keys on the bed that he shared with his wife. He sat down on the couch, staring at the television. The message on the screen read "Please Wait."

"What the hell does Sirus have to say about my wife?" Trevor's voice was loud and tense as he spoke out loud to no one. He could feel his anger building up, the adrenaline causing his body to shake. Slapping a hand down on the table, he screamed "C'mon and tell me what the hell is going on!" Nothing happened though. The screen didn't change.

He sat there, bouncing his foot up and down on the floor, a nervous tick he'd had since childhood. After three minutes or so, Trevor decided he was done waiting and would go down to the courtyard and check on his wife himself. Whatever Sirus needed to say to him could wait until he came back. He got up, got the keys off the bed, and started toward the door. Then it happened.

Someone popped up on the screen, but it wasn't Sirus.

"Hello, Trevor. I want to first say that I'm sorry we are meeting under these circumstances. Would you please have a seat?" The man on the screen had medium-length brown hair pulled up into a bun on his head. He had a clean-cut look and the bluest eyes Trevor had ever seen. Even on camera, they were shockingly blue. Trevor was sure he had never seen this gentleman.

After spending twenty years of his life in the Palace with the same people, it was easy for Trevor to remember faces, and this one was new. The man was not smiling, like so many in this facility tended to always be doing. His face was serious, and he looked as though he had something important to say.

Trevor made his way back to the white love seat and sat down, waiting for the stranger to begin speaking again. *How did he know I was standing? Can he see me?* Trevor wanted to voice his questions out loud, but he refrained for the moment. First things first.

"I want to let you know that I'm working with the government, or what you now know as the Order. My name is not important, so let's not bother. I'm contacting you to let you know about an event that occurred today with your wife, Amy, in the courtyard of the Palace. I'm not one for beating around the bush, so I'll just say it." Trevor's body went stiff as he waited for the words to come from the stranger in the television.

"Trevor, today in the courtyard we were alerted to the passing of your wife, Amy. She collapsed from a heart attack while walking the trail with a few others. Everyone in the area has already been questioned by teachers and other high-ranking members in the Order. They all say the same thing. Amy grabbed her chest and collapsed to the ground, where she kicked and screamed until her body went limp. No one had the ability to help her, so all of her friends waited until medical showed up. By then it was too late…" The stranger sounded like he was delivering lines for a TV show rather than telling a man he'd just lost the most important person in his life. Lack of empathy came to mind, but this didn't surprise Trevor. He was acquainted with this personality type.

Trevor had already checked out of the conversation. Every sound coming from the box in the wall sounded like jumbled nonsense. He saw red, and his mind became a puzzle that was impossible to put together. There was no anger though. He was calm as he just sat there.

At some point, the man went away and the screen went black, replaced by the normal message: "Please Wait." Trevor did just that. He sat there on the white love seat and waited for something to change. Waited for Amy to come walking into the pod.

That didn't happen though. No one came into the pod. No one even came knocking on the door. Trevor likely would not have heard or answered even if they did. Sirus eventually came onto the television to have dinner with every Palace member, as he did every night.

Trevor heard the prayer, but it sounded as though it were being said backwards, like those devil songs from different bands he and his buddies listened to in the Old World. Judas Priest had a song that seemed to tell fans to shoot themselves if you played the record backwards. Sirus sounded that way to him. Trevor didn't care about the Order, Sirus, the teachers, or the other ninety-nine point nine percent of the people in the Palace. His anger, hurt, and confusion were crippling.

He was in a shock, frozen in the moment by those six words: "…the passing of your wife, Amy." Trevor sat there all night, reliving that moment over and over in a nightmarish loop. The only other thought that came to his mind throughout the night: *I should have listened to her.*

CHAPTER THIRTY-FOUR

Sirus

"WE HAVE ALWAYS BEEN A WASTEFUL species, you know. Since the recording of history, it's kind of been our thing, and it eventually became worse. For every wonder created, every technological advance achieved, you will find waste in the background." Sirus stood with his back to the office door, speaking to the back of the gentleman's head. The man sitting at the desk was apparently too afraid and out of his element to turn around and look at Sirus, so he stared straight ahead at the seat Sirus had vacated.

Throughout his experience as Palace Program director, Sirus had developed a way of setting the mood, of saying the right things and creating an ambiance that suited the tone he wished to display. He placed his hand in the pocket of his black jacket as he puffed away on a cigar, allowing the smoke to create a fog-like haze in the office. Light filtered through the slightly opened curtains, the beams shining against the curling smoke.

"Do you know why we don't allow food or drink to be thrown away in the pods? In all my years here, I'm surprised that no one has asked me this question. So, I'll explain.

"The nutrition dispensary sends the uneaten food and drinks down to the basement level of our facility. This area houses the massive kitchen and other sectors that allow this beautiful building to provide all the things we need for survival, including the quarantine radius. Uneaten materials are saved and repurposed for other meals. The consistency stays the same, and it still makes a scrumptious meal for another Palace member."

The man's head dipped down, nodding slightly to show he was listening.

"I'm sure you remember that trash cans, dumpsters, and landfills were just a regular part of society back then. Throwing uneaten food and used materials in the trash was the norm. Mankind has always had this odd idea that things lose their value because YOU, as an individual, no longer have a need for it."

Sirus let out a hearty laugh that made his shoulders bounce up and down as he looked up at the ceiling. "Do you remember, Kyle? We would buy furniture or some other stupid object, get tired of it, and go waste money on newer objects. Then we'd just throw the old stuff away. We'd set it on the curb near the driveway, where it would get picked up by the trash trucks and just *disappear*! Right? Is that how it went? No, of course not. We had landfills to house all of our wasteful ways."

Kyle Hoffman sat with his back straight as a board in the chair, not daring to turn around and make eye contact while Sirus laughed like a maniac. Once Sirus got his laughing fit under control, he took a few steps toward Kyle's chair, kicking his feet out on each step like a nutcracker toy. He moved with the grace of a dancer. Not too shabby for a man of his age. "Not a talkative one, are you, Kyle? That's okay, because I like hearing myself speak, and I think you will get a kick out of where this is going."

Sirus slapped Kyle's right arm in an "ol' pal" gesture and laughed some more. He walked around the desk and ashed the cigar in a dark brown marble ashtray, then leaned against the desk and proceeded to finish his thought.

"You see, the majority of us thought there was a magical place where all of our trash would go to live happily ever after. 'Out of sight, out of mind' was the normal thought process back then. So, while the people of the Old World were out spending ungodly amounts of money on amusement parks, sporting events, and cheap little devices, all their trash was piling up and effecting the planet as a whole. Remember the landfills, Kyle?"

Sirus paused to allow Kyle to respond, but the man remained nervously tight-lipped.

"You may be a bit young to remember them, so I'll give you a spot of background on the topic. Landfills are places where waste material is stored, in most cases buried in the ground. A child could even figure out that it was a bad idea, but for thousands of years, this method of getting rid of waste remained." Sirus flicked more ash from the cigar into the ashtray as he sat on the side of the desk, crossing his legs in a relaxed, casual fashion.

"We all knew for years that it was a bad idea. We knew it, we just didn't care. In the Old World, problems were not problems until they were standing at your front door with a gun to the peephole, if you know what I mean, Kyle. Do you know what I mean, sir?" He squinted an eye at Kyle, moving a bit closer to him.

"Yes sir, I know what you are saying." Kyle moved around in his seat, the look on his face screaming his unease.

"I hope that you do, Kyle." Sirus got up from the desk and sat in his chair, putting the cigar out in the ashtray as he continued.

"Mankind has dumped millions of pounds of plastic into the oceans, lakes, and rivers. How counterproductive is that to sustaining life on your planet? Why would an intelligent species do a thing like that? They wouldn't." Sirus pounded his hand on the large desk, shaking a mug sitting on his right. The ring he wore with a golden emblem of the letter T made a clinking sound on the finished wood. Kyle jumped a little in his seat.

"I'm sorry, my friend, I did not mean to spook you. I tend to get a bit fired up when discussing the crimes of the planet perpetrated by my own era of humanity." He straightened out the folders and papers on his desk and sent a warm smile in Kyle's direction.

"My point is that an intelligent people would not do this, but in the

Old World, this was commonplace, as you know. I'm aware that you were in junior high when things...got flipped around. That had to be hard to deal with for a child your age. I did get a chance to look into your file before you got here." Sirus grabbed the top folder in the bunch and lifted it up over his head. "You were a middle child, correct? Middle children are always a bit more headstrong than the other two, right?"

"Yes, I'm a middle child. I had two brothers. Robert and Christen." Kyle nervously tapped the arm of his chair, looking like he wanted to run from the room. A bead of sweat slid down the man's temple.

Sirus plopped the folder on the desk, sat back in his chair, and put his feet up. His shiny black dress shoes were as pristine as the Palace he lorded over. Implementing procedures and enforcing the rules took structure and care, as did his neat appearance.

"Please sir, I mean no offense, but I'd like permission to ask a question." Kyle leaned toward the desk as he wiped the sweat from his forehead.

Sirus removed his feet from the surface and leaned toward the desk as well. He lifted his eyebrows in intrigue, as though he couldn't wait for Kyle to spill a secret. "You can speak freely here, I'm an open book." He winked at Kyle and sat back in his seat, kicking up his feet once more on the desk.

"What does me being a middle child have to do with anything? I was following what you were saying, up until that question." Kyle's eyes narrowed on Sirus.

"Of course, but I'll get to that point later. I did get a little ahead of myself, Mr. Hoffman. Would you allow me to digress and continue with my initial point?"

"Yes sir, Sirus, continue." Kyle kept his same posture, attempting to stick a pleasant look on his face and failing.

"I'm going to come at this a bit differently, but I can appreciate your to-the-point disposition. That's a great quality in a person," Sirus said, grinning. "One thing that people from the Old World wasted the most was right under their noses, and many never realized it. Human potential. For most people, this potential was never realized, the surface unscratched, and this was never viewed as a crime. My sensibilities would never be okay with such a thing, for potential is the bud of the most beautiful flower." Sirus stood up from his chair and stretched, reaching his long arms toward the sky. "Would you like a drink, sir?" he asked Kyle.

"No sir. We aren't allowed to drink in the Palace, sir. No one is." Sirus walked over to a small table near the grandfather clock. There were assorted bottles of liquor and two glasses. He shrugged his shoulders, pouring himself a glass. Sirus drank it all in one gulp, slamming the glass back on the table. He pointed to the side of his neck, grimacing. "It gets ya right there, ya know? Of course not, but maybe you will someday.

"You likely don't remember, but there were millions of unemployed people in the Old World, not working, not becoming more educated, nothing at all. The education systems that were set up were more or less in place to rob the masses of their currency, and in return, they got a poor education, and one they would end up working a lifetime to pay off the debt for. That debt was almost always necessary to even graduate from the institutions. It was wild, Mr. Hoffman. To live a lifetime in the Old World would have been a cumbersome thing for a man of your intelligence."

Sirus sat on the corner of the desk nearest Kyle. He smiled and cracked the knuckles on his aging but strong hands. "Which brings me to the reason why you are in my office today, sir."

Kyle crossed his legs, pretending to look unbothered by what was being said. Sirus saw right through it. The man looked guilty. He looked ready to explode with panic.

"It's been brought to my attention that for the last year you have managed to only show up for fifty percent of your morning enrichment classes and sixty percent of your lectures. And I'm being told that you have sent away multiple women for relations exercises without teacher approval. Now why would this be the case? Do you feel that you have reached your cap on knowledge and no longer need enlightening on the Old World or the New World to come?" Sirus felt his smile melt into a slight sneer. The mood in the room turned cold, which was his intention.

"No sir, I don't think that at all. I was not aware that I'd missed so many essential things this year. I've been suffering from small sicknesses, colds, sinus infections, things like that. So some mornings I'm not up to do things, and the last thing I'd want to do is get someone sick. I'm sorry," he said, giving the saddest face his features could muster.

Sirus glared at Kyle, unblinking. He cocked his head to the side, observing the body language of the man in front of him. "We did not think it proper to bring this issue to your attention right away. A pattern must be met before a problem can be identified. We are now in problem territory, thus your presence here today. All of your time in the Palace is to be spent making yourself a better person so that when it is time to move on to the next level, you will be ready. Not taking advantage of your time here is not recommended and works against your primary goal." Sirus wondered if the imbecile had any clue yet as to why he was here. They rarely ever did.

"Furthermore," he went on, "this behavior has the ability to rub off on other Palace members. No member has a working job, sir, but you do in fact have a job to do, and that's to follow your schedule and ascend to the next level, which is the Greater Understanding Program." Sirus got up from the desk corner and ambled back to his seat.

"I can and will fix this issue," Kyle said. "I appreciate everything you and the Order have done for me, sir. I've been feeling much better as of late, and I will not miss anything else on my schedule." Kyle spoke with uncharacteristic confidence and offered a smile.

Sirus smiled back, holding it for a few seconds. "Well of course we expect you to miss things every now and then. You are human, aren't you? Though I don't believe all of the absences are due to your health, as bad health has not been recorded by the infirmary or the teacher monitoring your floor. You can speak freely with me about anything you may be experiencing here. I like to know how Palace members are feeling." Sirus's mouth shifted from friendly smile to stern frown. He saw the panic return to Kyle's eyes before the man looked away.

"You really mean that I can say how I feel?" Kyle spoke in a low voice as he stared down at the desk.

"Yes, there is no reason to fear me. We are talking about an issue, we are conversing about an issue, nothing more." A glimmer of a smile appeared once again on Sirus's face. He bared his beautiful white teeth one instant, then tight lips the next.

"Okay...okay. I've been here for twenty years, sir, since I was twelve years old. I've heard every morning enrichment in every conceivable way it could be explained. I've sat in every lecture from every teacher time and time again. I've learned about the earth, new and old. I've learned about the faults of man.

"It's all very pertinent information as far as ascending to the next level, but it has become repetitive to me and others from the Old World. A lot of us feel like it benefits the Palace-born individuals more. It's hard to get up to go learn things that you could probably teach yourself at this point. Again, I'm not meaning to be disrespectful at all, I'm just being honest here."

Sirus nodded in agreement. "I see, I see. You say that others feel the same way? That is understandable. Yes, this was meant to be a temporary program, but things on the outside have not been as easy to fix as our scientists once thought. The particular bacteria that killed off much of the human life on our planet has proven to be a tricky bugger." Sirus snickered to himself and opened Kyle's file, staring inside for a few seconds before closing it.

"I'll answer your question from earlier, about you being a middle child, then I'll link that with my idea for you and the issue we have. As a middle child, you are naturally a seeker of new things. You are independent and always seeking to stand out in your own way. Middle child syndrome, my wife would say. I'm also the monkey in the middle, so I know this to be true. With an older sibling, you have to do more to get your parents' attention. And having a younger brother means you have to also lead and become independent. I get it.

"This very easily explains where you are in your maturation at the Palace. You have outgrown what we do here, in your own words as well as in my own observation. Which is why I wanted to pick your brain. I believe it is time you move on to the next level of your journey, Kyle Hoffman. The Greater Understanding Program."

Kyle jumped out of his seat so fast and with such excitement that he knocked the chair over. Fumbling to pick it up, he tried to speak but couldn't get the words out.

"Calm down sir, speak."

"I don't know what to say. I didn't think this day would ever come. At least not for me. I gave up hope long ago." Kyle pushed his chair into the desk and stood there with both hands on his head.

Sirus walked around the desk and dropped a hand on his shoulder.

"It's time, Kyle, it's time. You have earned it. There is nothing more we can do for you here in the Palace. You have met the limit of what can be learned here, and now it's time for the next challenge." He embraced Kyle, feeling the man's body shaking from elation.

"I'll get down to my pod and get my things together. Oh gosh, wait till I tell—" Kyle cut himself off, but Sirus didn't miss a beat.

"Wait until you tell who?" Sirus moved back and smiled.

"Uh, a few of my friends. They will be really happy for me. Forgive me, my mind is ice-cream right now." He laughed, unsure of how Sirus would take the lie, and extended his hand.

"I know you are excited at the moment, but you cannot return to your floor, Mr. Hoffman. Your things have already been retrieved and are waiting for you outside the room. Teacher Simon is waiting for you outside as well. He will be taking you to your next destination. For reasons that are obvious, we cannot allow you around the other Palace members right before you move on. You know that, sir."

Sirus shrugged his shoulders and put both hands in the air. "As you said, you were losing hope. You can imagine how it would feel for them to see that you are moving on and they still have work to do here. We will tell your friends about your departure via television announcement, as the ritual has always been. Do not worry about that." Sirus shook Kyle's hand and walked him to the door.

"Okay...okay...I understand. Well again, thank you, sir. I'll do all that I can with the Greater Understanding Program to make sure things become safe enough to release everyone in every Palace in the world." Kyle moved to open the door.

"Hold on, Mr. Hoffman. I have a question for you before you go."

Sirus's lips parted, and the corners of his mouth turned upward, creating a smile so big that a shark would be jealous. In the dim lighting of the office, he felt like a wolf, all teeth in the dark. "Why did you think I wanted to speak to you?" He felt his smile widen even more in anticipation.

Kyle seemed to be caught off guard. He responded with stuttering, messing with the doorknob while trying to find the correct words

"I, ummm, I had no idea. I...I honestly didn't know what this meeting would be about. I'm happy it happened though. Thank you, sir." He turned to the door, afraid to look at Sirus now.

"Teacher Luke happened to find a letter written by you. I've been shown said letter, and I must admit that you are quite the poet. We were impressed. I'm quite sure the young...man the letter was written for would have loved the sentiment."

Kyle didn't turn to look at Sirus. He continued to grip the knob of the door, not twisting it to open the door, but just to have something to do with his nervous energy.

"Seems that a lot of the time spent missing scheduled activities, you were spending with...what is his name again? Mason? Mason from the sixth floor, correct? But you know what? I think that deep inside, you remembered the rules of the Palace, and the very important rule about being honest and always being true to yourself, whoever you may be. I think that a part of you lost this letter purposely to be found by a teacher and brought to me. Sometimes the heart tattles on itself, ya know. The heart wants to come *bursting* out of the closet...if you know what I mean."

Sirus allowed silence to hang over those words. He loved the intensity of the moment, knowing that Kyle had no idea if he would be sent back to the Palace or allowed to leave. This filled Sirus with glee, and he allowed the silence to continue, certain that Kyle was too shocked to respond in any way.

"Get out of here, and good luck on your journey outside of the Palace," Sirus said from the dark corner of his office. Kyle opened the door, and just as he began to step out into the hallway, Sirus spoke once more.

"Kyle!" He paused. "Your secret is safe with me."

The newly ascending Palace Member turned his head slightly. "Thank you Sirus, sir." He then stepped out into the hallway, quietly closing the door behind him. Sirus grinned as he made his way back to the desk area and gave the golden globe on his desk a spin.

CHAPTER THIRTY-FIVE

Jacob

JACOB SAT, NOT PAYING ATTENTION TO his morning enrichment class, thinking about the plan he and Mary had been going over for the last few days. It was a no-nonsense plan, but it was something. They decided that someday soon, when the chance presented itself, they would leave the Palace area through the east exit. There were no security guards at that door, but there were some guards just outside of the courtyard. Mary had taken Jacob to the eastern side of the courtyard, where there was a cluster of trees near a small creek area. There was only one security guard outside of that area. In the evening, he would have an hour break, but no one took his place for that duration.

Yesterday they'd stayed in the courtyard for a good two hours, constantly going into the cluster of trees, waiting to see exactly when the guard would leave his post. The sun was just beginning to fall when the guard spoke into his walkie-talkie, gave a last few looks over the area, and then walked around to the front of the Palace.

From that area, they would be able to make a run past the red flag, past the quarantine radius. The darkness should shield them from sight, but even if they were noticed, it would be too late to be caught before they got to the forest area. Then it would just become a game of hide and seek.

Mary still seemed to be nervous about the entire thing, but that was to be expected. She had never been out in the real world. Everything she knew and understood of the world was fed to her in the Palace. When they went over their plan, she would hold on to his hand, and at times he could feel her tremble. She maintained that if he was going, then she was going with him.

The behavior of the guard in the central plaza had proved to Jacob that things weren't the way the teachers said they were on the outside. According to the Order, the people were here by choice because they wanted to stay safe, not because the Order would not allow them to leave. The two things were very different. Jacob felt if he wanted to throw his life away by walking past the quarantine area, then that choice should be his to make. But low and behold, a guard had stopped him from leaving through the main exit.

Jacob sat there as Teacher Andrew droned on and on about Mother Earth's love and how lucky they were to be alive today. He scribbled in his notepad, but not notes on the topic. Jacob instead wrote down the names of all the friends and family he'd lost so long ago.

From time to time, he would write those names, keeping them in his memory. It was easy to forget about the world before it all went to hell. He knew that his mother and father had passed, he'd been there to see that. There were others though. People whose fate he wasn't sure about. Leanne of course, and his best friend, Logan. Friends from school, people he didn't speak to much, neighbors. In his mind, he thought writing the names kept them alive in some shape or form.

It was a bad idea to keep your hopes up with things like this. The Order was misleading them about some things, but the ferocity of the sickness all those years ago was not one of them. He saw it with his own eyes. He remembered thinking he was the only living person on his street as he sat with his back to his parents' bedroom door, crying like a baby. It was still embarrassing for him to think about; he'd been a coward in that moment. He would not be a coward this time around.

He would risk trying to escape. The word sounded odd in his head: "escape." That was never supposed to be the case here, but Jacob now believed he was living inside of a well-kept prison that fed some desires while trying to rid you of others. It all felt wrong to him.

The enrichment class ended just as Jacob began to fall asleep. He didn't even care anymore to stay awake. Leaving the Palace was within his reach, and he would be leaving with Mary. He did love her—and they had made love every day since they'd both said the words. He taught her that phrase, "making love." She enjoyed saying it.

Jacob gathered his things and gave Teacher Andrew a wave goodbye as he made his way through the door leading out into the hallway. That's when he heard a voice that sounded like Trevor's. There were people running in the direction of a different morning enrichment class still in session. Jacob approached the crowd forming outside of the room. People chatted back and forth, concerned looks written all over their faces.

Making his way through the crowd of about twenty people, Jacob was able to get in the doorway of the morning enrichment class and found that it was just as he thought. Trevor stood in the middle of class, screaming at the top of his lungs. His eyes were burning with rage, his nostrils flared, and the veins in his neck looked as if they would burst through his skin if he screamed any louder. Jacob had never seen Trevor like this. Everyone in the room was backed against the wall. Teacher Paul stood in front of them with his arms outstretched, as if he could protect everyone with his own body.

It was hard to make out the words Trevor roared at the group. His anger wasn't directed at anyone in particular. Everyone who could hear was meant to feel his plight.

"What the hell is wrong with all of you people! Can't you see what they are doing to us? My wife is dead, and no one is doing anything about it." Trevor bounded around the room with his fist balled at his sides. He was so angry that steam should have been shooting from his ears.

Jacob moved through the doorway and stepped into the room. Trevor didn't notice him there; he just went on terrorizing everyone.

"They can just tell us whatever they want, and they know we will believe it. This is exactly the way the Old World was—we just began to believe everything the government told us, and they ruled everything with fear. You have to listen to me, I'm not crazy. I don't have a reason to live anymore."

Trevor stopped pacing and put both hands over his face, crying. "She's gone. I don't care anymore. I don't care what they do to me. They can kill me, they can banish me…what fuckin' difference does it make?" Trevor stood there, staring at Teacher Paul, pointing at him. "You know what's going on here, you bastard." He started toward the teacher.

"Hey there, buddy, are you okay?" Jacob stepped into Trevor's view with both hands up, his palms out in a non-aggressive stance. He knew Trevor was a military man, and he didn't want to set him off any more than he already was.

Trevor looked at Jacob and smiled, shaking his head as if he knew this would happen.

"This guy here, this guy is with me. This is my friend. He knows stuff is messed up here too. Just ask him, he'll tell you," Trevor said, pointing in Jacob's direction.

"I am most definitely your friend, Trevor. Can I get you to come out here with me? I'd like to talk to you about something. C'mon, man." Jacob took a few more steps toward Trevor, hoping to get an arm around him and lead him out of the area. Trevor was an older man and had lost a lot; he hadn't taken the losses as well as others in the Palace.

Shaking his head, Trevor started toward Teacher Paul again. "No, I'm not done saying what I have to say, old friend. I've been waiting to say this since we pulled up to this hunk of steel in those stupid white vans, and today is as good a day as any.

"You all think this is some kind of utopian place or something like that—you think it's so great, don't you!" he screamed at the people behind Jacob. "It's not. They are lying to us all. They set this all up, the US Government, probably with the help of the shadow government. Population control. Tell the truth, Paul. You know it."

He began wagging his finger at the small, balding man. Trevor was in such a rage, every word out of his mouth was followed by spittle flying off his lips. He looked like a rabid dog foaming at the mouth, snarling at everyone in the area. By this point, the crowd outside the room had doubled.

Jacob closed the distance between himself and Trevor, moving faster than he had since he was a young man. He needed to get close while Trevor's attention was on Teacher Paul. Jacob grabbed his arm. For a man in his late sixties, Trevor still had a sturdiness to him. Jacob could feel that. Trevor knocked his hand down and stepped back.

"Don't you put your hands on me. I told you that I'm going to tell everyone what they need to hear. Someone has to stand up against tyranny. DON'T TREAD ON ME!" Trevor yelled as he saluted Jacob. Tears spilled over his eyes, the wear and tear from the past years showing all over his face. The sight made Jacob feel terrible for his old friend. He didn't want people to see him that way.

"That's what the Old World was built on, at least in the United States of America. I have a right as a citizen of this country to protect the men, women, and children from all threats, whether those threats come from foreign or domestic parties. I TOOK AN OATH, DAMMIT!" Trevor snapped at Teacher Paul and the Palace members cowering behind him. The people looked on, horrified at what was transpiring right before their eyes.

There were older Palace members in the room who, while far removed from outburst and anger, seemed to understand Trevor's point as they looked on with knowing expressions. The younger Palace-born faces became masks of pure terror; this was obviously a shock to their system. Trevor seemed to be feeding on this fact. The more scared they became, the louder and angrier he got.

Just as he started yelling again, three security guards in black came rushing into the room, almost knocking Jacob to the ground. They had guns drawn, yelling for Trevor to get down. "Get on the ground, sir, or we will neutralize you! For the safety of yourself and everyone here, get on the ground NOW!" the guard in front said as he pointed what looked like a shotgun at Trevor's midsection. The man cocked the gun and took small steps toward Jacob's old friend.

One of the other guards grabbed Jacob roughly by the shirt and pushed him back toward the entrance of the room. "Get out in the hallway, right now!" the man screamed at him. Jacob didn't move; he was frozen to the spot. He had not seen a gun drawn since he was close to sixteen years old, when his grandfather took him to Target World to shoot a pistol for his birthday. *What if they kill Trevor?*

Jacob could feel someone pulling his collar and arm from the back. He didn't know who it was, and he didn't care to look. His eyes were fixed on what was happening in the room.

Trevor lunged at the first guard, the one with the shotgun pointed at his chest. The retired military man had a crazed look on his face, lips peeled back from his teeth like a wild animal going for the kill. Everything happened in slow motion: the other two guards moving toward Trevor, Jacob reaching out to try to help his friend as he was being pulled away by someone in the hallway.

Before Jacob was swept away in a sea of Palace members and teachers, there was time enough to watch his good friend get knocked out by the butt of a shotgun. He supposed that was better than the alternative. Things were changing in the Palace, and Jacob had felt it coming long ago. He was surprised it hadn't happened years before. *Better late than never*, he thought as he got lost in the screaming crowd of people.

CHAPTER THIRTY-SIX

Mary

THANK YOU FOR BREATHING LIFE INTO *every man, woman, child, and lifeform that you have deemed fit to walk on your skin, drink of your bosom, and eat of your fruit. We are thankful, and we shall never take your gifts for granted, O Merciful Mother Earth. Amen.* Mary spoke the prayer in her mind while walking down the hall with the others to the child center. She was in the back of the group, wanting to see the child center and wanting to run away at the same time. She knew it would be the last time.

Mary was not scheduled to come to the child center that day. She'd lied to Teacher Mathew, told him she needed extra time to observe behavior patterns among the smaller children compared to the older ones for research purposes. He had welcomed her with open arms.

The time to leave the Palace forever was coming soon, and a part of her needed this. A big part. She needed to see them one last time. She wanted to say goodbye to them and see how they were developing. This curiosity felt natural to her, almost as if she were looking over them as they grew...in the only way she could.

Mary didn't understand why this was important to her, but it always had been. She knew both their faces, the subtle differences in their hair color, the way their eyes sparkled—she noticed it all. A beautiful boy and a girl—they were a part of her, and that link seemed to be hard to break, at least in her head. They likely did not think of her at all. She never thought of her own birth mother or father.

After giving birth to each child, Mary visited the child center whenever she could, trying to memorize every aspect of them, giving them names in her head. She named them Todd and Nancy. She'd read a book when she was little that had characters with those names, and she liked them. It felt right to her, without even knowing why. She'd named them instinctively.

Now standing in the observation room, she knew exactly where both of her children were. They were always in the same groups, and rarely had she seen them play or communicate with each other. They didn't know they were siblings, just like any sibling in the child center. Keeping up with the goings-on of the children was a regular part of this morning enrichment class. Teacher Mathew spoke to the other Palace members about the different children and the strides they were making in the arena of self-confidence and independence.

Mary dismissively smiled at this notion, turning away from her group and gazing into the child center. She had grown up in this place and, even at her age, she remained a ball of self-doubt and anxiety whenever she thought back on her childhood. Jacob helped to make her feel whole; she felt complete when she was with him. This was part of the reason she enjoyed what they had together.

There was Nancy. Mary felt her knees begin to give, and she placed her hand on the wall, holding herself up. Looking at Nancy was like looking at a replica of her younger self. Long dark hair flowed and bounced behind the little girl as she ran and played. Mary couldn't see it today because of the shirt she was wearing, but she had spotted a shared birthmark on previous visits, the one on her daughter's right shoulder. Mary wanted to break through the glass and touch her, hug her, feel her. If only she could.

The tear forming in her left eye had to be held back, because she should not be emotional about this. If she became emotional about a random child, then Teacher Mathew and the others would think she were suffering from a stress attack. They would not be able to fathom that she loved the children that came from her own womb. Mary touched the corner of her eye, destroying the tear before it got the chance to escape.

Turning around to the opposite window of the survey room, Mary walked over and placed her face against the glass, hoping to see her son playing in the corner where he could frequently be found. He wasn't there. She looked at other areas of the child center, but still didn't see him. *What if I can't find him? Or what if he is sleeping or not feeling well?* she thought to herself, knowing this was her last chance to see them. Things could not be changed in the Palace, but leaving with Jacob could be the beginning of a whole new life. This provided a certain level of solace for her.

Just as Mary decided to stop looking and make her way back to the group before her poor body language and lack of interest became too noticeable, Todd came out of the cafeteria. She shared no birthmark with him, but he belonged to her...a mother just knew. Mary saw herself in his face and his eyes. Saw the features and mannerisms that he shared with his sister. His face was puffy and red, as though he had just finished crying. The sight of him being sad made her heart hurt. She knew how cruel some of the kids could be in the child center, especially when they didn't think the watchers were around.

Mary hastily moved back to the window area, placing her hand on it, longing to touch him. To wrap him in her arms, kiss his face, and tell him that everything would be alright. She could remember times in the child center where she felt so alone. Now she knew what had been missing from her life. It was having a mother, a father—someone who cared specifically for her. Not the group, but her.

Todd walked around the play area, kicking small toys as he moped around, trying to get someone's attention. But no one came. No one ever came. Like Mary had, he would soon realize that, and that's when the self-soothing would begin, which could manifest itself in harmful ways as he got older. These things were known in the Palace, people talked.

Mary watched him until he moved away from her field of vision, and even then, she lingered near that window, hoping he would pass by again. This was the last time, after all. He never did come back. He had probably already forgotten what he was upset about and was busy playing without a care in the world. That's what kids did though. Short memories were good for that.

Teacher Mathew was rounding up everyone in the survey room to begin taking inventory of changes they saw in each of the children since the last time they were here. Watching her children was great, and she needed to do this once more before she could leave. But too much watching could become detrimental; it was best to pull herself away from the glass windows before she dissolved into a crying heap of flesh for all to see.

Today was a sad day for her. But even though she knew she was leaving her only home, her two children, and every friend she had ever made, she still smiled as she joined the group. She was placing all of her trust with the one she loved. Regardless of what ended up being beyond the quarantine zone—whether it was a beautiful world or immediate death—it would be okay because it will have been her choice. In the end, that was all that really mattered.

CHAPTER THIRTY-SEVEN

Trevor

"WHO THE HELL DO YOU ALL think you are? You think you can just do whatever you want to us, and just because you hide behind the guise of the government, that we have to take it? Well, I'm not gonna just bend over and allow you to have your way with me. You are looking at a marine, sir. You will give me the respect that I deserve!" Trevor hovered above his seat, his hands gripping the arms of the chair so hard that his knuckles were white. He roared across the desk, aiming every ounce of venom stored inside of his heart for the last twenty years at Sirus.

"This place isn't exactly the utopia you all think it is. You believe you can house us all in this stupid building and boom, everything works out? Well, you have no idea how wrong you are. Most of these Palace-born folks are so messed up in the head that they could rival weirdos from the Old World." Trevor took a breath and sat back in his seat. Sirus sat across the desk, studying his face. He didn't speak or interrupt, and Trevor felt that was odd. He expected the program director to defend himself, the Order, and all that they were doing here.

"You know, I figured this out long ago. I won't lie, I still haven't figured it all out, but you can bet your ass it's not what you all say it is."

Trevor grunted in a dismissive way, waving his hand in Sirus's direction. Being watched the way he was now was beginning to make him feel...*observed*. "Why are you looking at me like that? Say something. You made them bring me here, probably told them to knock me over the head too."

"Oh no, finish speaking. I think every opinion in the Palace is important, and clearly, you are angry. So please...finish." Sirus moved his chair closer to the desk and placed his elbows on the surface, cheeks resting in his hands. His eyes flashed with interest.

Trevor pointed across the table at Sirus, narrowing his eyes. "Go fuck yourself, fella. Don't play games with me. I've seen things that would make your head spin, things that would keep you up at night, and I'm talking before the sickness. You sit across this big important desk, giving orders, believing you are better than the rest of us. You aren't though. DAMMIT, YOU AREN'T!" Trevor pounded the desk with a balled-up fist, causing the golden globe in the center to shake.

"I hate to interrupt, Mr. Cox, but can I ask a question?" Sirus raised an eyebrow and leaned back in his chair. "I will most definitely allow you to finish your thought, but I'd like to know something."

Trevor smiled, keeping his rage just beneath the surface. For the moment. "Sure, it's your place."

"Thank you, sir. Why are you so angry with me and what we have created here? When there was no hope, the surviving members of the different governing bodies around the world got together and rescued the people from eventual demise, and yet you seem unhappy with us. Were you forced to come here? The quarantine security team was instructed to only bring individuals in need of saving. If you expressed to them you did not want to be saved, they should have allowed you to stay wherever it is that they found you." Sirus gave a sympathetic look.

"No, I wasn't forced to come. My wife wasn't either. But what else were we to do?" He threw both hands in the air.

"Whatever you wanted to do. The decision was yours. You opted to come here, and now you spit in the face of the people who made that happen for you."

Trevor started laughing. "Are you fucking kidding me? Listen, don't do that egghead double-talk nonsense with me. I'm not as dumb as the other people here from the Old World or the idiots who were born here, so you can drop the 'who me?' act right now, because it doesn't play with me at all."

Sirus looked at Trevor in a surprised but impressed manner. The way you look at someone when they pull off a feat you didn't expect them to accomplish.

"Look at how nice you are living up here, Sirus. Done real well for yourself, haven't you?" Trevor winked at him. "Tell me though, how much does it cost to kill most of the human race? Must be a good gig. Bet you didn't lose anyone all those years ago. Your children, wife, friends—they are all alive, I'm sure. Maybe living here in some secret area, I bet. Laughing at us the whole time, huh? Is that how it is?" Trevor laughed again while looking around the office.

"Look at all the nice shit you got in here. Only color I've seen in this building. How's that? We get hospital hallways and some weird post-apocalyptic pods, and here you are, living like Scrooge McDuck. How much did that big grandfather clock run ya? I'm guessing free, swiped it from some dead guy's house. A bunch of crooks, all of ya." Trevor stuck his nose up at Sirus. "Tell the truth. You guys created this pandemic to control the population. I know you did. Look at how you monitor the reproduction of women here, how you have your hands in every little thing we do."

Sirus's eyes gleamed. He looked far too amused for Trevor's liking. "I think that is so interesting, Mr. Cox. I've always thought you were an interesting man. I've been watching you for some time now. I watch everyone—it's my job—but you more than the others. You have some grandiose ideas about the Palace Program, and you seem to believe that for some reason, we created all of this...to lower the population? That's silly of course; there was enough room on the planet for five to six times the amount of people than there were at the time of the sickness." Sirus rose from his chair, sticking his hands in the pockets of his jacket and walking over to the window. He opened it, allowing a small amount of light to shine in. The day was dreary and rainy.

"The hell you watching me for?"

Sirus tapped his finger on the window and exhaled deeply. "I just think you are interesting, is all. Like now for example. Most Palace members who are brought to my office are nervous, and they allow me to lead the conversation. Look at you though, sticking it to the man with that good ol' Kentucky accent of yours." He chuckled as he turned away from the window and looked at Trevor again.

Trevor stared at him inquisitively, caught off guard. "Don't mess around with me," Trevor stated. "You know that I'm right about what I'm saying to you. My wife and I want to leave this place. I don't care if it's not safe out there, I know it's not safe in *here*. We are never getting into the Greater Understanding Program, so we would like to opt out of the Palace Program as well."

"You *and* your wife, huh?" Sirus raised his eyebrows. "I hear what you are saying, and of course we will allow you to leave if that's what you wish. You do know that once you go outside of the hundred-yard radius, that we can't help you again?" Sirus walked over to a box sitting on a small table near the grandfather clock in the darkened area of the office.

"Lived through it once, we can live through it again. Besides, at this age, you tend to not give a flying hell. Don't got much longer anyway. If we are to go, I'd rather it be on our own terms," Trevor said.

Sirus opened the box and pulled out a cigar. He lifted it to his nose and inhaled the smell. Clicking the box closed, he asked, "You smoke, Mr. Cox? I mean, did you smoke before...you know."

"I did. That was a long time ago though. If you are offering, I'll pass."

Sirus pulled a lighter from his back pocket and lit the cigar, puffing on it continuously. The smoke added a haze to the room. "I wasn't offering a cigar, Mr. Cox, that's not allowed here." He took another puff and walked back into the lighted area of the room, leaning against the desk.

"I'm asking for a reason. In the Old World, you did smoke. Why though? What did it do for you?" Sirus asked as he flicked ash into the tray on his side of the desk, curiosity glowing in his eyes.

"Because I wanted to. Ya see, back in those days, we did things because we wanted to, not because we were strongly suggested to. I mean, that's what you guys do here, right? Suggest things? And we can either do as you say or risk punishment—or banishment, which is as good as death. That's what you would have us believe." Trevor looked up at Sirus with a sneer. His disgust for the program director felt thick and tangible.

"Because you wanted too, huh? Quite the rebel you are, Mr. Cox. I like it. I'm glad you answered honestly. Though I knew you would. And you make my point for me. All too often in the Old World, we all did things only because we wanted to. In fact, the majority of the things that took up our lives brought no real value to them. This place should have been a great tool to teach you to think deeper into things. I know it's helped for me. I was flawed too, like you and everyone else in the Old World. Not because I was inherently bad, but because that was the society in which we were born.

"Granted, this program was not meant to go on as long as it has, but the positives of that meant that you would have extensive time to self-assess and become better at this faulty decision-making from the Old World. But look at you, Mr. Cox, ready to throw your life away. Over what? Conspiracy and a shitty day?" Sirus took a long puff of the cigar, blowing the smoke in the opposite direction of Trevor. "You will have no part of reasoning though, will you?"

Trevor stood from his seat and got face to face with Sirus. "I can't be controlled. My life is my own, I'm a free man. You and no one else get to decide what's a good or bad decision for me and my wife." Trevor looked Sirus up and down. "The way I see it, we all have a life to live, for better or worse. Allow me to live mine the way I want to. Doesn't have to make sense to you."

Sirus put both hands in the air, as if he were being robbed, and backed away from the desk. His eyes were wide, and there was a smirk on his face. "Tough guy over here. I'm sorry if I offended, that was not my intention. I'm just asking a question. Sometimes I forget that most are a lot more emotionally sensitive than I. I just find it odd that you would be willing to put your wife in jeopardy to prove a point to the Order. And I'm still confused on exactly what that point would be, but sometimes you just gotta rebel, so there is that. Old dogs aren't good at learning new tricks though. That's how that saying goes, right? Or something similar."

Trevor sat back down and shrugged his shoulders with a defiant smile on his face.

"I can only be me, Mr. Program Director, sir."

"Touché, touché. I think I'll grant your wish. No point in having you here if you don't want to be here, right? This is and always has been an at-will program." A quick smile appeared on Sirus's face and retreated as fast as it came. He put the cigar out in the tray and sat down in his own chair, grabbing a folder in front of him. Sirus opened the folder, read a few lines, then stuck it back into the pile. Trevor rose to his feet.

Sirus put his hand up, motioning for him to wait. "One last question before you go though. This has been itching at me for quite some time, and I'll have you answer before you leave."

"Go on." Trevor put both hands on the desk and leaned toward Sirus, staring directly into those icy blue eyes.

"I've watched you through this window for twenty years now, Trevor, and I've witnessed plenty of odd behavior during that time. You taking flowers to random women in the garden, talking to yourself, pretending to hold someone's hand...Have the mental evaluations and counseling not served you at all, sir?" Sirus spoke gently, sounding as if he actually cared.

Trevor squinted his eyes at the strange man. "What do you mean? I don't do nothing like that. My wife is out there, I'd lose an eye if I gave flowers to another woman. And I don't talk to myself, so I don't know who you been stalking through that window of yours, but you got the wrong guy." He nodded his head in the direction of the wide window behind Sirus.

"Just think for a minute, Trevor. Why did you even go to that room to scream at the teacher and everyone in class? What drove you to alert everyone about the Palace and our 'evil ways'?" Sirus made air quotes with his fingers. "You were screaming about something awfully loud. Try to think about what that was, Trevor. It's important."

Trevor blinked at the man before him and felt his face fall. He suddenly felt every bit his age. As he tried to remember what led up to his outburst, he became suddenly confused. Feeling so lost frightened him, and his heart raced. He stood straight up and put both hands on his head, turning in a full circle as he looked around the room.

"I uhh, I was mad about something coming on the TV. Something about my wife getting hurt or..." Trevor tapped on the desk with his index finger, trying to remember those lost moments. He shook his head hard from left to right.

"Calm down, calm down, Mr. Cox. Now, if something happened to your wife, how would she be able to leave with you? You were saying she was dead. Isn't that right? You always say that about her, usually only in counseling sessions. But lately, you seem to be getting worse."

Trevor thought that maybe Sirus was trying to trick him or play some kind of game. Maybe to keep him in the Palace. That was it. The director was trying to trip him up.

"No, no...I remember now," he lied as he pointed at Sirus and wagged his finger at him. "I got angry because something came on the TV saying the Order was trying to kill everyone, something about you all working with Iraq. Yeah...that's what it was about. I remember now. That's why I got all upset. Don't bring my lovely wife into this, trying to get me off my game. You done already said we can leave. Be a man of your word, Sirus, don't play ga—"

"Mr. Cox!" Sirus screamed at him from across the table but remained seated. "Amy died in that house with your children twenty years ago! She is not here now, and she never has been. You know that already. We have been over this many times. Why do you insist on doing this?"

Trevor shook his head, refusing to give in.

"From everything we have learned about you, we can surmise that you are not clinically insane. We know this. So please, stop this now, and explain to me why you pretend that she is alive, then create situations in which she dies, then recreate her all over again? Why replay this pattern over and over?"

Trevor dropped his hand to the side and took two steps back. "My wife isn't dead. Don't you say that. The kids died, not Amy. She's here with me...yeah, she is here with me, and she always has been. I don't want to hear anything else about it. Just let us go where we gotta go. We have been waiting for this moment for twenty years—don't you back out on your word." Trevor began to tear up, his voice breaking over the words.

"But Mr. Co—"

"Shut up! Right damn NOW! I don't want to hear another word about it! Just let me go. Please...just let us go." Trevor wiped tears from his eyes, then he straightened up and stared at Sirus, pleading with his eyes. He was done talking, he was done with everything. "Well, you gonna let us go? Me and Amy? We can go?"

Sirus stared down at his desk and seemed to be thinking it over, shuffling the folder in his hands. He looked up and regarded Trevor with a soft smile.

"Teacher Simon is outside the door there with your things. He will prepare you both with protective suits. The Greater Understanding Program is in your future. While I do not agree with much that you have to say, I do recognize the leadership and free-thinking qualities that you possess. Furthermore, there isn't much more you could offer for the Palace Program. The only purpose you would serve in staying with us here would be distracting others and fearmongering. I'm certain that once you see the world outside of this place that we built for you, you will see the fault in your thinking. The work in the field is hard, even for a young man. You have all the answers though, so I wish you the best of luck." Sirus nodded his head in the direction of the door. "Get going, Trevor Cox. I do wish you could have stayed with us longer. The Order, and the Palace Program, does appreciate what you have contributed. I hope the Greater Understanding Program is to your liking."

Trevor turned to face the door, then stopped and looked back. "So, Amy and I are in the Greater Understanding Program? No bullshit? We can just leave now?"

Despite Sirus's smile, the expression on his face looked almost painful. "Yes, you and Amy can go."

"What if we don't want in the program? What if we just want to be free and go?"

"If that's what you choose once you are on the outside, then that's an option. I can assure you that you will not choose that option though. I've been out there plenty of times and...its bad. But again, the choice is yours. The first step begins with Teacher Simon outside the door there. But something tells me you know what you are getting yourself into."

"I do, and I couldn't be happier." Trevor waved without meeting Sirus's eyes and exited the office.

CHAPTER THIRTY-EIGHT

Dwight

THE WHITE COMFORTER WAS BEGINNING TO have a vile smell independent of the body underneath it. Dwight lifted and fluffed the thick material in the air, the same way you would over your bed when it was time to make it up for the day. The comforter fell over Michelle's body. This was the third time he'd been back to her pod to do things that would be frowned upon in the Palace. Things he had only dreamed of doing.

Dwight looked at the lump of the person beneath the cover. He couldn't believe he had three whole days to explore every wild thought to ever pop into his terrible mind. It was coming to an end now, and the thought of that made him feel miserably sad inside. Based on the decomposition, he knew he only had one more day at the most to spend time with her.

He stepped over Michelle and turned on the shower. Then he undressed, laying his clothes on the toilet seat. He caught a glimpse at himself in the mirror and stopped. Dwight never looked at himself in the mirror. In every counseling session he'd had here, he was told that he had a mental break when he climbed through his parents' window and witnessed their bodies splayed across the bed, covered in vomit.

Dwight still saw a ten-year-old child wearing pajamas staring back at him, his face thin and hungry. This image had not changed in the last two decades. The years had passed, but his reflection in the mirror didn't show that. His mind was still stuck in that trailer park somewhere in Ohio.

That gruesome scene was too much for a child to deal with, and he never had. The glitch that he downloaded that Monday morning was there to stay. The crumpled body of a female child lying there on the floor was evidence of that.

The last few days had brought eureka moments in droves to him. He was at least grateful for that. So today he would take a nice long shower. He would clean his body, because he knew what needed to come next. Tough decisions had to be made, and he was the man to make them. Doing this, coming back here each day, had changed the plan.

Dwight touched the mirror, seeing himself and not feeling ashamed of the boy staring back at him. For the first time, he was okay with accepting what was. He did not ask for any of this. Didn't ask to be born to dopeheads. Didn't ask to be born at all. He didn't ask for Mother Earth to decide to kill off everyone else and leave him alive with a mere five percent of the planet. He should have died in that crummy excuse for a home with his parents.

He smiled at himself for the first time in a long time. Now that the shower was hot enough, he got in and closed the shower door behind him. Dwight let the water rain down on him and pretended that it was a warm day in his old trailer park with his friends. They were friends whose names he couldn't remember, but that was okay. He would make up new ones for them.

For an hour Dwight stood in the shower crying. The tears were for the young version of himself. The kid in the mirror, trapped in the past without an afterlife to go home to. That child resided in his mind and would not allow him to be a man, to mature in all the ways necessary. It had been twenty years, and still he felt the same.

He had always preferred boys, and if he was honest with himself, in his heart of hearts he knew he was a homosexual man...or boy. That was another thing he had come to grips with in the last couple days. Before he could actually rape Michelle, he needed to cut her hair short. He did this without even thinking. In the moment, he didn't realize it, but when he got back to his pod that night, afraid, scared, slamming his head against the wall, it hit him. He was a gay man, among many other things, and it was the first time he could accept this.

It made sense though. He remembered games of hide-and-seek turning quite frisky with Billy and himself. Nothing too wild, a little touching was all that happened. As he aged, he tried to write it off as youthful curiosity. He'd pushed those thoughts to a hidden cavern deep in the back of his mind, locked the door, and swallowed the key. And when something caused him to remember, he'd plug his ears and pretend he didn't hear the memories knocking at the door.

The frequent visits to the child center—the lying, conniving, and jumping through hoops with teachers just to get a look at a young boy —had become tiresome. A part of himself was ashamed of his behavior. He knew that what he was, what he had become, was wrong. Being sorry didn't change it though.

Now that Dwight no longer felt a need to fit the mold of a perfect little Palace member, he was able to accept what was to come. He didn't know what was going on in this place, but he did know the government was up to something. However, last night, he'd decided that it no longer mattered to him. He was only a small man, in a world that was becoming increasingly smaller by the day. He could not change anything, and he would not play the conspiracy idiot like his father before him. That world was gone, those ideas laid to rest with everything else meaningful. But there was something else he could do. And it would make his father proud.

Dwight turned the shower off and just stood there, allowing his body to drip water. He looked through the steamy shower glass and onto the white bathroom floor, admiring the reason for his most recent realizations. She looked peaceful under that comforter, and it wouldn't be long before he joined her. Good thing for Dwight that new Palace members were allowed a week of nesting time before they were required to adhere to the daily schedule. Had that not been the case, a teacher would surely have come looking for her after a day or so. Lucky him.

Dwight walked out of the shower, made his way through the living area, and over to the nutrition dispensary. Coming into the fresher air of the living area reminded him of how bad the bathroom smelled. At this point, the entire pod smelled of death, but the bathroom was on a different level. Still, he preferred the bathroom. The smell of it would just quicken his decision.

He opened the dispensary, ignoring the bagel, butter, and orange juice he'd ordered last night while spending time with Michelle. He swiped the knife and closed the dispensary door. Turning to his right, he unlocked the pod door before opening it slightly, leaving it cracked just enough. Dwight walked past the broken television screen, not forgetting to flip the bird at it. "Fuck you all," he said in a calm voice.

There was a wastebasket near the toilet. Dwight grabbed it and used the object to prop open the bathroom door. He would allow the smell to fill the entire pod. It made him happy to know that he would be responsible for this entire place burning down. His actions would be the spark to begin the great fire.

Dwight got on his knees next to Michelle beneath the comforter, placed the knife on the floor, and clasped his hands together for a prayer. The last prayer he would give, and this one he would deliver out loud. He wanted to make sure whichever GOD was responsible for this life could hear him. There would be no mistakes about who was speaking, and whom he was speaking to.

"O Merciful Mother, you evil vindictive bitch, and you too Jesus, or God, or whatever you go by these days. I'd also like to address any of you other gods that lived in the past and are maybe still out there, being worshipped in the world today. I want to give a royal *fuck you* to each and every one of you. You childish, petty children.

"If you are even real, you'd have to be evil. No decent human being would commit the crimes on humanity that you have, so I find it hard to believe an all-perfect deity would do so. I doubt that you are even real at all, but just in case you are…fuck you. And I can't wait to see you soon, so I can tell you in person.

"All that I am, all that I've ever been is because you willed it into existence. They say that God has a plan for everyone, so I guess I shouldn't feel bad about the things I've done to others, because it was your plan, right?" Dwight abruptly burst into laughter but kept his eyes closed and hands clasped in front of his face.

"It's all a big cruel joke, right? Of course it is. And I'm here to tell you that I will no longer play along. I never asked to be born, so I'll veto your choice to create me. See you soon." He lowered his hands and grabbed the knife from the floor.

Lifting the comforter by the corner, he slid inside and cozied up next to Michelle's body. Same way he had done for the last three days. She was fully dressed; he'd put her clothes back on after the day he allowed his compulsions to take over and did the unthinkable. Since then, there'd been no more of that. He had returned to this pod every day, but not to harm her. He only came back to lie next to her beneath the covers, to feel her skin, to put his arm around her and just be close to someone in that way.

Dwight would stay in Michelle's pod until late at night, then go back to his own to eat and show face for the teachers on the floor. In the daytime, he'd come back and lie with the decomposing body.

Getting closer to her, he felt her leathery skin on his arm and again felt guilty about what occurred here. But he was going to make it right. Rigor mortis had set in, so her limbs did not move as he maneuvered around her body to create what resembled a soft, caring moment. Dwight was able to keep the hand free that held the knife, and he kissed the back of Michelle's head, feeling the soft hairs tickle his lips and nose.

He closed his eyes, took a breath, and slit his own throat. Dwight did not scream, he did not fight to live. He choked, held her closer, and drifted off, escaping the Palace forever.

CHAPTER THIRTY-NINE

Lonnie

L ONNIE STEPPED OFF THE ELEVATOR AND made his way to meet his friend at the gym. Everyone seemed to be on edge lately, and it was definitely time for him to release some stress with an intense workout. People were getting into the Greater Understanding Program left and right, seemingly for no reason at all. A guy almost got shot by a security guard in the central plaza a week or two ago, and then a raving lunatic had lost it and nearly attacked a teacher in class today. People were beginning to talk about things he'd never heard them whisper about before. Sirus and the Order would eventually deal with this, and Lonnie didn't want to be on the chopping block when that happened.

He'd had an interesting morning enrichment that day. Jacklyn, who had been the bane of his existence since their time in the child center, had the entire session in a frenzy. She was just saying what everyone was thinking, and they were told not to lie. But everyone knew that was a crock of shit, all you ever did here was lie. Whether or not you were good at it was the question really.

She had interrupted class and unexpectedly asked, "Are we free to leave here whenever we want? All of us, could we just walk out the front door if we wanted to?" Teacher Peter's face did everything but fall onto the floor. He transformed from a well-spoken, articulate scholar into a bumbling, mumbling idiot before their eyes. If Jacklyn blurting out the question did not make people feel uncomfortable and disturbed enough, Teacher Peter's response finished the job.

Lonnie passed a few friends in the long hallway who were just coming out of a pod, where they most likely were having a study session. After a few pleasantries and forced words, he continued making his way to Coleman's pod. Coleman was his best friend here. They were not allowed best friends, girlfriends, boyfriends, or anything of the sort, but it still happened. You could only change so much in one generation, especially with the people from the Old World living there with them. People talked. Other people heard.

Teacher Peter's reaction was scary. It had scared Lonnie, and he could see that it had scared others as well. Everyone was talking about leaving and whether or not they could leave prior to getting into the Greater Understanding Program. Without a protective suit, you could not hope to live outside of the red flags. Even the people from before said that; they lived through the sickness. Lonnie was confused about everything. So much had changed in the Palace so fast. There was comfort in repetition, and he wanted things to go back to the way they were.

Jacklyn was still doing what she'd done in the child center when they were children. Not thinking before she spoke and causing a shit-storm at someone else's expense. Lonnie really hated her. She was intelligent and a good learner, but something inside of her wasn't right. She was different, and she had zero empathy for anyone.

He still remembered how she would tease him and get others to do the same thing when the watchers weren't looking. She knew all of the blind spots and quiet areas of the center. She verbally tortured him, and the worst part was that people he thought were his friends would laugh too. No one thought to stop her.

"Why's your skin so black?" she would say. "You are the color of mud, and your lips are so big. Why does your hair not look like ours? Were you born with an affliction?" She would make jokes and tell people that he needed to shower more, to clean all the dirt off his face.

Why was she like that? There was no reason for it, no one had taught her to be this way—they'd all had the same upbringing in the

239

child center. In the last six or seven years, he had accepted that some people were just screwed up. For others who didn't know that side of her, he understood how it could catch them off guard. Not him though; he had seen beneath her mask. They all wore one, but Jacklyn's mask came off all too often.

In class, Teacher Peter ended up telling her that the topic was not deserving of an answer. Everything the Order did was for the survival of all humanity. "Wherever you heard such rot, you should leave it there, and never speak such nonsense in these walls." His face turned the color of a ripe strawberry and his voice became high pitched. Everyone in class noticed that he did not answer the question.

Jacklyn had simply given a smug grin, sat back in her seat, and went back to doodling on a notepad. For the rest of class, things were very quiet and awkward. Everyone could feel it, including the teacher, which was probably why he let the session end early.

It was a few more doors before he reached Coleman's pod. *They need to build another elevator in this place. The walk from end to end is becoming so long.* Then something grabbed his attention.

A foul odor washed over his entire face so rapidly and with such strength that he had to grab at the wall to keep from falling over. Lonnie's eyes began to water, and he bent over, hands on knees, dry-heaving and coughing. It was all he could do not to vomit right there in the hallway. "What in Mother's Earth is that smell?" he choked out, looking up and down the corridor. No one was there but him.

He looked up at the ceiling to make sure he was not beneath a vent that, for whatever reason, was blowing out such a smell, but there was nothing. Then Lonnie noticed that the pod door to his right was open a crack. He stepped closer to the door, placing his hand on it, letting his nose sniff at the air coming from the opening. The scent was potent enough to knock him out cold, and it nearly did. It was putrid, the odor of rotting fruit being stewed in a pot of excrement.

Lonnie covered his nose with his blue shirt and stepped into the pod. There was no one there, but still, he would leave the door open just in case a teacher came up this way. Trying his best to breathe as little as possible, he noticed a waste basket propping the bathroom door open.

Peeking into the bathroom, Lonnie at first saw nothing at all. But the smell was so thick there, it just about took on a shape of its own. Then he looked down at the ground and noticed the dirty lumpy white comforter lying there. There was something else...thick blood, so dark it almost looked black, pooled around the white cover. Lonnie took off running back into the living area, bursting out the door and screaming like he had never screamed before. No words, no direction—just blood-curdling, nerve-shaking, horrified screaming.

CHAPTER FORTY

Jacob

"ARE YOU SURE YOU'RE READY TO go? When we go through with this, there is no coming back. There is no other option. The second we run past the red flags...that's it." Jacob took both her hands in his and kissed them. Her small hands were like those of a child captured within his huge, scarred, aging ones. The contrast between the two spoke volumes to him, but what they felt for each other was more authentic than anything he had ever known in his twenty years at the Palace.

While her hands were quivering, her expression was all business, driven and confident. The inner struggle she was jostling with was apparent to Jacob. She was trying to be strong for him so he wouldn't feel bad for convincing her to come with him, but the teachings were there in her mind. Days, weeks, months, and years of indoctrinating couldn't so easily be thrown by the wayside, not even for love. She was trying though, and for this, Jacob cared for her much more deeply.

"Yes, my love, I'm ready to go. I've taken care of all that I needed to, and I've gone over the plan more than a few times. We are set to go tonight." She looked deeply into Jacob's eyes. "There is no turning back for me. I've never been more sure about anything in this life," Mary said, sitting on the white love seat with him.

"Okay, good. We will go through the remainder of the day normally, and around seven p.m., we will meet up by the trees outside of the courtyard. I need to find Trevor first. I'm sure I'll run into him today. Maybe he's still in the infirmary. Everyone has been talking about what happened with him and security the other day. I'm sure he will want to go with us." Adjusting his sitting position on the couch with her, he began rubbing her leg. They were speaking in whispers. There were ears all over this place, possibly even in their pods.

"Do you think he will be up to it though?"

"I have to try. We came into this damned place together. He has been through a lot, and I couldn't leave without telling him and at least giving him a chance to go with us," Jacob said.

"You are right. Something bad is happening here, even I can see that. Margaret said something bad happened on the fourth floor earlier today. The entire floor was blocked off." She lowered her voice even more as she spoke.

Jacob stood and led her further from the door, over to the bed. They sat down, Jacob never letting her hand go.

"What happened on the fourth floor?"

Mary paused, nibbling on her bottom lip. "Well, Margaret thinks that Lonnie—you don't know him, but a guy that we grew up with in the child center—went insane on that floor. He was found on his hands and knees outside one of the pods, screaming. She told me that he either would not or could not stop screaming. He was taken off to the infirmary that way. He doesn't even live on that floor, so that was weird too. No one knows what happened to him or what caused it, but someone was saying maybe he saw something that caused him to lose it.

"Everyone's been talking about it; my morning enrichment session was canceled. I spent that time in the central plaza, finishing up a novel. I'm surprised you didn't hear about it." Her eyebrows knitted as she glared at Jacob.

Jacob's eyes moved to the ceiling as he dropped her hand and began tapping his shoe on the floor—an anxious habit carried over from a lifetime ago.

"I skipped out on my morning enrichment class. For all I know, it

243

was canceled as well. But I wasn't in my pod this morning to get any announcement. I was checking up on something. There is one thing I need to do this afternoon before we make a run for it. I've always wondered about the Palace and where Sirus is located. Is he here, or in a different Palace? He's never been seen here by anyone, but it's possible he stays here, right?" Jacob looked at Mary with hesitant hope in his eyes.

"Sure. Why not? I think it's a long shot, but it's possible."

"I thought it was a long shot as well, until this morning when I got in the elevator and tried a few things. I've been thinking for some time that he is here, at least sometimes. You can see the black helicopter coming in and out from the Palace—I think that's him. I'm not talking about the gray choppers that bring in supplies, but the black one. It must be landing on top of the building on a helipad."

"Okay," Mary said, blinking at him with questioning eyes. "What about it?"

"We know that the first eighteen floors are for pods, sessions, and activities. There is no talk of offices or any area for Sirus. Which made me think that there could be another floor. Like a hidden floor. Most commercial buildings like this one back in the Old World had floors like that. They could be in the basement, hidden between existing floors, or even above the top floor. In this case, a nineteenth floor." Jacob got excited and rose from the bed with a grimace. His knees popped. They both heard it, but Mary smiled and waved him on to finish his story.

Jacob fought through the embarrassment of his body showing its age and continued to talk. "Anyway, I got on the elevator this morning and messed around with the buttons in there. I held down on the 'close door' button while constantly pressing different floor buttons. I didn't think anything would happen at all, but figured it was worth a try.

"After hitting buttons like a child for a few minutes, I sent the elevator to the eighteenth floor. Once there, I tried some more button mashing. I pressed the button for the first floor while holding the 'close door' button. I wanted to see if the elevator would go all the way down to the first floor without stopping for anyone that may be calling it. Then it happened. The elevator started moving up, not down." Jacob felt his face light up with a grin that would put a clown to shame. "Do you understand what I'm saying, Mary?"

"But...but how could it go up if you were already on the top floor?" Mary was looking at Jacob, but also looking through him. He could see the cogs turning in her head. Puzzlement was written on her face, then the sparkle in her eye came shining through, and her gaze met his. "What happened when you got to the higher floor?"

Jacob grabbed her face with both hands and kissed her lips. "I love you, darling. It went up to the hidden floor, the doors opened, and the halls were no longer white—"

A loud voice came over the intercom suddenly, cutting off his words. "MAKE YOUR WAY TO THE FIRST-FLOOR AUDITO-RIUM. AGAIN, MAKE YOUR WAY TO THE FIRST-FLOOR AUDITORIUM. THERE IS A PALACE-WIDE MESSAGE TO BE HEARD. DISCONTINUE ANY LECTURES, ACTIVITIES, AND MEALS. THE MEETING WILL BEGIN IN FIFTEEN MINUTES. THANK YOU."

The booming, unfamiliar voice went away as suddenly as it had arrived. All was quiet in the room. Neither of them spoke.

There had never been a meeting pertaining to all Palace members at one time. There were very few meetings in the auditorium to begin with.

"What the hell is going on?" Jacob finally said, looking at Mary in disbelief. "What are they planning?"

"I have no idea, but it sounds like we are both about to find out." Mary rose from the bed, put her arms around Jacob's neck, and kissed his lips again. "When this is over, let's meet back here and finish our talk. No matter what's said at this meeting, we still leave tonight. It's time to go, I can feel it, and I know you can. I'm sure the meeting is about the fourth floor incident. I told you it was the talk of the Palace this morning."

He wound his arms around her, pulling her closer and taking in her scent. Jacob wanted to throw her back down on the bed and slide deep inside of her again—that would make the tenth time this week alone. Since confessing their love to each other, they'd had a lot of sex. Enough for them or for anyone in this place, he would wager.

There was no time for that right now. He settled for another kiss, but this time a longer, more passionate one. He took her bottom lip fully into his mouth, tangling his tongue with hers while holding the side of her face just beneath the jawbone. He'd missed this feeling with a woman, this closeness. He thought that feeling from his old life was gone forever, but he was wrong.

"Let's go," Jacob said to Mary, grabbing her hand once again and leading her out of his pod. They joined a line of other Palace members making their way to the elevator.

CHAPTER FORTY-ONE

Mary

S HE SAT NEXT TO JACOB OF course. They stopped holding hands the second they left his pod, but sitting here next to him in the auditorium, she wanted to hold his hand more than anything now. That was looked down upon here—no connections allowed. No one held dominion over another. He did though; she belonged to him, and she loved it.

Jacob looked worried, as he should. This had never happened before, so clearly something terrible had gone down, or was about to. There was loud chattering all throughout the auditorium.

"There was a fight."

"Someone got killed, and the killer jumped out the window."

"I heard two teachers beat each other up."

So many stories were flying around, it was hard to take any of them seriously. But something must have happened that the Order felt very strongly about, or else they wouldn't all be there.

Mary noticed Jacob's eyes darting from one person to the next, picking up pieces of conversation on the way. His foot was tapping the floor, as it always did when he was worried. She leaned over and hit his shoulder with her own. Jacob snapped out of his eavesdropping trance and looked at her.

"Relax, Jacob," Mary said as she touched his knee firmly to stop it from bouncing. She lifted her eyebrows and grinned at him. He smiled back and nodded his head.

The auditorium began to darken as the wide, bright circular lights in the high ceiling softened. This was the clue for everyone to be quiet and sit down. The room was so quiet you could hear people breathing. From outside the door to the right, footsteps could be heard coming toward the entrance.

The door crept open, and a man stepped into the room. He wore a black suit, nice shiny black shoes, and a shiny watch. Mary had never seen anything so shiny in her twenty years of life, nor had she ever seen this gentleman who was now gliding to the podium. He held his head high and had a certain air about him. He seemed unbothered, unfazed by anything around him.

The man's blond hair was short, styled in a buzz cut. He had skinny eyebrows from what she could see, a clean-shaven face, and a strong chin. His features were...eccentric, feminine in a way, but he was a very good-looking man. Mary wondered why this was her first time seeing him. She knew it was a bad sign.

"Who is that?" Jacob whispered and looked at her, confused.

Mary shrugged her shoulders.

"This isn't good, Mary. I know this isn't good." Jacob began looking around the auditorium, trying to see if everyone else was as worried as he was.

"We are about to see." She grabbed his hand now that the room was dark and no one could see.

As the stranger walked up to the podium, a massive projection screen came sliding down the huge wall behind him. The man paid no attention to it. He stood straight in his spot, looking out into the crowd of over two hundred and fifty Palace members, twenty teachers, and assorted watchers and security guards. Not all the staff were here, but a good amount of reps from each sect were present. The strange man waited patiently as the screen moved slowly down the wall. He did not speak as he turned his head from left to right, regarding the crowd.

"Hello everyone. I'm David. Most of you don't know me, but I work closely with Sirus and some of the other higher-ups in the Order. I did just arrive mere minutes ago via helicopter to this beautiful Palace facility. I'd like to say you all have a beautiful and thriving community here."

Mary thought that the gentleman spoke well and said a lot of nice words, but his eyes...they were not kind, and they did not seem to agree with his mouth. She felt as though he were eyeballing them all with disgust while his mouth was busy flattering them.

"Why's he here? And why have we never seen him?" Jacob murmured in her ear, trying not to move too much.

"Just listen, Jacob. I'm sure we're about to find out," she responded.

"I'm not one for beating around the bush," David said. "Something of enormous consequence has happened within this Palace. To those involved and others who witnessed it, I'm sure some of you already know what I'm talking about. Rumor is commonly worse than the actual story, so I'll be honest and explain what did occur on the fourth floor of your facility."

David leaned forward against the podium, speaking at them rather than to them. He sounded seasoned in the art of explanations and taking control.

"There was a situation on the fourth floor. A newly appointed Palace member was raped and killed by a long-time Palace member."

There was a chorus of exhales and screams, a flutter of hands shooting toward faces to cover mouths in appalled outrage. Mary had never heard so much noise in the Palace. "Sweet Mother of Earth!" and "O Merciful Mother, save us!" were some of the phrases being shouted throughout the auditorium. Teachers were trying to get order in the room, trying to calm everyone down. The whole time, the stranger called David said nothing. He simply scanned the crowd from left to right, just as he had when he first stood at the podium. He seemed to be allowing everyone to finish their rants and screams.

"What the hell is going on here?" Jacob said in a loud voice as he stood up from his seat along with everyone else in the auditorium. Mary sat there, pulling at his hand to get him to sit down. He looked at her, and she could tell that he suddenly remembered what she hadn't forgotten. None of it mattered, and they would be far away from this place by morning.

Jacob sat back down. "But who would kill someone here? And rape? Why? Sex isn't hard to come by here. And where is Trevor? Do you think he could be involved somehow?" Jacob was whispering all this into Mary's ear, not stopping to pause.

She turned her head so that he was no longer talking into her ear, but kissing her lips. No one noticed amidst all the crying and chattering taking place. It was a quick, soft kiss, nothing long or drawn out, but her intention came through in the electric spark that passed between them. "It doesn't matter, Jacob. None of it does. You will find Trevor after this nonsense is over, and we will be long gone after that."

Mary turned her head back to the stage and waited for David to finish what he came to say. She was trying her best to be strong in this moment, hoping that Jacob noticed. He seemed to, because he relaxed back into his seat and reached for her hand.

"I know," David finally said. "We know this news is troubling for you all to deal with right now, but we must endure." The crowd quieted down and took to their seats as David's voice filled the room. Small chattering ensued but soon faded as he continued to speak. "The one who committed this incident against a female Palace member was from the outside world, like myself and many others here. Please do not allow this fact to cause unkind or harsh thoughts against us. The victim did not deserve what befell her."

His voice was calm and direct. Even though he sounded as if he cared, there was no actual empathy there. His words were flat, like his eyes—business as usual almost.

"This is an uncommon thing here, or anywhere in the world today. We are beyond these savage ways of behaving. This is what the Order has worked so hard to obliterate among our kind, and yet these...these terrible things slip through the cracks." The word "things" fell from his lips with disgust.

"How do these things slip through the cracks?" he seemed to be asking himself in a low voice, looking down at the podium beneath his chest. David was silent for about five seconds, then snapped back to the matter at hand. "We do not want anyone worried about safety. This was a one-off. There is no danger or anyone to fear. To ease tensions, we are bringing in another security unit, and they will be going around questioning Palace members from the fourth floor. Nothing to worry about—we are just making sure nothing is left to chance."

Jacob smacked his lips and smiled. "And this is how it begins, Mary. This world will soon become what the Old World came to be." Shaking his head, he squeezed her hand.

Everything Mary had ever known now seemed to be untrue, or at the very least skewed. She knew that the end of her time in this place was near, but what about her friends? The people she grew up with, the children in the child center? They wouldn't just run away, like she was going to do later tonight.

"Seems that way," she said to Jacob.

"For the next few days, we are suspending all morning enrichments, lectures, activities, and access to the central plaza. It's best if everyone remains in their respective pods as the unfortunate event is being investigated and we attempt to put this all behind us." David grabbed something small from the podium and pointed it in the air. The projection screen suddenly flashed with the message: "Please Wait."

While they waited, some blather could be heard flowing throughout the auditorium about canceled activities. The teachers were silent and the watchers said nothing (but watchers hardly ever said anything, so that wasn't surprising). None of the staff showed any emotion on their faces. They didn't seem as surprised or alarmed as the others. *Maybe they knew ahead of time. I'm sure that's the case, but still, how could they look so indifferent?* Mary wondered.

"Our leader and program director, Sirus, has some words that he wants to share with everyone. Refrain from speaking while he is talking. That is your warning, do not be disrespectful," David snapped with authority as he placed the small object back on the podium.

"Warning?" Jacob glared at Mary, scrunching his eyebrows into an angry, animated face. She said nothing back; she did not know what to say.

This was all unfamiliar territory for everyone. Mary felt guilty...at least she had an exit plan. The plan may or may not work; for all she knew she and Jacob would drop dead in a fit of vomiting and choking the minute they passed the flags. But just the chance to be free and with him out in the world was good enough for her. And with recent events, she no longer felt staying inside the Palace was the safer option.

The projection screen changed from "Please Wait" to Sirus in a white room, sitting about ten feet away from the camera. The room was empty except for him and the chair in which he sat. Sirus had his hands clasped together in his lap and one leg crossed over the other. He wore an inviting smile, like nothing at all out of the ordinary had happened that day.

"I was listening in to David giving you the news about the happenings on the fourth floor." Sirus put his head down, staring at his lap while making a sniffling sound. "It's truly an unfortunate day in our Palace. We all—I mean the teachers, security, the watchers, and every other member of the staff—have done everything in our power to make sure nasty, unclean things like that NEVER happen in our facility!"

Sirus uncrossed his legs and stomped his foot on the ground to emphasize his anger. He then took a deep breath and leaned back in the chair, seeming to collect his thoughts. When he spoke again, it was in a softer voice. "Not to worry though. We are on the job and making sure we get to the bottom of this. You see, we did a fantastic job of quarantining the sickness from this place. We've managed to keep everyone safe for the last twenty years or so. Twenty years, right?" he said to someone off camera. "Give or take? Regardless, we have had a great run without having to come face to face with this behavior." Sirus leaned forward in his seat with elbows on his knees and legs spread apart, eyes gleaming in the camera as it panned closer to his face.

"But it seems we may need a few more restrictions, or, might I say, surveillance. The better to keep the peace for all, of course. Extra security is en route and locking down all portions of the Palace. There will be guards walking the corridors at all times, making sure that everyone is following the rules and doing what their schedules entail.

"It has become obvious that our lack of attention to detail has put Palace members in jeopardy. I'm personally saddened by that. I'm taking the blame for what happened. The gentleman that perpetrated this situation was a mentally ill individual. We knew that, but he was able to...pretend well enough about his level of sanity.

"Believe you me, that is not the correct thing to do, because as you can see, the lies, self-hate, and insanity came bursting out, and someone was violated and murdered. Never again...not on my watch. Never again." Sirus shook his head as he stared into the camera. His eyes appeared wet, as if he were going to cry, but the corners of his mouth lifted just a bit. Mary thought she saw a hint of a smile.

"The problem now is the same problem that we have always had. The deepening desire of wanting a thing is all too easily extinguished by receiving a thing. Therein lies the flaw in our kind. No matter how good things are, or how much we say we would be content if we just had A, B, and C—the second we receive those things, we go looking for D, E, and F. Even if it's at the detriment of others."

She always thought Sirus was...different, flamboyant, even an oddball. Clearly, he became even more so when anger and embarrassment were mixed in with his natural disposition.

"You will be released to return to your pods. Please stay there until you get word over the speaker that it's okay to come out. In the meantime, if you hear a knock at the door," Sirus popped up from his intense leaning position, smile and all, "just open the door and answer questions from the security team. We do not tell falsehoods in the Palace, so keep this in mind. Wouldn't want to have to banish some poor soul for not cooperating...Let us all say the prayer before dismissal. All together now."

David still stood at the podium, unshaken by Sirus's words. Mary noticed that he hadn't even turned around to view the projection screen. Instead, he stared out at the Palace members in their seats, the auditorium dark and full of doubt, fear, and confusion. He did recite Mother Earth's prayer with everyone. Like a choir, they spoke the words in perfect unison. This made Sirus smile as the live feed faded out and back to the "Please Wait" screen.

"Screw that. Come back to my pod, we need to talk. We have to leave sooner." Jacob got closer and spoke into Mary's ear, "We have to go now."

CHAPTER FORTY-TWO

Jacob

"TRUST ME, HONEY, WE HAVE TO go right now. I'm not sure what we will do about the guard near the exit, but I'll figure it out. I'll take him out if I have to, but we have to leave now. I know what this story shakes down to, I've seen it a million times in the Old World." Jacob paced near the bed while Mary held her hands close to her mouth like she was praying, clearly upset and afraid. "Get away from the door, come over here. We can't risk someone hearing you." He nodded at the floor near where he was standing.

Mary moved away from the door, looking at it skeptically, like she could see the teachers standing outside of it. "Are you still going to try to find Trevor before we go?"

"Yes. I think you should stay here though and wait for me. If someone knocks, do not answer the door. The extra security squad shouldn't be here for a few hours, so I should still be okay to move around for a bit. I'm gonna go check the infirmary and a few other places," Jacob said as he placed his hands on her waist and pulled her close for a soft kiss. Mary wriggled her lips and nose, he knew that his beard tickled her there.

"Okay. I'll stay here and wait for you to get back. Please be careful, Jacob," she said with a worried look on her face. Mary rubbed her hands through his hair, allowing her fingers to get lost in it as she stared into his eyes.

"I'll be fine. And I'll be back in no time, hopefully with Trevor."

With another kiss and a long hug that he wished could go on for years, Jacob exited the pod, making his way to the staircase. He thought it too dangerous to take the elevator. The infirmary was only one floor below his own, on the tenth floor.

Jacob waved casually at the medic as he walked into the infirmary. There were usually two of them sitting around, not doing much of anything, but today there was just Roxanne.

"Hey Roxanne, how are you doing today?" he said, trying to appear natural.

"Been dealing with...you know. So, yeah, I've had better days. But what can I do for you, Jacob? You aren't due for a refill on your blood pressure meds yet." Roxanne sat at her desk, typing on the massive computer, not looking up for more than a second.

"No, I'm not here for that, I just had a question for you. I was looking for my buddy Trevor. Wanted to see if I could bring him lunch or something before the big lockdown and all." Jacob looked down the right side of the infirmary, where the white beds were. All empty.

"Is Trevor here? I know he was brought here after getting into a fight with security." Jacob began scratching his head. "He should be here," he said, looking baffled at Roxanne the medic.

"I'm sorry, Jacob, but Trevor was taken to speak with...Sirus, I believe." She looked around the infirmary, which was big enough to house ten beds. Jacob wondered why there were so many beds; this was a place of safety and peace.

Focusing on her face again, Jacob moved closer to her desk, resting a hand on the solid wooden surface. "What do you mean he went to talk to Sirus? How do you know that? Who took him?" He asked the questions in a single breath. Jacob had a tendency to spout off multiple questions in a row. His mom would call him the question machine when they drove about town, stopping at different shopping plazas and picking up Starbucks frappés.

"Teacher Simon came to get him. Didn't say much, just said Sirus was looking to have a word with him." She buried her face back in the computer screen so that she would not have to look at Jacob. He got the feeling she knew something was wrong. "If you need more information than that, you need to speak to someone else," Roxanne said, flipping her strawberry-red hair. Hair like that was a bit much for a woman of her age, but she seemed to like the color. Even wore matching lipstick. Jacob liked her, and it was weird to see her so nervous.

"Okay, I think I'll try to find Teacher Simon to see what he knows about Trevor. I may find him on the first floor near the central plaza, so I'll just make my way down there. I've seen him down there a lot." Jacob waved a hesitant hand in her direction as he walked away, moving along the white linoleum and through the exit door of the infirmary.

Jacob walked around the corner and back into the stairwell. He stood with his back against the door to think. He'd been able to avoid any teachers so far, but he didn't want to make a bad situation worse by being found wandering the Palace after the weird meeting in the auditorium. An early lockdown situation could prevent them from leaving tonight. It was around 4:00 p.m. right now. He knew they should leave before 7:00 p.m. The extra security squad may arrive by then.

What about Trevor though? It just didn't make sense. Jacob had been in this Palace for a long time, and he'd never seen Sirus in real life. Was he even here? After speaking to Roxanne, Jacob was certain the mysterious man was in fact here. She had no reason to lie. *I need to talk to Mary.*

Jacob started up the stairs to his pod, all the while wondering what was going on with Trevor, knowing that he couldn't leave without finding out what happened to his old friend. If Sirus was on the premises, Jacob knew where he could be found.

CHAPTER FORTY-THREE

Jacob

J ACOB MADE HIMSELF SKINNY, SLIPPING INTO the room like a house burglar just beating the spotlight of a cop's telescope. He closed the door behind him as quietly as he could. *Not bad for an old man.* Mary was lying on the bed, on top of the covers, staring up at the ceiling. Jacob thought she was sleeping, but as he approached, her chin dipped down as she looked at him.

"Tell me you have good news," she said as she pulled herself up on her small bony arms, letting her back rest against the white faux-leather headboard of the bed.

Jacob sat on the bed next to Mary, and before speaking, he touched her face and kissed her lips. For him, that was the easiest thing to do at this point. He wished that those kisses could make the world disappear. He wished they could make him forget about the present as he had forgotten about the past. Leanne, to be specific. He did forget about her sometimes. That was for the best though; she was gone and would want him to move on.

"Something is very wrong. I don't want to lie to you, and I see no reason to do that. Roxanne in the infirmary told me that Teacher Simon collected Trevor to go speak with Sirus."

"Hold on." She paused. "Sirus? So, Trevor was taken somewhere to meet with the program director himself, and no one saw him leave? And plenty of people would have noticed him due to the commotion he caused before." Mary straightened up, letting one leg dangle off the bed while she curled the other leg underneath her.

"That's a thought but...I think Sirus is here. Maybe Trevor never left the Palace," Jacob said, raising both eyebrows and giving her the "never say never" face.

"What? How?"

Jacob grabbed her hand; he enjoyed having a reason to touch her hands. They were so soft, and the way they felt inside of his own made him feel strong, needed, craved.

"Remember when we were talking earlier, before the voice over the intercom called us to the auditorium? I was telling you about the secret floor?"

Mary blinked her eyes hard. "With all the commotion, I'd almost forgotten," she said, tugging at her hair nervously. "How does that tie in to everything?"

"When I got up to the hidden floor, it was pretty dim. There were no lights, but I could see enough to tell that it wasn't white. I took a look up the hall and came back down, because...well, because I wanted to come back and talk to you before I did anything I would regret. It was dark, but I know what I saw." Jacob's face was serious, unflinching, and he gripped her hand harder. "I want to go back before we leave."

"How do we get there? And what if the teachers are on the elevator or monitoring it?" Mary said, beginning to raise her voice.

Jacob put a finger over his lips, signaling for her to stay quiet. "Same elevator trick I did to get there. I know how to do it again. We gotta go up there, Mary. I think Sirus is there, or at least his office is. Maybe we can find something there that we can show people here, some evidence against the Order. Maybe he is busy with the issues here and not in his office. We can go looking...or I can go looking, and you can stay here and wait for me."

Mary's face grew somber. Her grip on his hand loosened and she let his go. "Jacob, I'm never leaving you again. When you left to go to the infirmary, I was afraid the whole time and wishing I'd gone with you. If you are going, then so are am I." Mary got up and walked toward the door. Jacob watched her for a moment, in awe of how much she cared for him. The young woman was willing to risk capture, banishment, death, whatever. He knew that she was in on this with him.

"Okay, let's go then." Jacob took his time getting up, feeling the anguish in his knees. Sometimes he wished he were a young man again, but he knew if that were the case, then he would not be here in this moment with her. He thought that the Order, Sirus, and maybe even the teachers had done something to hurt Trevor. Or maybe they moved him somewhere else. If the answer could be found, he knew that it would be in Sirus's office on the nineteenth floor, if there was an office.

In all honesty, Jacob didn't know what awaited them there. For all he knew, the hidden hallway could lead out to a helipad. It could lead to a super-secret cafeteria for the staff or a parallel universe. There was no way to tell without going up there.

"Listen, Mary," he said, placing his hands on the door over her head, trapping her between his body and the door. "We go there, look around, and then we leave and head straight out to the courtyard if we don't find anything. Or back to the first floor if we do."

She nodded, unblinking.

"I'll deal with the guard, if there is one to deal with at all. For all we know, he was sent to a new spot to guard because of the incident on the fourth floor. I'm almost sure we will find something though. You can wait by the door and be the lookout while I try to find something to blow this whole place to smithereens."

Jacob rested his forehead on hers. They kissed one last time and vacated the pod. The door slammed behind them, leaving the white room to itself, everything looking just as immaculate as it did on the first day he came walking through the door with nothing but a book bag and a mind full of terrible images that twenty years of counseling couldn't stop him from seeing every time he closed his eyes. The TV still displayed the same message that it always had..."Please Wait."

CHAPTER FORTY-FOUR

Jacob

THEY BOTH STEPPED OFF THE ELEVATOR together, not quite holding hands. But they were close enough to do so if need be. The corridor outside of the elevator was exactly as Jacob remembered it: darkness, no white, no sounds, no teachers, no life. The corridor felt dead. Very dim circular lights were installed in the walls, set about six feet apart.

"Just stay close to me, honey. I'm not going to let anything happen to you," Jacob said, not looking at her. He was paying attention to the lights cascading down the walls, leading to a big door on their right and a smaller door across from that one.

Once they reached the doors, Jacob saw that the smaller one led to a staircase. But to where? He opened the door and looked. Like the corridor, the lighting was almost non-existent in the stairway. Jacob closed the door and turned to the bigger one behind him.

The door was made of thick, glossy wood. The knob looked antique, unlike the rest of the Palace. He hadn't seen a door like this since his old life. Jacob touched the door, feeling the smooth wood. Even just a touch could bring back memories of his past life. He remembered getting a million splinters in his fingers from trying to build tree houses with the neighborhood kids.

He thought it funny that something as simple as seeing or touching an inanimate object could pull memories from the back of his brain, shuffle them, then display them as clear as day.

"Are you okay, Jacob?" Mary asked as she grabbed his arm.

"Yeah, I'm okay. I was just thinking about something."

Jacob grabbed the knob and turned it clockwise. They heard a small click and then an abnormally loud creaking sound as the door slowly opened. Maybe it just seemed loud to Jacob because he had not heard that sound in so long. He grabbed Mary's hand as they both stepped into the room.

The smells, the objects, the colors—it was all so nostalgic for Jacob. He hadn't seen items like this in so long. The office was dark, but there were candles in different spots illuminating certain things. The carpet was a dark brown, almost black. There was a coffee table off to the right near a huge grandfather clock. A smaller table sat beside that with what looked like bottles of expensive liquor. Jacob thought the room looked like the study of some old college professor of an Ivy League school.

Mary walked into the room behind Jacob, closing the door quietly. When she turned around, Jacob saw her mentally wrestling with the full culture shock. He knew she'd heard about things like this, but she had never seen them.

The room smelled of old leather, wood, and old books. Jacob noticed a bunch of folders and books on top of the desk at the back of the room. He began walking toward the desk, feeling the soft plush carpet beneath his shoes. It reminded him of his parents' house. Walking out of the living room of their home to go outside and enter the big white van was the last time he had felt such soft carpet beneath his feet. Jacob wanted to just pace the room, the feeling brought back so much. That hurt though, because it was all gone now. What point was there in remembering when you could do nothing but relive the moments inside of your own spotty memory? It would never be real again.

Mary walked over and touched the big clock, feeling the carved wood as she watched the pendulum swing back and forth. She seemed to be in love with it and regarded the clock as some kind of dinosaur fossil. The items in this office had to appear otherworldly to her.

She walked over to a bookshelf on the wall, scanning all the books briefly. Jacob watched her reading the spines and smiling. She was so impressed by the items before her that she seemed to forget the risk of the situation.

Jacob turned away and looked at the desk's surface. It was covered in folders. He couldn't help but wonder if there was a file for him. And if there was, what would it say? He had to find out.

He moved a few of the folders around and noticed the name "Trevor Cox" written across the top of one. The name had a red slash through it. This filled him with dread, and he could feel his heart quicken and his stomach fold in on itself. He grabbed the file and whipped it open. He scooped all the papers out and flung the folder carelessly to the side.

Rapidly flipping through the pages, Jacob tried to find something incriminating. He noticed all of the papers had a footer at the bottom labeled "NCP Corp." Jacob wondered if he had ever heard of that before, but he was sure he hadn't. He continued trying to find something alluding to where Trevor could be.

Mary started toward Jacob just as the office door made that same creaking sound. He looked up from the papers in his hands to see the door slowly moving.

Jacob blinked. Sirus seemed to be in the room without ever walking into the room. The door opened, and there he was on the carpet, staring at them both. He didn't look angry or threatening, more so bored and expectant. Mary stumbled over her own feet upon seeing him there, coming close to falling. Jacob dropped the papers on the desk but did not move.

He was as tall, handsome, and well dressed as he appeared on the dinnertime videos. Jacob watched Mary stare at Sirus, looking him up and down. She looked as though she had seen a ghost. Jacob had no idea what to say. The only thought that came to his mind was, *How did he get in the room so fast?*

After a time of awkward silence, Sirus turned around smoothly and pushed the door closed with his hand. He turned back around and leaned against that door, crossing one foot over the other. He looked like some model from one of those GQ Magazines, only older. Mary began backing up. Sirus had a carefree demeanor, and based on what he'd just walked into, that was cause for concern.

"Do not move, Mary. I'd prefer you go back to the corner there, check out the books once more." Sirus nodded in the direction of the bookshelf. "Seems Jacob here has an interest with my belongings at my desk. This intrigues me much more."

Mary did not move; she appeared too afraid to take a step in either direction. "I will not ask you again, Mary. For now, you are not in any trouble, nor am I agitated. But let's not change these things. Go," he said, snapping his finger once and pointing to the corner. Mary managed to make her way there this time. Slowly and hesitantly, but she got there.

She stared at Jacob. He could see the fear all over her beautiful face. Her lips were shaking, and she had begun to cry. She looked as though she wanted to run away. Jacob noticed a tear run down her face.

Sirus walked in her direction, locking eyes with her as he made a shushing sound with his finger to his lips. He reached into the breast pocket of his jacket and pulled a white handkerchief out, then extended his hand to give it to her. He moved in closer after she took the handkerchief and whispered in Mary's ear, "Wipe your face clean, there is no need for that." Then in a swift motion, he was facing Jacob again. Sirus made quick strides to the desk area, where he pulled up short and sat down in the seat that was normally designated for visitors.

A bright grin came over his face. "I would say that I'm surprised to see you here, Jacob, but I'm not. I also doubt that you are surprised to be here." Sirus crossed his legs and placed both hands on his knee. "So, what brings you to my office today? No, tell me something else first. How did you even find this part of the Palace? I have a bit of bet going with Teacher Simon." The grin on his face somehow got bigger.

"I...well, I was messing around with the buttons in the elevator, and it brought me here," Jacob said. He could feel his posture falling, like he was visually submitting to the man sitting before him. Jacob suddenly stood up straight, lifted his chin a bit, and spoke louder. "I just found it. That's beside the point, sir...Sirus. Where is my friend Trevor, and why is this room hidden away?"

"Hold on with all the tough questions, Jake. There will be plenty of time for that."

Jacob felt the corners of his mouth turn down. No one had called him Jake since he'd been with his best friend from the Old World, Logan. It made him angry to hear it come from Sirus.

"I told Teacher Simon that someone would one day stumble upon the nineteenth floor, just as you have. Honestly I'm surprised that it didn't happen long ago." He looked up at the ceiling, thought for a moment, and then said, "Twenty years was a good run."

"What are you talking about?" Jacob asked, trying to keep his cool. "What does all this have to do with Trevor?"

"We will need to come up with something better in the future, but that's another talk for another man. To answer your question, Trevor was admitted into the Greater Understanding Program. He outgrew the Palace—his mental stability waning in the end there proved that." Sirus twirled one finger around the side of his head in a circle. "Aren't you happy for him?" Sirus asked, opening both arms like he was expecting a hug. "No, you aren't happy because you don't believe me, correct? You are an easy read, Jake." He brought his arms back in and rested them on his knee again.

"Stop calling me Jake. My name is Jacob," he said with authority in his voice.

"Calm yourself, let's try to be civil...Jacob. Better?" Sirus said with a wink.

Mary was in the corner, still wiping her eyes and listening to their conversation. She had not moved from the spot Sirus had ordered her to stand in, near the bookshelf.

"I asked you," Jacob said, "where is Trevor? I'm not going to ask again. I just found his file here, and you were looking over all this information on him. What's that about?" He shot Sirus an annoyed look. He was beginning to feel his temper rise, the initial surprise and fear slowly being replaced with rage.

Sirus got to his feet faster than anyone Jacob had ever seen, and by the time he noticed it, he was face to face with the program director, who was still smiling. Mary let out a small cry from across the room. Jacob instinctively jumped back, lifting an arm to block his face, but Sirus didn't make a move to strike him.

"Tell me, Jacob, what happens if you have to ask me again? I'm a tad confused by this statement. Is that a threat? Of what, I wonder?"

His head snapped over to Mary, and he pointed at her. "Did that sound like a threat to you as well?"

Mary sobbed. "No, he was not threatening you. Please, Sirus, can we just leave? We are sorry, and we will never return to this floor," she said, crying while holding herself up by gripping the bookshelf with her right hand. She looked as though her legs would break beneath the weight of her body.

Still looking at Mary, Sirus continued talking. "I don't wish to take those words as a physical threat, but I have no issue with things escalating to that point." He looked at Jacob again, glaring into his eyes. Jacob felt like Sirus could sense his fear.

Without thinking, Jacob took a step back to make space for a right hook. He swung and fully missed Sirus as the program director swiftly moved to the right, causing Jacob to stumble forward and hit his hip on the side of the desk. Before he could register the pain reverberating through his side, a quick jab crashed into his right jaw. He heard a cracking sound.

Jacob went down to one knee, spitting out two teeth on the carpet along with a mouthful of blood. Even though his right ear was ringing, he could hear Mary yelp in fear. He felt ashamed at that moment. True enough, he hadn't been in a physical altercation since he was seventeen, and the older Sirus had just reduced him to a child...and in front of Mary.

"We are so much better than these violent acts, Jacob. Stay on your knee until I tell you to get up. If you choose to rise, I'll take that as an aggressive act and strike you once more...or twice more." Sirus leaned against the desk next to Jacob, shaking his head at Mary and her cries. "Don't do that."

Jacob heard Mary stifle her sobs and quiet down immediately.

"Do me a favor, Jacob." Sirus began to move around Jacob. "Switch me sides of the desk, please. This is actually where I sit, and you sit—look at me!" Sirus raised his voice, causing Jacob to jump. Jacob looked at him warily. "You sit in that seat." Sirus pointed at the seat he'd been sitting in moments ago.

"You are not doing a good job of leading the conversation, Jacob. If violence is the only language you speak, this will not last long. Get up and go to your seat. I'm sure you came to talk. Go on." He waved Jacob away. "Ah, no place like home, right?" he said as he plopped down hard in his chair. "Well, I didn't mean that the way it came out, but yeah. Get comfortable. Let's talk about Trevor. Mary, you stay right over there, I'll dismiss you soon enough. You need to hear this though." Sirus straightened his suit jacket and adjusted the sleeves.

Jacob sat across from Sirus. Mary stood behind him in the corner, no longer crying but seriously distraught. Wiping blood from his mouth with the bottom of his shirt, he now understood that using his words would be more useful in this situation. *How is a man of that age so fast and powerful?*

"About Trevor...Trevor was an older man when he arrived here; close to my age, actually. He suffered from small mental issues even then, but the death of his children and wife did the remaining damage. For the last twenty years, we have been trying to rehabilitate Trevor, but his brain fights back. He is...was, quite the powerful soul. You were friends, so I'm sure you can attest to that. He was able to accept that his children had passed when the sickness came for everyone. The fact that his wife died with them was not something he was ever able to accept.

"I'm quite sure you have seen him speak to himself, pretend to hold hands with someone behind him? Of course, we wouldn't be able to see the person behind him, but to him, she was very real. Reality is only what you can see, hear, and feel. Not what others perceive. Do you understand?" Sirus grabbed a pen and began tapping it on the desk, waiting for Jacob's response.

"Hold on, are you saying that Trevor believed that his wife was still alive? We were close for the last twenty years—I think I would know if that were the case. He never even wanted to talk about her."

"Well, for obvious reasons, Jacob." Sirus laughed a bit. "Had he brought it up, you would have forced him out of his fantasy. A part of your friend knew that he was lying to himself. Not speaking about it was...shall we say, a preemptive defense mechanism.

"Before he spoke with me, he came up with some story about one of the teachers telling him that his wife was killed here in the Palace because she saw something she shouldn't have. That wasn't the first issue he's had with wild stories that had a tendency to send him into a frenzy, but he was getting worse. Walking up to women in the court-yard and forcing flowers on them, calling everyone Amy. Trevor was tortured by the past, and he needed to be set free. Maybe you hadn't noticed his behavior until the classroom blowup because you have been busy screwing with that sweet thing in the corner over there." Sirus winked at Jacob.

Jacob's face scrunched up as he tried to understand how that made any sense. "Even if I did choose to believe that, you are telling me that because Trevor had mental issues, which the Order failed to fix, that he was rewarded by being promoted to the next level ascension? I just don't understand the logic."

Sirus leisurely tossed the pen into the air, letting it fall onto the carpet near his chair with a dull thumping sound. He then laughed, almost uncontrollably.

Jacob turned in his seat, looking over at Mary. She looked just as confused as he was by what was happening. Sirus slowed his laughter. "You are good, Jacob." He looked over to Mary. "I see why you love this one—he's good looking, and with investigative skills beyond any before him to enter this room. My excuse would have worked on you, I bet."

Sirus placed both hands onto the desk, tapping his fingertips one after the other. "How about some truth? Haven't played that game in quite some time, but I feel you both deserve it. I mean, look how far you have gone to speak with me. Things are changing here in the Palace, and honestly, there is no place for you here.

"You already know too much, and I can't possibly allow you to go back into the population here. I know why you are here, I know what you have found out—I know it all. Not because we are watching you in particular, but because we are charged with watching everyone and everything, Jacob. There are over three hundred bugs in each pod, video and audio. Microscopic little things, but the video comes across in amazing clarity and the audio is astounding." Sirus lifted both hands and gave Jacob a double thumbs-up. "What happens or doesn't happen in the Palace is decided by the Order, and we have our reasons. One man could...ascend, for talking too much about the old ways, while we may allow another Palace member to go as far as he can...even to kill."

"But why?" Jacob said, so softly the words barely came out.

"Why, why, why...always a 'why' with you people. Okay, I'll explain everything before I allow you both to scatter off into the great beyond like the new modern-day Adam and Eve." Sirus looked over at Mary, Jacob thought maybe to make sure she was still paying attention. And she was.

He then focused his attention back on Jacob. "No interrupting, okay? Once we are done speaking, Teacher Simon will show you both out through the door across the hall. By the way, the guard outside of the cluster of trees has been removed. See, I'm not so bad. Your escape was to be unimpeded. We knew you were leaving and planned to allow that."

"Just like that, you would have let us leave? If so, why did the guard get so aggressive with me at the front exit?"

"Well, we couldn't have you influencing the crowd to...think the same way. All influences are meant to serve a purpose, even the ideas you believe you come up with on your own." Sirus sounded proud of himself.

"Anyways, I'd been watching your friend Trevor since he got here, that is true. It's also true that he had severe mental issues and couldn't accept that his wife died twenty years ago. The deeper we got into his psyche, the more he saw us as the enemy. Then his military back-ground kicked in, allowing him to create this narrative in which we, the government, were doing crazy things behind his back. Which is not one hundred percent false. We will get there though.

"Trevor began to lose his way, and at one point he became a phys-ical threat to everyone around him. You are from the Old World, just like I am, Jacob. What do we do with rabid dogs in the Old World?"

Sirus's eyes narrowed as he pointed to Jacob. "C'mon, c'mon, I know you know the answer."

"Put them down?" Jacob said. He sounded unsure, even though he knew it was the correct answer.

Sirus's lips curled downward into a sad face. "Aww, don't be so somber about it. Death isn't so bad, trust me. Maybe he will do better in the next lifetime. But yes, you are right. We put them down for the better of the group, and the group is us, sir, the Palace members."

"So, you killed him?"

"Well, yeah. I had Teacher Simon take him out back and terminate him," Sirus said nonchalantly with a wave of one hand as he sat back in his chair. "If it's any consolation to you, I think he was okay with it. The man was being tormented by a past he couldn't escape. It was for the better. His purpose was served."

Jacob could hear Mary crying in the background. "You people are monsters. What the hell is going on here?" Jacob said.

"Oh hush, don't be dramatic. Preservation is going on here. There are things worse than death, you know that, you saw it. You still see it every night when you sleep. Tossing and turning, kicking the covers off, waking up in a sweat and still seeing your folks covered in their own mess. I know these things," Sirus said as he raised a hand at Mary over in the corner, motioning for her to be quiet. She complied.

Jacob was fuming; he wanted to say so much, but he also needed to hear whatever information Sirus was willing to give. He swallowed his pride and stayed quiet. "Mary, let the man speak without interrupting. I know it's hard, honey, but we do need to hear this. I need to hear this."

"Good man," Sirus said. He reached out and gave the golden globe a spin on his desk, never breaking eye contact with Jacob. It made Jacob uncomfortable as he spun the globe like he was God or something. Jacob felt like a mere piece in a grand game played by Sirus and the Order.

"Let's be honest here—there is no Greater Understanding Program." Sirus looked to Mary again. "If you make a peep, I will have Teacher Simon come in here and remove you." He turned his attention back to Jacob.

"The Greater Understanding Program was always a goal for you to reach, to keep you focused on something. God knows you people can't focus for longer than a few seconds if there isn't an apple on a stick in front of your face. I'm surprised that the guise worked as long as it did, but all good things come to an end, right?"

Jacob held his head in his hands, unable to believe what was being said to him. This was all much worse than he'd thought. *Why are they doing all of this?*

"There are no people on the outside trying to fix the world. That's not a thing, Jacob. Mary, it's not real. It never was. You people did in fact bring on this sickness though. That much is true," Sirus said while straightening the folders on his desk. "Feels good to be honest about this." He paused for a second. "Also, I'm tired of eating dinner with you," he said as he stacked the folders in a neat pile, casually explaining that everything in their lives was a lie.

"Why? Why lie about all of this? Why would the government do this?" Jacob said.

"There is no government as you remember them. Everyone died for the most part. Including them. Do you really think that you could put together something like the Order in a few days with remaining members of governments from all over the world?" He laughed.

"You are smarter than that, Jacob, I know you are. Look at all that I've explained thus far. Now be creative. Tell me what you think this is. Why this is."

"To lower the population?" Jacob was so perplexed by what he was hearing, he couldn't see straight.

Sirus laughed again, close to spinning around in his chair. "Of course not, don't be silly." He pressed his fingers to the bridge of his nose, contemplating something. "But...it depends on which revolution we are speaking of. This is the fourth revolution of Planet Earth."

"Revolution? What are you talking about? Speak plainly, Sirus!" Jacob smacked several items off the table, hurting his hand in the process.

"For a man of forty years old and twenty years of intense learning, you are still as dumb as the day you arrived here." Sirus leaned closer to the table, turning his head to the side and giving Jacob the eye. "I think you know who I am, and who we are. What we are attempting to create, and with whom." He nodded at Mary.

"I don't. Call me stupid or whatever you want, but I'm lost. Just tell me what the hell is going on," Jacob screamed. His voice echoed throughout the room, making Mary jump.

"This one does not have a flair for theater, it seems," Sirus said, pointing at Jacob but speaking to Mary. "Okay, I'll make this as simple as I can for you. We have always looked over what you all called Planet Earth, as it's a creation from our...area of the universe. This planet has been here longer than you could even imagine—your brain couldn't possibly fathom it."

"What..." Jacob tried to find the words—any words. He couldn't be hearing this. But Sirus went on before he could think of how to respond.

"For that amount of time, we have been here, watching, visiting, testing, starting, ending, starting over, then starting over again. This is the fourth revolution, meaning the fourth time we have had to forcibly instill order on this particular planet, and for lack of a better term, start over. To you this sounds heartless, but you have yourselves to blame."

Universe? Created this planet? What the hell is he talking about? Jacob rubbed his eyes with the palms of his hands, unsure if any of this was real. He had gone from reliving the same weeks over and over for the last twenty years, to now being told it was all a lie and the person in front of him was...not from the same planet as him.

"No matter what we do, you people find a way to screw things up. We let you live near each other, you kill everyone you can and wage war. So, we split the planet up into continents. Think that will stop your kind? Of course not; you find ways to meet up and begin the killing again." Sirus's voice began to show his passion and resentment as he spoke.

"And it's not enough for you animals to just kill each other normally. No, you sit around thinking of more fantastic and amazing ways to kill each other in droves. Guns, bombs, drones, nukes, and other things that we stopped from happening." At this point, Sirus was yelling. "There are only so many great floods that the planet can take!

We already did three of those, and forty percent of the planet is now below sea level. You monkeys think that Atlantis was an underwater city. But no, it was above ground to begin with. Much like your society, the people there became greedy and murderous beyond repair. So, they needed to be 'put down.' We wanted something different this time around.

"We thought to ourselves that we could try something that allowed the planet to stay as it was, but also leave some of you alive, meaning we would not have to fully start mankind over again for the fourth time." Sirus began to calm down. "Pressing the reset button comes with a price to our planet."

"So...you all created the sickness to get rid of us?"

Sirus stared at Jacob. "I've overestimated you, Jacob. I thought you more intelligent than this. Maybe she is the smart one. You are an old man with a failing body and high blood pressure. That is all."

"I'm not an o—"

"Shut up, I'm speaking! I'll tell you when it's okay for you to speak again. I'll take a phrase from your book. I won't tell you that again. This is no longer a conversation; I'll finish what I have to say and then allow you both to leave." Sirus wiped his brow and slowed his breathing.

"We allowed some of you—people from the outside—to live and come into this amazing experiment we built. We wanted you here so that the Palace-born humans could learn *some* things from you all; a certain amount of you were allowed to survive for this reason. We wanted the Palace humans to be born of man and woman, not a test tube, as you all were so many millions of years ago."

"And this is why my children were taken away from me?" Mary said. Even though she spoke in a voice as small as a mouse, her words surprised Jacob. Staring down at her feet, Jacob could see she was afraid to look at Sirus, or whatever this man was.

Sirus smiled and applauded loudly. "Look at you, Mary. Your children, huh? Now where did you learn something like that? Jacob, have you been manipulating our subjects?" Mary didn't speak again, just continued staring at the ground.

Sirus focused his attention back on Jacob. "We knew that you would eventually die off from old age, or from your own meddlesome ways. Behave and live in the Palace until you die of old age, or become bothersome and get into the Greater Understanding Program, which of course was a bullet to the back of the head. In hindsight, be happy that you never ascended." Sirus chuckled. "It was not quite the golden ticket you all thought it to be."

"What's the point though? In all of this, why are you, whatever you are, going to such extremes to make us behave the way you want us to?" Jacob said as he rose to his feet. "If you have such power to do all the things you say you have in this world, the universe, and so forth, why not just force us to behave the way you want?"

"Does a father walk away from his children just because they keep making mistakes? Of course not. You teach them, you nurture them, you show them different ways. Would your father, Mathew, have left you? For any reason at all?"

Jacob shook his head no. A single tear formed and fell into his beard as he backed up to where Mary was. He retrieved her shaking hand.

"You humans are the only species that we cannot seem to get right. No matter how much gene splicing we do, no matter how many safe-guards we put into place...you end up being dumb killing machines, and any intelligence you do have is used to persecute your fellow humans and create different religions, which you all use to kill even more.

"So, tell you what. If you both want to go out into the world, be my guest. But it's not what you think it is. You were smart enough to figure out that the sickness is no longer a threat, but other threats have surfaced. You won't last longer than twenty-four hours outside of our protection here, but I know that doesn't matter to you, so I'll allow you to leave. Teacher Simon is outside that door waiting to take you to a secret exit where you can leave this place forever. So go...you will wish you hadn't though." Sirus got up from his chair and walked over to the window that overlooked the courtyard. He opened the curtain, allowing sunlight to fill the room. He kept his back to the scared and confused couple.

"Jacob, Mary, before you leave, I want you to know something.

Here, you must deal with rules, morning enrichments, the watchers, security, and our other staff. Out there though?" Sirus pointed out past the forest area. "Beyond those trees there, lies something worse, something we are struggling to get ahold of. You were warned. Goodbye, my children," Sirus said in a calm voice, never turning around to regard them or watch them exit.

CHAPTER FORTY-FIVE

Jacob

TEACHER SIMON LET THEM OUT ON the eastern side by the courtyard area. No one was there, which felt weird to Jacob, but the excitement and fear took over, and he barely noticed.

He and Mary took off running. He felt her fingers touch his as they made their way beyond the cluster of trees, and he grasped on to her hand. There were no guards patrolling the area, just as Sirus had promised. They ran faster than they had ever run, faster than the wind would allow.

They crossed the red flags in the grass, legs pumping, running hand in hand. The forest was just ahead. Mary tripped while running, but Jacob pulled her up by the arm. They continued on, Jacob looking back to make sure no one was following them. The Palace stood behind them, as defiant and sturdy as ever. Watching them...

"Not much longer to go, honey. Keep running, we're almost there," Jacob said between heavy breaths.

Nothing stood between them and freedom but the forest ahead. They were free, and whatever was out there waiting for them could not be worse than the Palace. "We did it...we did it," Mary was saying through tired breaths as she struggled to keep up with him. He wouldn't let her fall behind though; he would pick her up if need be.

The world felt huge to Jacob now, bigger than it had ever felt before. The air smelled sweet; it burned his lungs because he was so tired, but he loved every moment. They were not far from the forest.

And so they continued to run.

CHAPTER FORTY-SIX

Sirus

"ARE THEY WATCHING?" SIRUS SAID WITH a phone to his ear, speaking to someone in the Palace. He paused while the person on the other end spoke. "Okay, good. Make sure they have a good look at this. It will serve as the new standard for those who do not understand that what we have here is no longer on an at-will basis. Do it."

Sirus hung up and slid the phone into his pocket. He turned away from the window, walked over to his desk, and grabbed every folder there. He dumped them all in a large wastebasket near his desk. At that moment, a roaring sound filled the Palace. It could be heard everywhere—the courtyard, the child center, the space between the red flags and the forest...

CHAPTER FORTY-SEVEN

Mary

AND HE LET GO OF HER hand...

She ran a few more steps before turning around to see why he slowed up. Mary was running so fast, and the wind was flashing by her face at such high speeds—she never even heard the shot go off.

What she saw when she turned around was enough to drive anyone mad. Her life, her future, her love, lay there in the grass with a small hole in his back. Blood spurted from the hole like a weak sprinkler. Jacob tried to crawl, but he was barely able to move his limbs. He reminded her of a dying bug, slowly moving its legs, trying to fight the inevitable.

She ran over and grabbed his hand. She pulled with all her might to turn him around. When she finally got him to turn over, he was looking up at her. Their eyes met, and she could see nothing but those eyes. She dropped down to her knees and began kissing his face, asking him to get up. They were so close to the forest. It was only fifty yards away. Their new life was just fifty yards away.

He pushed her face away while she was trying to kiss him and encourage him to get up. He turned his head and threw up an ungodly amount of blood and what looked to her like organs. After that, he was able to get out one word: "Go."

Jacob's eyes met Mary's one last time right before his pupils made a beeline to the clouds above. He was no longer breathing.

She began to hug and kiss him, trying to get him to wake up. Mary touched him below his neck, and her hand fell into the messy gulf that was once Jacob's chest. She didn't even notice it before. The hole in front was ten times the size of the one in his back. She hadn't seen death like this in all her twenty years of life, but she knew enough to know that he was gone.

Mary kissed his forehead one last time and screamed to him that she loved him and always would. Then she dragged herself away and disappeared into the trees, leaving his body behind forever. Leaving everyone behind.

No one came after her.

CHAPTER FORTY-EIGHT

Sirus

To: NCP Group
From: O'Sullivan, Sirus
Date: May 14, 2040 08:14:48 EST
Subject: Experiment 48, Phase 2 Initiation

I CONTACT YOU WITH EXCITEMENT TODAY. Experiment 48 has advanced to phase 2. We have made great leaps with the Palace-born adults. Today, Palace member Mary, acting on her own accord, planned to leave the Palace with the help of a human from the outside world. Mary showed decision-making skills, and most importantly a desire to live. She was allowed to live and escaped into a nearby forest area. She will exit in the 23rd sector of this area, very close to experiment or Palace 114. Please contact the staff there to be on the lookout for her. She is not to be hurt or stopped. Let's allow this to play out.

I've copied statistics from the Palace Experiments. Updated last night.

218 of 919 Palaces: Offline.
345 of 919 Palaces: Online in Phase 1.

187 of 919 Palaces: Online in Phase 2.
169 of 919 Palaces: Taken over by rebel forces.

Thank you, gentlemen.
Sirus

CHAPTER FORTY-NINE

Mary

MARY SLEPT IN THE FOREST THAT night. There was an endless number of trees and no path to take. After stumbling and falling for hours, she finally gave up and decided to sleep. She found a small cave area that she could use for shelter. The night was beautiful though, and she laid there all night and cried for Jacob. She stared up at the stars through the cave's opening and realized it was the first time in her entire life that she'd ever done that—stared at the stars.

The next morning, she woke up nauseous, feeling like she had to vomit. She did not move though. She did not get up and rush off because there was nowhere to rush off to. She lay there on her side, listening to the birds sing their songs while thinking of the man who had bought her freedom with his own life, rubbing her belly the whole time.

EXCERPT FROM TOMORROW'S WRATH

Lonnie

THIS MADE THE 4TH DAY IN a row. In the beginning, it was hard for him to deal with. No, maybe that's the wrong word, it was sad for him, he felt empathy for them. From what Lonnie could see, it was hard for all of them. They had never seen anything like that. Not even close. Rules were rules though, and the balance of the very planet hung in the balance. Sirus said so.

It all happened so fast. One day everything was business as usual. Same old Palace schedules that had long become repetitious to everyone there, then it all changed with a boom and a body lying motionless in the field.

The last of the Palace-born individuals were trickling into the auditorium and taking their seats. Everyone was dressed in the white uniforms they had been given a few days ago. All of the women had their hair pulled into tight ponytails, the men were sporting short buzz cuts. Lonnie didn't understand why the change in hair and clothing, but he was sure The Order had their reasons.

He sat there, daydreaming about the events that had transpired after they all watched that old guy, Jacob, get shot down outside of the Palace. Everyone was made to come to the central Plaza and watch through the glass as Jacob and one of the Palace-born women made a run for the forest. She made it, but he didn't. *Her name was Mary, she was probably dead by now...or taken and enslaved by the others out there.*

Lonnie still remembered the screams of everyone in that moment. In unison, there were rounds of panicked gasps, hands covering mouths and eyes, outright blood-curdling screams. He noticed that the teachers and security didn't budge, they didn't seem to be surprised at all. Like they expected it... he supposed they did. Especially considering what happened next.

He sat in his seat and stared up at the stage, as he watched the Old-World individuals on their knees, hands tied behind their backs, with white blindfolds over their faces. It made him feel...indifferent. On the first day he was empathetic, now he felt as though it was simply another session. A lesson to be learned about how things worked. Sirus and The Order were calling "this" the beginning steps of Phase 2.

Lonnie looked away from the stage and noticed the person to his right. Melinda was a few years younger than him, maybe 15 years old. Her hands were placed on her knees, visibly unsettled. He saw she was trembling in fear of what was to come. Her right hand shot up to her face to wipe away a tear, then back down to her right knee.

He leaned in close to her so not to be loud as he spoke. "You have to relax, they won't like to see you crying. Calm down."

Melinda straightened up in her seat, sniffled and looked straight ahead to see more Old-World palace members being lined up in rows on their knees. There were three rows of them at this point, and more were being brought in from behind a theater curtain from the stage area—all of them blindfolded. There was no sound but that of their cries, mumbling pleas for mercy, and negotiations to be banished from the Palace. Speaking to no one, because no one was listening. They were the enemy.

"You remember the video they showed us. They are not good people and must be eliminated if we are to go back into the world and start anew. We all saw the video." Lonnie whispered to her, being quiet enough to not be noticed by anyone.

"I know... I know, it's just so sad. I know those people up there." Melinda held her eyes open as wide as possible, Lonnie believed she did that to keep the tears from dropping. Knowing that if she were to only blink, the tears would come streaming down once more. Maybe someone would notice and believe she felt bad for the criminals up there... then maybe she'd end up on the stage next?

"You saw how they were all trying to corrupt us. They showed us on the television. You even saw that guy Jacob confuse the Palace-born woman and use her to leave this place. We watched it. Those people up on that stage are not the people you thought they were." Lonnie said as he sharply moved away from her, returning to a straight position. The last of the Palace members were in their seats, and the Old-World members were in four rows on the stage now. It was time for another cleansing.

"I know" is the last thing he heard from Melinda before the lights in the auditorium went dark.

Security came in through the back exit, in a single file line. They walked up to the first row of seats of Palace-born members in their white uniforms. They hadn't had a chance to cleanse a group yet. Lonnie did though, on day two. The security team placed a gun into each of their hands. Same as yesterday, and the day before that.

The security team split into two groups and made their way to opposite sides of the auditorium. They placed their hands behind their backs and stood, staring up at the stage of crying, blindfolded Old-World members.

Just then Lonnie felt Melinda's hand graze his. She seemed to be trying to hold onto him, to brace for what was to come. Even though he felt annoyed with her and the crying, he allowed this kindness and took her hand.

Even though he felt annoyed with her and the crying he allowed this kindness and took her hand.

The first row of Palace-born members got up from their seats, guns in hand, and walked up to the stage, also in a single file line. They made a circle around their blindfolded friends of the past. People who were once seen as loved ones and comrades were now targets to be shot down.

Lonnie could hear the guns being cocked back, a bullet moving into the chamber ready to be disengaged. Melinda's small hand squeezed his, and he felt his own hand give a firm grip in return.

He and hundreds of others were sitting in their seats, eyes fixed upon the dark stage as if they were watching a Broadway musical from the Old-World. They watched, half in amusement and half in eagerness, to see problems from that past be extinguished. Some faces were smiling, some looked distraught, much like Melinda next to him. He felt nothing and that bothered him. He wanted to feel something.

It didn't matter either way. He and Melinda held hands tightly as the stage lit up with gun-fire. A strobe light show of sparks, smoke, blood, and smiles from the shooters. *They were smiling...* And still, he watched...and felt nothing.

YOU CAN READ the rest of the story in Tomorrow's Wrath by J.M. Clark

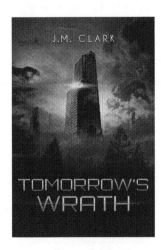

Join the mailing list and receive free giveaways and exclusive content:

WEBSITE: http://www.writtenbyjmclark.com
     Email: writtenbyjmclark@gmail.com

ABOUT THE AUTHOR

A SELF-PROFESSED OUTGOING PESSIMIST, J.M. CLARK is a word enthusiast, and an up-and-coming science fiction author in southern Ohio. J.M. studied English literature and writing at Northern Kentucky University. Now, a member of Cincinnati Fantasy-writers and Sci-fi and Fantasy-writers of America, J. M. indulges in his passion for writing and critiquing work in the realm of fantasy fiction. An avid reader, and transitional professional from lyricist to author, J.M. loves interacting with friends and other writers. He continues to deliver hesitantly optimistic advice, and produce work that keeps fans constantly wanting more.

Join the mailing list and receive free giveaways and exclusive content.

Website: http://www.writtenbyjmclark.com
Email: writtenbyjmclark@gmail.com

   facebook.com/writtenbyjmclark

   twitter.com/jmclark35

   instagram.com/writtenbyjmclark

ALSO BY J.M. CLARK

THE ORDER OF CHAOS SERIES

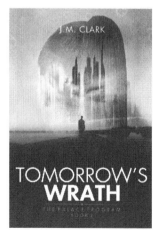

Join the mailing list and receive free giveaways and exclusive content:

Website: http://www.writtenbyjmclark.com

Email: writtenbyjmclark@gmail.com

Made in the USA
Middletown, DE
17 August 2020